BEST LESBIAN EROTICA 1999

Selected and Introduced by Chrystos

Tristan Taormino, Series Editor

BEST LESBIAN EROTICA 1999

Selected and Introduced by Chrystos

Tristan Taormino, Series Editor

CLEIS
PRESS

Contents

Acknowledgments

I would like to thank the following people for their contributions to the book:

To Frédérique Delacoste, Felice Newman, Don Weise, and everyone at Cleis Press for continuing to make this one of the most exciting, stimulating projects to work on. To Peter London of Avon Books and Leigh Davidson at Down There Press for help with permissions. Extra special thanks to Stephanie Gilman for typing services and to Clyde for important courier services.

To Chrystos for all her hard work, generosity, late night phone calls, and her care and nurturing of me and this book. To Heather Lewis, Jewelle Gomez, Jenifer Levin, and all the contributors of the 1996, 1997, 1998 collections for continuing to be part of the BLE Family. Special thanks to the folks at bookstores, especially the independents, who continue to support, promote, and host events for the book. A huge round of applause to the incomparable Hannah Doress and everyone at Hanarchy Now Productions for consistently supporting and promoting my work, the anthology series and its contributors, past, present and future.

All my gratitude, devotion, and appreciation to Toni Amato, Tom Bates, Kathy Blenk, Teresa Cooper, Bree Coven, Tim Driscoll, Michelle Duff, Morgan Dunbar, Gerry Gomez Pearlberg, Stanley Kent, Joan Larkin, Robert Lawrence, Ron Lieber, Lori & Nicole, Reggie Love & Jordan, Peggy Munson, Bryn Pryor, Carol Queen, Russell & Martin, Janet Schomer, D. Travers Scott, Michael Selditch, Don Spargo, Jr., Jill Muir Sukenick, Matt Bernstein Sycamore, Cecilia Tan, Mikel Wadewitz, Winston Wilde, and my mother for their ongoing support, encouragement, love, inspiration, and understanding. To Jenny Robertson for all of the above, and more, and for letting me dance for her.

Foreword

This has been a year full of sex. And as we all know, some sexual encounters are better than others.

I'm sure by now you've heard about the powerful man in a high-profile leadership position, the perky young intern, and their semi-steamy affair at the office. The cum-stained dress, penetration with a cigar, blow jobs under the desk while he was on the phone to important people...they are the makings of a cheesy porn pulp novel sex scene. We have been drowning in the details of the sexual encounters of Bill Clinton and Monica Lewinsky. And, sadly, the specifics were pretty uninteresting. As if the mainstream media weren't already obsessed with sex, it has become completely overloaded, saturated with who-did-what-to-whom-how-many-times. We don't need to go to the local video store's back room or call up to pay per view, we can now get pornography for free—thousands of pages of transcripts, hours of videotape—compliments of network television, the *New York Times*, and the Internet. Dr. Susan Love brilliantly satirized the scandal during a performance at The World Pornography Conference. At a mock ceremony, she presented Kenneth Starr with an award for creating the most expensive "porn production" ever made (and, she wryly noted, the only porn production ever paid for by the government)!

In addition to the Clinton sex scandal, we've been barraged by plenty of other sex in the news, from the goofy clips and outrageous sales of the homemade Tommy Lee/Pamela Anderson Lee sex video to the Viagra craze, prompting news articles about senior citizens becoming nymphomaniacs. These are merely a few examples, but the overall trend is enough to make us sick of sex. Are we there yet?

At the same moment when sex is the nation's top news story, one of our nation's most sinful cities (and my home) is being de-sexed. New York City mayor Rudy Guiliani began a surprisingly successful "Quality of Life Campaign" in 1998, which resulted in the closing of dozens of strip clubs, adult video stores, and other dens of pleasure. In the *Village Voice*, Richard Goldstein aptly asked, "If a legal business can be driven to the brink of extinction in the name of development, what else can be shut down? What passions will be sacrificed, what sins will be policed?"[1].

Have no fear. There is some good news to report from the fringe. The return and relaunch of the lesbian sex magazine *On Our Backs* has marked a new era in lesbian porn. When *On Our Backs* debuted in the early 1980s, it was *the* document of a liberated lesbian sexual revolution. Now that the revolution is in full swing and the antiporn feminist wing seems less of a threat, it will be interesting to see how *On Our Backs* positions itself. Fatale Video, one of the only companies to offer lesbian porn actually *produced* by lesbians, has been revived with the release of its latest feature *Bend over Boyfriend*, a guide for women who want to strap it on and fuck men in the ass. As kinky as this topic is, it does lack a lesbian focus. Producer Nan Kinney explains, "My main desire with Fatale is to keep doing lesbian videos, but our titles like *How to Female Ejaculate* and *Bend over Boyfriend* cross over into the sex education market. They sell better and help finance the other projects. *Bend over Boyfriend* fits into Fatale's mission: it tries to present sexual practices that are authentic, alternative, and not normally seen in mainstream porn."[2]

Kinney was among the scholars, producers, and veteran porn stars who sat side by side this summer at the World Pornography Conference in Los Angeles, sponsored by California State University at Northridge. Georgetown professors, hard-core directors, and professional dominatrixes debated such topics as feminism and porn, the emergence of the "gonzo" genre, and a history of fetishism in porn. *Time* magazine even covered the conference in its feature "Porn Goes Mainstream," in which writer Joel Stein noted that porn has come out of the closet, becoming more Hollywood all the time: "For big releases, there are screenings and premiere parties. VCA, one of the four big adult-film companies, has put promotional billboards along Sunset Boulevard in Los Angeles, and Vivid has placed ads at the Burbank airport as well as along Sunset."[3]

And if you think sex is happening only on the two coasts, think again. The International Sex Worker Foundation for Art, Culture, and Education (ISWFACE) purchased its own piece of history in 1998: the Dumas Brothel in Butte, Montana, the longest-running brothel in the United States. Big Sky Country may seem an unlikely place for a pro-sex worker movement, but Butte was once home to the second-largest red-light district in the United States. "Unlike New York, where Guiliani is trying to get rid of us, Butte residents are tolerant and open-minded— the town wants us here," says ISWFACE's director, retired sex worker Norma Jean Almodovar, who believes the attitude of the town is overwhelmingly supportive. Almodovar traveled to Butte at the end of August, where she received a special commendation and witnessed an important ceremony: the town dedicated Copper Block Park, located in the heart of the once-famous red-light district, to the prostitutes who worked there.

Along with these significant happenings in the world of "alternative" sex this year, and, perhaps, in response to the banality of sex in the mainstream, the explosion of lesbian erotica anthologies has continued to gain momentum. This new abundance has caused some editors, booksellers, and readers to cry overkill and overstimulation. Is there too much lesbian erotica? Are lesbians bored with sex too?

My experience working on *Best Lesbian Erotica 1999* suggests quite the opposite. This year, the guidelines for submission decreased the number of different pieces one writer could submit from five to three, yet we actually received a hundred more submissions than the previous year. This notable increase signals that more writers are choosing to write lesbian erotica *and* to submit it for publication. Both the *Best Lesbian Erotica* series and other erotica collections continue to hold strong places on the bestseller lists of queer bookstores; readers are hungry for erotica, consuming it at an alarming rate.

Compared to previous years, I think the hundreds of submissions we received this year, overall, were the most ambitious in form and content. Of course, some worked better than others, but the ambition was there. Writers took more risks with style, language, and genre; there were more hybrids of suspense/erotica, mystery/erotica, sci-fi/erotica. They also braved the erotics of underexplored territories: new and future technologies, love and romance, sickness and disability, craft and craftsmanship.

I was so excited about some of the submissions that I actually brought them over to my lover's house, read excerpts out loud, and had some pretty amazing sex. Remember, I've read lots and lots of erotica, plus I'm not in the habit of discussing manuscripts with others while they are under consideration, but some of these stories just begged to be shared and, well, enjoyed. In fact, I am as excited about this year's collection as I was about the very first anthology: the increased number of submissions, the quality of the work, and the people and places I had the privilege and pleasure to read about. I was going to come up with a Top 10 List of why lesbian erotica is thriving, but I suggest you look at the table of contents—there are twenty-eight signs that lesbian erotica is alive and well.

Tristan Taormino
New York City
October 1998

Notes:
1. Richard Goldstein, "Porn Free," *The Village Voice* (September 1, 1998): 34.
2. Tristan Taormino, "Naked Ambition," *Paper* (July 1998): 44
3. Joel Stein, "Porn Goes Mainstream," *Time* (September 7, 1998): 54 - 55

Introduction
Chrystos

When I was fourteen, I read *The Well of Loneliness* for the first time. Girls at school had been shouting that I was a lezzie, and I got suspended for beating one of them up—the irony of which I did not appreciate until much later. I understand now that I was passionately in love with my best friend Karen Rose. I didn't buy *The Well of Loneliness* because it was about lesbians—the title appealed to me because I was excruciatingly lonely. The contents were a revolution that cannot be understood by anyone not my age. The early sixties, even in San Francisco, were deeply silent about lesbian sex. It didn't exist in any of our lives.

Later, at seventeen, I went searching desperately for lesbian bars with another girlfriend whom I loved. We didn't find any. My coming out process was long, painful, and confused. I had no one to talk to as a teenager—there were no Lesbian Resource Centers, no women's bookstores or publishing companies or concerts. There was just loneliness. I write about this faded part of my past to place this book in a matrix which we often forget. We've only had lesbian books—as a plurality, with many choices—for the last twenty years. This birth has profoundly affected how all young girls on the continent come into adulthood. Now, we have young lesbians going to proms together—an act I find magical even though I don't like proms (haven't been to a queer one despite my enchantment with ball gowns).

I didn't even learn how to make love to a woman until I was twenty-nine. (My first four lovers were stone.)

The controversy about lesbian porn is essentially a war between bad girls and good girls, a war I recognize, sadly, from high school. Those of us on the bad girl side want as many books and as many voices for lesbian sex as we can create. We claim lesbian sexual images as radical acts of freedom. We celebrate our existence in the one (and only) common ground we share—the love of pussy. I use that word *pussy* deliberately, reclaiming it as we have reclaimed *dyke*.

The good girls apparently think sex is dirty or ought to be contained or is private (simple answer to the privacy issue—don't read it if you don't like it) or that men will abuse us by enjoying our porn. I'm sure they will and do. That's not a reason to stop fighting for our visibility and our freedom, which was the original purpose of feminism.

It was called Women's Liberation.

These stories are liberating. I wish all of you the enjoyment which the selection process has brought me. Not all of these stories "turn me on" but I could see how they could turn others on. Putting aside my personal taste as much as possible (not entirely accomplished, as you'll notice a repast of delectable butches) in the interest of a widely enjoyed collection has dramatically changed how I think about my sexual choices. I know on an even deeper level how mysterious sex is.

The stories I've chosen spoke to me as a writer and as a sex maniac. They celebrate butches (still the most hated woman on earth, unfortunately, often by other lesbians) and trouble and humor and the games we can't figure out how to stop playing with each other. If you don't get off on these, get busy writing your own. The erotic is a source of our power as women. We live in a colonizer culture which continually uses that power—women as producer—for its own ends. Lesbians are the only women with a possibility of using this power for ourselves. In celebrating the joy of pussy, we change the world we live in. Somewhere a young girl will pick up this book and learn what it took me years to find out. Darlin', I embrace you. Don't be lonely. Have fun, use latex and stay wet.

juba
Letta Neely

for Renita

u be a gospel song
some a dat
ole time religion
where the tambourine git going
and the holy ghost sneak up
inside people's bones and
everybody dancin and shoutin
screamin and cryin
oh jesus, oh jesus
and the people start to clappin
and reachin back to african rhythms
pulled through the wombs of
the middle passage
and women's hats start flying
while the dance,
the dance they do gets hotter and holier
and just the music has brought cause for celebration

yeah, u be a gospel song, girl

like some a dat ole back in the woods, mississippi river kinda
gospel
and i feel the holy ghost when you is
inside me
and the tambourines keep goin
and folks is stampin they feet
and oh no,
it's the neighbor knockin on the door
askin is we alright
say we was screamin
oh jesus, oh jesus
and i heard us but i
didn't hear cuz
i was bein washed in the gorgeous wetness of
your pussy
being baptized w/ ole time religion
the oldest religion there
is
2 women inside the groove
of each other
we come here
we come
we come here
to be
saved

Notorious
Alison L. Smith

She was best in the flickering light of a movie theater, our faces
turned away from each other, our hands following their own
course downward. She fumbled her way from the top button of
my shirt collar to my skirt, parting its damp folds with her hands.
She coaxed me, with whispers, with small noises, as if she were
begging a dog out of the road. Our eyes never left the screen; we
stared at the narrow ribbon of flesh between Ingrid Bergman's
halter top and the waist of her palazzo pants, that one inch of her
enlarged on the dust-speckled screen.

We were fifteen when we met in Sister Bartholomew's English
class. My desk was pressed up against the back of her chair the day
Sister's habit caught the late-summer breeze from a low window
in the first-floor classroom at Our Lady of Perpetual Sorrow
School for Girls. As she turned away to adjust its tight band at her
neck, the girl in front of me tilted her head back. A strand of her
strawberry-blond hair fell between the open clasps of my binder
as I snapped the metal fasteners together. The straggled ends
caught there, pulled taut; she gasped. I curled that long strand
around my finger, kissed it, and released her. Christ stared down

from his station on the powder-blue wall, his loincloth slipping.

The next year she cut it off with her mother's kitchen scissors. Her shorn hair fell in kinky strands over her father's shaving brush, her older sister's neat zip bag of eye shadows, the opaque whiteness of her mother's Ponds cold cream jars.

"Do you like old movies?" she asked, one hand following the line of her cropped hair along the dome of her head, the other hooked into the clasp at my locker's handle.

"I don't know," I told her, school books pressed against my chest, my hip slung out, leaning into the locker's cool metal surface.

All I knew was that I wanted to press closer to her than I thought was possible, that my clothes felt too small in her presence and my skin itched with an ardent, heated rash as if I were allergic to my school uniform, its soft weight against my breasts, the skirt falling in even, pleated lines over my thighs.

In the balcony of the old Tower Theater on East Avenue, next to the glass-walled Cadillac dealership, catty-corner from King Prince's diner on a crisp November afternoon, she showed me *Notorious*. Ingrid Bergman, Cary Grant, Brazil, 1946. The theater swelled with the odor of mildewed carpets, moth-worn upholstery. The ancient hinges on the seat bottoms whined as they yielded to our weight. My hands wrapped around some iced drink, my mouth poised on the sharp edge of a straw, we sat in the balcony and abandoned our school bags to the dark recesses of the littered floor.

Even before the opening titles finished, she moved her thigh up against mine, let her left hand fall across my knee. With her right, she caressed my mouth, ran an ink-stained thumb over my chin. Her fingertips rested in the small dip at the base of my neck. Our eyes darting across the lighted screen, her hands traveled to the rounded Peter Pan collar of my blouse. The small buttons, pearlized, caught in the screen's dim light, glowed beneath her fingers.

One button at a time, she moved my blouse out of the way, whispering in the darkness "Please, please, please." Her mouth, hovering above mine, that even, repeated tone on her breath, the words barely audible, over and over she said it to Ingrid Bergman, to Cary Grant, to the half-empty theater.

She found her way from the flat disk around my nipple to its rising tip, ran her middle finger along each rib. Her hand paused at the white edge of my underpants. Then, traveling the circumference of the worn, elastic waistband, she played along that edge till she got up the courage to pull me to her. One arm around my shoulders, guiding me over, she settled me between her thighs, my back curving into her chest. Our eyes fixed on Ingrid Bergman's full mouth, her hand slid down farther, squirreling in between the worn elastic and the untraveled skin below.

When she entered me I gasped. The couple in front of us stirred, the man, his brush cut tickling his girlfriend's cheek, turned around, squinted back into the shadowy darkness. She put one finger in, then pulled it out, returned with two fingers. She pulled out again. I followed her fingers down as they left me. She returned with three, stretching the untried muscles, her thumb on the outer rim.

I knew nothing of the wetness. I had never heard of it before, never felt such a rush of it. I thought it was menstrual blood, my period come early, or a kind of internal bleeding, her hand at the sight of the wound, cutting in. I filled her palm with it, spilled over, rivering into the narrow line between my buttocks, pooling on the cracked, leather seat. Her uniform skirt gone damp, its even pleats wrinkling under us, she added and subtracted her fingers into me. Three, two, one. One, two three. Working faster, she matched her rhythm to the increasing speed of my breath. All the while her small whisper continued, like a ticking clock at my ear, "Please, please, please."

Her thumb traveled to my clitoris, running over that elongated spot with a flickering exactitude. I arched into her hands, my breath came hard. Then, a catch in my throat; for one long moment I could not breathe. I felt something buzz around me, something almost tangible, a cloud hovering over me, waiting to descend. As Ingrid Bergman leaned over to the airplane's small window, her lips parting, the Brazilian landscape opening out beneath her, it fell and I came for the first time.

It's five years later, it's seven, it's ten, and still when I walk into a theater I walk into her. My scalp tingles, my hamstrings contract. The air, close around me, opens up to her form. The worn wood of the seat arm softens into the edge of her biceps. Already her thigh presses tight against mine. Already she is descending on me, her mouth at my ear, her hand between my legs, the fingers adding and subtracting into me. One two three. Three two one. I arch back, spread my legs wider. There, in a high corner of the balcony, the safety bar cutting the screen in half, dividing Ingrid Bergman at that flash of white skin, I remember the mottled and flickering light on my classmate's face, Ingrid Bergman floating out of the screen, her mouth on the lip of my mind, the edge of that white abdomen, that narrow ribbon of flesh, like a road, a rope, a signal light flashing, flickering in the half-empty darkness.

Meeting Halfway
Peggy Munson

This is because she likes to be protected, I think to myself, stretching the belt taut between my hands and pressing it flat over her mouth, to hold her lips shut and her head to the pillow. This is because she likes to be protected, I think to myself, as I buy her bondage bracelets, a dog collar, as I ease my hands into leather gloves. This is because she likes to be protected, I think to myself, as I hold her down on the bed.

This is because she needs me as much as I need her, I think to myself, as I pull into the parking lot of the hotel. I hate arriving first, worrying she won't show up. All I can do is think of ways I would like to remind her of what I can give her that nobody else can. When she finally pulls up, late, I want to punish her for making me wait. All I can say when she taunts me in the room, though, is "Fuck you," like some monosyllabic child whose parents cuss around the house. I repeat it again and again, "Fuck *you*," with different emphasis, until she finally taunts, "So, why don't you fuck me, then?"

I circle her a few times. I know she dressed for me, even though she's tried to look like she pulled something off the floor just to cover herself. She gives me her cutest hangdog expression because she knows she has pushed me just as far as she needs to. I pull her to me, kiss her roughly, unbutton the fly of her Levi's with my thumb and forefinger, let her stand there for a minute while I examine her. We know neither of us will be satisfied sitting around talking. We've been waiting. My hands shook in anticipation when I took the keys from the desk clerk.

I push her onto the bed, yank her down over my knee, and pull down her Levi's. I stroke the softness of her underwear, the cottony, well-washed softness of it. She wants the reprieve of exposure. She wants me to know her quickly, forget formalities and bring the secrets of her blood tingling to the surface. But first I stroke the cotton, as if I were getting myself off in a fabric store imagining a wealth I never had, fondling the finest velvet, the tightest weave of silk, the frivolity of gingham. I bend down and kiss her where her spine starts to curve inward, then lick the top of the elastic. She moans quietly. I move my hand in slow circles on the cotton, over the curvature of her ass, down the quiet ravine into the warmth of her cunt. I hold my hand millimeters away, just thawing myself there, and then press slowly against her cunt to see how wet she is. I bend down so my lips are right over her ear. "I know what you need," I say to her. "I can make you wet just by telling you." She groans slightly, and I say to her, "You need to be exposed." I position the knee of my bent leg so it is pressing into her clit and lifting her ass slightly. "Don't you?" I ask, grinding into her there.

She doesn't want to say anything. I press my knee in a little harder. I want her to feel a dull ache but not too much, not enough. She doesn't want to ask for more but I know she wants it, she wants it quickly, her cunt is salivating for my hand.

"Don't you?" I ask a little more firmly, pressing my forearm down on her head to hold her there. "Don't you want to be exposed?"

"Yes," she answers. Before she can even breathe through her

quivering lips, I yank her underwear down so I can look at her ass. It's the color of sand, perfectly windblown and smooth from a distance and slightly rough closer up. Her asshole is a purplish-brown around the edges, puckered. Her cunt is open like a hungry animal and visibly moist. I stroke my hand down the crevice of her ass, then run one finger along the darkened edge of her asshole, just inside the line where the skin tone changes, up and down, so slowly she is lifting her ass into the air unconsciously, wanting more. When her back is arched and her ass is lifted high enough for my taste, I give her a very quick slap on the highest, palest point of the arc so that her spine quivers and she moans. The echo stays in the room with a kind of tension. Her body is tight as a spring. Our ears are perked up, both of us waiting for that sound again. I knead her ass cheeks and then squeeze them together, between my other palm and my body, so that the flesh is gathered close for my hand, and I spank her hard, several times, so fast she doesn't have time to gasp. I release her and her reddened ass relaxes over my legs.

"Did I say you could stop lifting it?" I snap. She curls her ass upward, obediently. I examine it with my gaze for a minute, though I know she wants my hand. I look at the blotches made by her blood rising to the surface. I look at the way her asshole seems to be widening like the pupil of an excited child. I look at the downy hairs that grow deep in her crack. I look at her cunt, staring up at me, the nectarine of a thirsty summer. I slap her cunt lightly, making the wet *thwap* sound of a snapped towel. Then I slap her inner thighs, the edges of her labia, the spaces close to her asshole. These are gentle slaps, growing slightly harder and louder as I progress, falling into a simple rhythm so that she knows what to expect. And then I surprise her, slap her hard on the fleshiest part of her ass, so hard she falls forward from where she was lifting herself, and her open mouth moans into the pillow where it lands. Then I resume the gentle slaps, this time spreading the cheeks of her ass with my left hand and spanking her right on her asshole, trying to make it open up for me, making her tremble involuntarily, her ass pulsing towards my hand in expectation.

"Your ass is so red," I tell her. "And warm. Touch it." I pull her hand forcefully down to touch the warm, puffed skin where my hand has fallen, then spank her hard where her hand isn't, so she collapses onto me because she cannot brace herself.

"That's it," I say. "Relax." I spank her hard and fast repeatedly, all around her ass, varying the tone, the way I cup my palm, the way it lands, until it sounds like a kind of applause.

"Do you like doing this?" she asks, insecure, timid, when I have stopped to catch my breath.

I spread her cheeks open again and stroke one finger slowly up and down the crack. "Oh, yes," I say. I feel myself getting wet. I feel the heaviness of her vulnerability and the weight of her trust. My cunt hovers on air above her like a thundercap.

I lean down and move my tongue around her earlobe, into the shell of her ear, through the tiny labyrinth at the top. Her ear becomes moist with my breath and my tongue, and I feel the heat and condensation of my words when I speak. "I want so much to go inside of you," I say.

She moans. Her eyelids tighten.

"Oh, please," she begs.

The room we are staying in tonight could be anywhere. It has the standard two beds, the nightstand with a Bible in the top drawer, a round table and two chairs, a television in a cheap particleboard TV stand. We've turned the TV on to mask the sound, because somebody might wonder, somebody might knock when they hear the echoes of my hand. A cooking show is on, and interspersed with my slaps rises the voice of the chef. "The inside should be tender and pink…" he says. Slap goes my hand on her ass. "They can bite when they're alive…." Slap on the tender skin around her asshole, slap on her quivering cunt. "Cook until moist and the outside is lightly seared…." Slap on the back of her thighs, her ass, her cunt, her ass. She is moaning deliriously and then I fuck her, my finger sliding slowly into her asshole, in and out. The sounds of the TV rise in the background, and I imagine someone watching us, I imagine the voices are people watching and her ass is pointing to the camera, wide open and exposed. Her asshole puckers around my finger, squeezes, then widens. "Oh, honey," she says. I give her more then, two fingers, sliding gently in and out and then harder, with the full force of my weight, the crook of my arm working like a fulcrum.

"Too much?" I ask, spanking her hard while I'm penetrating her. She doesn't answer, so I spank her harder.

"Too much?" I ask again. She shakes her head. I spank her harder. She is biting the sheets. I spank her again and again with my fingers thrusting into her. Then, in a moment of pause, I gently pull myself out. "Don't move," I say to her. I untangle myself from beneath her and she keeps her ass up in the air, waiting for me.

"Beat them into soft peaks…" the TV chef is saying. Her red ass is high in the air like a cherry lollipop while I strap on the dildo I have brought. "Don't move," I order her when I see her flinching in discomfort. She wriggles her ass higher for me and I adjust the dildo in the rubber ring. I climb on the bed behind her and grab her hips with both my hands to pull her ass back and higher into the air. I spread her knees apart slightly. Her cunt hangs down heavily from the weight of its hunger. I rub the dildo against her wet labia so gently she thinks it's my hand. "Close your eyes," I say to her, and when she does I open the lips of her cunt with two fingers and press the dildo up inside her, quickly, so that her body almost buckles. She is so moist and ready it slides right in, and I move it in and out until her sounds get deeper, her mouth widens as if on the same circuit as her cunt. Her throat opens too, so that her sounds are more hollow, deeper, as I thrust into her. I feel the flat end of the dildo pressing against me, too, and it makes me want to fuck her harder so I can feel it pressing into me. I grab at her hair like a mane, ride her bareback for a while, reaching around and squeezing her breasts while I push into her. We fall into the same rippling motion for a while until I feel like we are on the same carnival ride, the same garish, cheap ride.

I'm sure sleazy things have gone on here, in this room. It is a bargain-traveler, lunch-hour-with-your-secretary kind of place. The Bible hides in the drawer like a silent witness, recording stories. We've been in other places like this one, meeting halfway between our homes, in the middle of nowhere, because we might get caught by those who really own us. I can't help it; I kiss her on every elevator, sticking my tongue into her wet mouth, then walking off when the door opens as if nothing ever happened. Of course, it is those who try to be the Easy Riders of sex who always capsize, and it is like that with us. When I am inside her in this room, I want to stay inside forever. I want to quarantine in her body.

When I thrust into her one last time, she starts heaving out noises I don't understand. At first I think she is laughing, then I realize she's crying. "Oh, sweetie," I say to her. "Honey." I stroke her back while I pull gently out of her. "What is it?" I am concerned. She falls onto her side and I am next to her, pulling her to me, squeezing her. "Oh, God," I say. "What is it?" For a minute she is sobbing too hard to talk, and then she pulls me closer to her, sealing all the seams of our two bodies.

"I feel so naked," she says to me. "Will you cover me?" And I do, I pull the blankets over her, pull her close, press my body into hers, stroke her gently and say, "Sweetie, I'm here." This is because she likes to be protected, I think to myself, holding her against me. And whatever I fucked out of her pours out for a good ten minutes while the cook on TV whisks, beats, purees, and tastes the "exquisite balance" of what he has created. Meanwhile, we enjoy our symbiosis for a minute, the flow of her tears against my chest where I'm holding her, the intertwining of our legs. I think how I'd like to walk up to her on the street, where we would pretend we're not together, then drag her into an alley, press her hard against a brick wall and kiss her there, feel the friction of her leather jacket against my breasts, the warmth of her flesh beneath the tough hide of her, the softening of her body beneath mine, time and distance melting away.

The cheap hotel has a certain neutrality, like household objects that are as basic and complex as the wheel. And she, too, has spanked me here with belts, with lobby magazines, with a single calloused hand. She and I like to switch our power game: we like to meet halfway. And I can tell, once her tears relent, that she is creating castles out of garbage again. She scans the room. I can almost see her mind concocting beautiful, B-movie fantasies.

"That table," she says to me, pointing to the corner of the room. "I plan to bend you over that table and take you later. If you're lucky."

She and I, we like the simple pleasures.

I give her a conspiratorial smile. Then I kiss the moistness off her cheeks, counterproductively, as my lips make her wetter and the tenderness makes her cry more. Finally she just pulls me into her with our full bodies pressing tight and says, "I can't believe I let you see me like this." And then I think I love her.

Alchemy
Toni Amato

Alchemy. The mystical art of turning rough stone into precious metal. There are pure and good reasons why I love this woman. And there are other reasons. Personal reasons.

Here's one.

Valentine's day. I love her, truly I do. My wrists ache every time she walks into a room. But I'm bad with dates, and I'd been working my ass off, and I was so tired I could barely remember what day of the week it was, never mind if it was special or not. Two hours before she was going to come home I heard an advertisement on the classic rock station I was listening to. Don't forget that special girl on Valentine's Day. Shit. I forgot. What to do? I'm so in love, and I can't blow this, can't let her down.

I decided to do what any red-blooded Sicilian butch would do: make her a dinner that would roll her socks down. Exquisite. I can make a spaghetti that makes you want to weep, or fuck. Both, really. I'd fill the kitchen with flowers and music and delicious aromas. Then make love to her for hours. Good old-fashioned lover boy.

When she came through the door, the air was filled with the aromas of melted butter and roasting garlic. The soundtrack from

Diva was playing, because she loves opera and I love to hear her sing. Wine and roses on the table. Only, she'd come home early and I wasn't quite ready. Not finished with all I had to do.

Have you ever tried to keep your mind on cooking when there is a gorgeous woman in the kitchen with you? Ever tried to not cut your finger, drop the spoon in the sauce, just let the whole damn thing burn?

She stood in the doorway. Actually, she leaned against the doorway, shoulders back, head tilted, eyes scanning the scene. She didn't say a word. And she didn't look at me. What she did was open her lips just wide enough to release sound, and begin to sing.

She sang along with that beautiful diva, and I had to stop chopping because I had to close my eyes and listen. Listen like I was drinking it , like every pore of my skin could take in sound. I stood and let her voice fill the room, wash over me, and I knew she knew what I was up to. I knew she knew that I could not hear this without wanting to make her sing another kind of music, just for me.

"Open your eyes." She'd never interrupted the music before. Sacrilege to disrupt. But there it was, I'd heard it. "Open your eyes." And I did, because her voice had gone deep and strong, and in that voice she could tell me to step in front of a truck, and I would.

She knew this, too. I opened my eyes and looked down at the scattered onions, the pile of grated cheese. The smells were still there, still overwhelming. And there was another scent, then. Her.

"Look at me."

I lifted my head, and as soon as I saw her, she started to sing again. But she'd let her hair down, and her hands were slowly unbuttoning her shirt, pushing aside silk fabric to show me what I live for, what I really would die for. She was stripping for me, this woman. To opera. I told you there were reasons why I love her.

Breasts and belly and that sweet, sweet ass. Have you ever watched what singing opera does to a woman's face? Really watched it? I could no longer handle the knife. I could no longer stand. I had to sit down and watch, because this was definitely a command performance.

She had never done this for me. I had begged her a thousand times to do this for me and she had always demurred. I understood this was my Valentine's gift. I understood that dinner would just have to wait.

She was stripping, but beneath her office clothes she was not naked. A red lace bra and red lace thong. She knows me. She knows the sight of her ass is divinity to me. She knows this, and I could not believe the things she was doing. Could not believe this could be done to opera. She moved across the room and stood in front of me. Stood in front of me and lowered herself to her knees as the music ended. I wanted to stand to applaud, but her hands were on my belt.

Have you ever noticed the way a singer's eyes shine after a performance? Ever noticed how full her lips become with the swelling of the song?

Her hands were on my belt and she looked at me. Looked at me and said, "I'm so hungry," as she loosened the buckle. I wanted to die. I wanted to fall through the floor and die. Every butch's worst fear. I wasn't ready. I was not ready for this woman's desire. I took her face in my hands, all remorse and regret.

"Oh, baby, I'm not wearing it. I'm not wearing it right now. I'm so sorry. I got so busy with dinner, and I…" She didn't let me finish. She put a finger up to shush me and as it came to rest on my lips, I caught the scent of her.

"I know that," she whispered. "Don't worry. I'm not waiting for that. I was so excited coming home…I was so excited to see you that I took care of things." She smiled shyly at me. She smiled because she knew I didn't understand. Smiled and leaned back on her heels as she began to show me, began to show me exactly what she meant.

And I have begged for this performance, too. Have pleaded with her to please God, just once, let me watch her get herself off. Just once be an audience to her solo. She never had let me. Until then. She leaned back and dropped her hands to her cunt. One hand spread her lips while the other moved in slow circles, moved and dipped through shining wetness. And I knew that this, too, was part of my present.

Have you ever watched a woman get herself off? Have you ever watched a woman make love to herself? Ever had a woman make love to you with the rhythmic motions of her hands on her own body? She rocked back on her heels and spread her legs wider, let her head fall to the side. I watched as her thighs shook and belly arched and she sang out again and again for me.

"I took care of things, and now I'm so hungry." She sat up and reached for my belt, sliding the leather out through the loops. She laid the belt on the floor and slowly pulled my zipper down.

"Oh baby, did you hear me? I'm not ready for you, baby." I put my hands over hers and tried to stand. She pushed against my hips and shook her head.

"No. I think you are ready. I think you are very ready, and I'm so hungry." She looked up at me, all expectation and desire. "I'm so hungry, and I think it's time for my present, now."

Caught. I was caught. She'd given me so many things I'd begged for, given me so many of the things she'd always said she was too shy, too afraid to do. Such a big heart. And now I knew it was my turn, knew she knew that, too.

"It's your turn to sing." Her voice was thick and low and I couldn't deny her, couldn't fail to return the gift. I sat back and sighed, as she asked, "Don't you want to feed me?" Her hands tugged my jeans down and she lowered her face to my briefs. Warm breath through damp cotton. The pressure of her mouth. Her fingers traced the edge of the waistband.

"I want to go down on you. I want to make love to you, right now."

The heart is a place of courage as well as a place of love, and mine was full to bursting. Full the way my cunt felt full, the way I'd spent years denying it could be. And my girl, my sweet, sweet girl was on her knees, begging for this gift of taking. I nodded, and she bent her head.

Fingers pulling my briefs down, brushing gently through the damp hair beneath. Fingers laying softly to each side and opening me. Stripping me to where I'd never been naked. I had to close my eyes. I sat, trembling, waiting for what would come next.

"God, you're beautiful," she whispered, "I want to look at you. Want to just look at how beautiful you are."

Have you ever had your mind blown open by a gust of breath on your most private parts? Have you ever felt what it is to have your secrets exposed? I felt tears start behind my eyes. Real men don't cry, and I started to weep as I felt her mouth on my lips, her mouth loving my own swollen lips. Her lips on mine. Her tongue, and her breath and even a nip of teeth and I don't remember what else. Don't remember anything else but the music in my head and the sound of her murmuring and my own breath raging.

I don't remember when her mouth became her hand and I felt myself opening to the inconceivable. I don't remember when it happened, but I remember it happening, I remember the feeling of her hand entering my body as if she were reaching right straight up into my heart and squeezing it, hard. Squeezing and releasing. Again and again and even my breath was in her control and I don't remember if I was sitting or standing or lying on the floor. Don't remember the words to the song she taught me. But I know I sang. I know I sang and she joined in. I sang to the tempo she was teaching me, squeezing and releasing, until there was only the music and the rhythm of her hands conducting me. I don't remember when the music ended. But I remember looking down at her when it was over. I remember looking down at her and thinking that if I could ever speak again, I would sing songs of praise, sing my own psalms, until there was no more breath in my body.

Have you ever seen a woman's face after she's made love with her mouth? Ever really seen the way her lips are swollen and her eyes shine? I looked down at this woman kneeling naked at my feet and realized I would spend the rest of my life hoping to keep her well fed.

What more could a red-blooded Sicilian butch want?

Jimmi Veneer
Andrea Tetrick

The other night around eleven at the Fallopian Lounge, Jimmi Veneer pulled her left breast up tight to the bar and asked me to join the band. I didn't expect the offer, so I gulped my beer to cover my surprise. I killed the pint and said, "Sure, why not." Not so much because I believed like religion in the band and the idea of the band—the way Jimmi did—but because I liked Jimmi Veneer's hows.

How she held her tangy cigarettes, pinched between one long finger and thumb. How she chewed her whiskey before swallowing. How she rolled her sleeves something like a million times when she was thinking about something really important, which was most of the time. How her crooked smile made me feel in my middle when she flashed it at me.

For three fat seconds (which is a very long time when you've been drinking) she stared at me with that smile, taking me in. My face got hot. She bought me another beer. She laid out the practice schedule. Then Jimmi gave me a homemade tape with four songs the band wanted to record, plus her calling card, just in case I "needed to get in touch." The card was something else:

JIMMI VENEER

FORWARD IN ALL DIRECTIONS

1(800) GRL-N-GRL

While she kissed me goodnight on the forehead I started hoping real hard I wouldn't fuck things up by breaking out in another tragic and damaging crush. Sure, I wanted her. But I didn't need to go falling in love and all.

She left me there with my pint, her empty glass, and a smoke still burning in the ashtray. Picking up her cigarette, I twirled it over my fingertips, then took a hit. I held the smoke in my lungs for a long time, like I would marijuana. I exhaled, carefully stubbed it out. When nobody was looking I put the butt into my own cigarette case. I returned the case to my pocket, along with her card and the practice tape. Then I let myself touch the spot on the bar graced by Jimmi's long-gone breast. I didn't get home till five in the morning, groggy and pretty drunk, but I decided some bass practice wouldn't hurt. I busted the E string and passed out on the couch.

The next day I hauled myself from the couch, changed my shirt, and brushed my teeth. I didn't have time for much grooming. I rode the Metro to the National Gallery and waited for Jimmi to show. I'd heard she was working on some project and was hanging around the museum a lot. Waiting for my hangover to clear, I sat on the rim of a fountain, taking in all the bellies and thighs of the naked statues in the entryway.

I wandered into the hall with all the postimpressionists to look at a couple van Goghs. In one of the rooms I found Jimmi Veneer, standing jaunty and cross-legged in front of a canvas layered with paint. A damn fine sight she was, in a long coat and boots, with a scarf pulled back to show her throat. I walked up behind her and coughed. She whirled around, her eyes going wide before kissing me hard on the mouth. "What was that for?" I asked, covering my lower lip with three fingers. A few people turned to gawk, but Jimmi didn't seem to mind. She didn't seem to notice I was following her, either. Maybe she didn't care. She kissed me again, this time running the tip of her tongue over my incisor. Swollen and stuck under my ribs, my heart jerked out a crazy pattern.

"I'll show you," she said, straightening her scarf. Jimmi fished around in her coat pocket, pulled out some paper, and unfolded three typewritten pages. "See these?" she said, holding out the paper. "These are notes." She waved the pages around so I couldn't get a good look at them. "About what happened the last time I was here. Conducting a study for a magazine article." Jimmi raised her voice a notch. "About women and public sex." She smiled her crooked smile, refolded the paper, and returned it to her pocket. More people looked our way. I wanted a cigarette.

She told me I looked like shit. I agreed in a loud voice, and that finally upset the speech of a tour guide jawing on about orchards and asylums and fragments of ear. The guide, a pear-shaped lady with varicose veins, glared our way. Jimmi grabbed my hand and we scrambled from the room. She aped the guide in a pinched British accent. I just laughed, scared to say anything that might break the spell.

We ended up in the modern wing, surrounded by ridiculous paintings done all in one color and deformed plastic sculptures. I wasn't into this shit, but Jimmi was fascinated by the larger paintings, the ones that took up entire walls. "The scope," she kept saying, "The scope. Most people don't think this big. But I do." She pulled the typewritten notes out of her pocket again, handing them to me. She asked me to look them over, let her know what I thought. "The writing's rough, but I'm gonna fix it up and send it to this sex mag I read. I know one of the editors," she said. "I think I can get it published."

I nodded, slipping her words into my breast pocket, near my cigarette case. Jimmi took my arm and steered me toward a huge mural by a guy named Rauschenberg. She stared at it for ten minutes or so, absorbing every inch of it. I couldn't breathe for her hand on my arm.

The second I got home, I cleared a pile of newspapers, some empty soup cans, and a broken clock from the kitchen table. I pulled out Jimmi's papers. I lit some candles and incense, locked the door, and sat down on my only chair. Smoothing out the pages, I began to read:

> *A lot of fucked-up feminist thinkers believe that women who engage in public sex are involved in a complex control dynamic, attempting to claim the inherent power of a traditionally "masculine" sexuality. They associate all sex with power and then go further by assigning sexual behavior—especially public sex acts—to the sphere of men, since men have historically held exclusive sway over this domain. I myself tend to think these feminist thinkers are full of shit, mainly because they are thinkers and not doers.*
>
> *During my most cynical hours, I often want to pose a set of questions to this particular brand of abstract feminist: "Why trouble yourselves to live as powerful women, unafraid of the rules of conduct established by men? Why go that far, when all you really have to do is call yourselves "feminist thinkers" and lay out your own set of restrictive rules, spend all your time labeling behavior and cataloguing types, categorizing every last creature who has the misfortune of being sucked into your clinical little world...until you don't have any energy left for sex*

and you've alienated all your prospects, anyway?" At the same time, I say to myself, "Why not?" And so, whenever I can, I go out and have sex. In public.

The first time I sought out public sex was at the National Gallery of Art in Washington, D.C. To gear myself up, I half-heartedly cruised art students for an hour or so. Soon growing bored, I took on the challenge of older women of leisure.

When positioned in a social phalanx, these ladies are unapproachable, impossible to pry apart or distract with small talk. The only thing for me to do was herd one away from the gaggle, into a far corner of the museum, and engage her in discussion about a particular artist's brush strokes or sense of light. Separated from her familiars, a woman of leisure grows attractively vulnerable, suddenly removed from the stabilizing forces of place, caste, propriety. I particularly liked playing games with these stranded creatures because insecurity and lack of control seemed to bring out the life in them, to conjure up their humanity.

Accordingly, I noticed a lovely olive-skinned woman in her forties, flecks of silver in her dark hair and a slightly pink bloom to her mouth. She scrutinized a Cezanne with such passionate reverence that I thought perhaps she was conscious enough to notice a bit of flirtation. Deciding to forgo the verbal angle, I gently brushed against her flank. She stepped away sharply. I grabbed her elbow and begged her pardon, smiled and let my hand caress the soft inside of her arm before I removed it. She smelled good.

Puzzled, and a bit alarmed, she nodded at me and moved with great dignity to another painting in the hall. She was well bred, this one, I could see. She didn't wish to reveal how flustered she might be. I stayed where I was for a few seconds, then walked behind her to position myself at a painting to her left. I noticed she stiffened a bit as I passed behind her. She watched me from the corner of her eye as I pretended to contemplate the artwork before me. I stared straight ahead but very slowly moved my hand to my throat and began to unbutton my blouse. First one, then two buttons. I had her full attention. She faced me, instead of her painting. My chest heaved a little from the excitement of being watched by this stranger. I parted my blouse a bit so she could see the curve of my breasts beneath the cloth. I dropped my hand to my side and continued to study the painting in front of me.

I let it go on this way for another minute or so, then turned toward her, desire etched on my face. I smiled, then ran my eyes down the length of her body. She flushed, glanced at a guard whose back was to us across the way, looked at me with a mixture of confusion and horror, then slowly backed toward the doorway leading to the neoclassical rooms. I didn't follow. I knew nothing would come of it, but I was impressed by how well she bore the strain of another woman's public pursuit. I walked to another hall as if nothing had occurred. I alighted in the modernist wing, still a bit aroused by the thought of a woman's gaze upon me, the thought of this beauty knowing I had eroticized her while I touched myself. I told myself I would soon return, perhaps with a more willing subject.

I was pretty worked up after I read through the notes. I wanted to read more. I wanted Jimmi Veneer rubbing up against me. I wanted sex or a cigarette, maybe even a drink. Anything, really, to occupy my mouth. To get my mind off sex, I put on the band's tape and listened to it a few times before plugging in my bass and playing along.

I spent most of the night learning the bass part to the songs. I wanted to be ready for my first practice the next day. Later, around midnight, I checked in at the Fallopian, but none of my crowd was in sight. Neither was Jimmi. I took my usual spot at the bar and Maude, the bartender, slid me a beer.

A cute little dark-haired thing (my weakness) got to flirting with me. She kept asking me to dance. I told her I didn't go in for that stuff, so she started calling me butch. I said she didn't know what she was talking about. She tried to buy me a beer, but I caught Maude's eye and threw a bucket of water on that fire. The little charmer wouldn't go away. I thought about breaking down, but I didn't want word to spread that I was fooling around with some little tart. Just in case Jimmi heard about it.

Now, I don't like stirring up things, but between her tapping on my shoulder for an hour and continuing with the butch thing, I finally had enough. I swiveled my bar stool around to face her. She moved in, running her nails up and down the length of my thighs, pressing hard enough to leave lines on my jeans. Then she started kissing on me. Shoving her away, I took a good look at her. Smeared makeup and glassy eyes. I told her to beat it. Maude chimed in too, cutting off her booze.

The girl stood there pouting, then started yelling and calling Maude names. Maude is a gentle woman. But she's big, and if she wanted she could toss you around like nothing. So once she headed around the bar toward the girl, I thought it was all over. My admirer lit out of there pretty quick after that, though. Good ole Maude. She looks out for my interests. I swallowed the last of my beer and stood to go. As I walked toward the door, Maude called after me, "You got lipstick on your chin, kid."

I showed up at Jimmi's place on the corner of M and 9th Streets with my bass slung over my shoulder. I was a little early, so I sat on the curb across the street and smoked a cigarette. Jimmi lived in a drooping old row house with five other dykes. They had two stories, an attic, and who knows how many bedrooms. The attic, soundproofed with thick foam pads stuck together with duct tape, was where the band practiced. I'd been up there once before when a friend of mine took me along to photograph the band for the cover of their second record. I stood there, holding the camera bag and lighting equipment. It was the first time I laid eyes on Jimmi Veneer. She was the only member of the band who talked to me that day. In my own way, I'd been trying to talk to her ever since.

Before I went up to the door and rang the bell, I opened my cigarette case. Jimmi's old cigarette butt was still there. I gave it a little squeeze, for luck. A girl in the band named Ginger answered the door. She was dressed like a go-go dancer. She let me in. I'd seen Ginger around but I could tell she didn't like me much. Jimmi used to date her and I think she still had a thing about anybody prowling around her ex. We climbed up the stairs to the attic, where the rest of the band waited.

Jimmi Veneer leaned against the far wall with one bent leg tucked behind her. She wore her shin-length jacket over a white blouse, with black trousers tucked into motorcycle boots. She clicked a pair of drumsticks together and introduced me to the band. There was Angel, who sat behind her drum set, sporting a pompadour and the beginnings of a goatee. Nice eyes. Two women dressed alike in sweatshirts and jeans sat holding hands on an old car seat, propped against a wall. The lovebirds turned out to be Molly and Jane, the guitarists. Viva, a girl I knew from high school, played violin. "And I guess you know Ginger," said Jimmi, strolling over to Angel and handing her the drumsticks. "Our keyboard player." Ginger made a little curtsey in her miniskirt and sneered.

We plugged in, tuned up, and started out with the hardest number, a song called "Valerie S.," in which the drummer sits out and the bass and keyboard act as the rhythm section. Jimmi walked over to a microphone, set down a tempo, and off we went. Everything started out fine, until Ginger decided to get cute and speed up the pace to throw me off. I didn't pay any attention, laying down my baseline to match Jimmi's vocals. Finally, Jimmi stopped and told Ginger to quit fucking around so we could get some work done. We ran through the tune again and my part came off without a hitch.

We practiced for an hour or so. When we finished, Viva and Jane told me I sounded pretty good for my first time. Angel handed me a beer. We wandered downstairs and talked for a while before I got up to go. Jimmi walked me to the door. I told her I liked the stuff she'd written so far for her article. I was going to give her back the notes but changed my mind. I lied. I said I forgot them at home. "No problem, I have another copy, " Jimmi said. She rolled a sleeve. "Will you meet me at the Fallopian Lounge tomorrow, around two?" I nodded and then, right there in front of everybody, she pressed me against the door and gave me a long, delicious kiss.

That night at my kitchen table, I dug out Jimmi's card and stared at it for the longest time. I thought about calling her, even dialed her 1-800 number, but I hung up after one ring. I didn't want to push too hard. Opening my cigarette case, I picked out Jimmi's cigarette stub. A bit of tobacco fell from the end onto the table. I brushed the brown flakes back into the case, wedged the butt back in, and closed the lid.

I don't know why, but Jimmi's cigarette reminded me of this crazy queen I used to know. I guess I didn't want to turn out like him. He was in love with that guy from REM, Michael Stipe. That was all he could talk about. Michael this, Michael that. I was over at his house smoking dope one day, when he asked me if I wanted to see his prized possession. I didn't really care but I said sure, since he was getting me high and all.

He sorta skipped over to this little table in the corner, covered with REM stuff. In the middle, in front of a white candle that he never blew out, was something wrapped in foil. This guy picked up whatever it was with both hands and brought it over to me. He slowly unwrapped the foil and held out a hard piece of buttered bread, a perfect bite taken from the middle. "Garlic bread," he said breathlessly. "Taken from Michael's plate at a restaurant in

Athens, Georgia."

I didn't believe it at first, until he told me he knew some girl that worked at the restaurant. After Michael left, she bused the table, saved the bread, and sent it to him. I asked him why he kept it on the table, where it would disintegrate or something. His face lost color. I told him he should freeze the bread so it would keep. He rewrapped the bread, rushed to his refrigerator, and lodged it between some ice trays and a bottle of tequila in the freezer. I never went over to his place after that. He had good smoke, but he was just too freaky for me.

In the morning, I called in sick to work. I went back to bed for a couple hours, then got up and played my bass for a while. I ate some cereal, smoked a cigarette, and ran some water for a bath. I had to clean up for Jimmi. Taking my time, I clipped my nails and rubbed lotion all over my body. I even put on a little cologne, this stuff called Drakkar Noir that some girl I dated gave me once. I dressed in my best pair of black jeans, a clean white shirt, and a gray silk vest. Grabbing my jacket, I left for the Fallopian. I felt pretty good.

Jimmi Veneer was already sitting at the bar with a beer when I showed. She tried to buy me a pint but I refused. I wanted a clear head. Clarice, the daytime bartender, poured me some coffee. We didn't say much, just sat there sipping our drinks, staring straight ahead until Jimmi turned to me with a wild glint in her eye. "I want you to fuck me," she said, studying my face, "at the museum." I'd figured it was coming, but I flinched a little, anyway.

I took my time answering. I reached for my cigarette case. Jimmi bummed one, too. When I flipped open the case, she noticed the cigarette butt. "What are you, on a budget?" She gave me one of her lopsided grins. "If you're that hard up for cash, I'll buy my own pack." I grabbed two cigarettes and shut the case— quick. Jimmi took one, slid it between her lips, and patted her pockets for matches. A flame jumped from the end of my lighter.

Eyes on me the whole time, she steadied my wrist and lit the end of her cigarette.

While we smoked I asked Jimmi how she came up with the idea for her public sex article. She ordered another beer and a shot of whiskey from Clarice. "I couldn't sleep one night, so I started writing in my journal about some things I didn't like about feminism," she said. "The movement is so politically correct you can't get anything done, can't tell the truth with any passion just in case you offend somebody. It's obscene." She pulled out a small black notebook from her jacket pocket, flipped through it for a moment, and shoved it back in her pocket. "I figured public sex was a big enough topic to make my point. I wanted to write about something with scope. Something over the top."

Stalling for time, I decided to order a beer. I burned bad for Jimmi, but I wasn't too sure I wanted to end up a statistic for her notes, either. I asked why she didn't like feminists. "Not all feminists. Just the ones who use feminism as a political platform to ram their own morality down our throats." She finished her first shot and asked Clarice for another. I had never seen her drink so much before. Jimmi slammed her whiskey and said, "Well? Are you in or what?" Sitting there, hands curved around my beer, I made up my mind. I took a breath and said the word I'd wanted to say for so long. "Yes."

We didn't waste any time once inside the museum. Jimmi led me to the room I'd found her in last time. Five people wandered from painting to painting; a young couple, two ancient ladies, and an art student working on a reproduction of an ugly Gauguin. Removing her jacket, Jimmi walked over to the leather bench in the middle of the room and draped herself across it. She wadded up the jacket and shoved it under her head, for a pillow. "Come here," she whispered, unbuttoning her shirt. I did what she said. Removing my own jacket, I climbed on top of her long body. We kissed. Her lips tasted like whiskey and smoke. We kissed some more, I don't know for how long. I forgot about the people in the room, until out of the corner of my eye I saw the old ladies scuttling out of there. Nobody else moved. The couple stared down at us, horrified. The student snapped out of it and took out a sketch pad, following our movements with a pencil. Jimmi giggled.

I pressed my weight against her and slipped my hand under her open shirt. Her bare breasts on my palm made me wet. Fingering her thick, rosy nipples, I began to grate my pelvis against Jimmi. Underneath me, her body rose and dipped in time with mine. Beyond the reach of my teeth and tongue, from the back of her throat, she made a little sound. I pulled a little on her nipples with one hand and started to loosen her jeans with the other. I wanted my hands on her, everywhere at once, and then my mouth. I didn't care where we were, who was watching. I wanted her.

After I pushed myself up to straddle her belly, I slowly worked Jimmi's pants down to her knees. She wasn't wearing underwear. I fell on her again, sucking and biting her stiff nipples, while rubbing my thigh between her legs. Her juices glistened on my jeans. One of the spectators said something I couldn't make out. I looked up to see the couple leave in a hurry, the man dragging the woman by the elbow. It was just the three of us, now—Jimmi, me, and the student making wild scribbles on her pad. But I could hear loud voices coming our way, and footsteps.

It didn't take very long after that. With my mouth, I worked my way down Jimmi's body until I planted my face in her crotch. She shivered, then grabbed my hair and forced herself against me even harder. I licked at her and sucked like crazy, feeling her thrash on the bench. She pressed her thighs together so tightly I thought my head would burst. Without taking my tongue from her skin, I drove three fingers into her and twisted inside. Then, right there in the National Gallery, in front of the art student and a stunned security guard who appeared from nowhere, sputtering into his walkie-talkie, I made Jimmi Veneer come all over.

Jimmi heaved me off of her, squirmed into her jeans and leapt to her feet. She backed toward a wall and pointed behind over my left shoulder. Trouble. Picking up my jacket, I turned around to face the security guard and one of his buddies. They were multiplying. As the two guards closed in on me, Jimmi whooped and grabbed a statue in the corner, making like she was going to push it over, rip off an arm or something. "Split up!" she shouted, as the guards, three of them now, charged her. "Meet you at the bar." Just as one of them, a brute with a nasty mug, was about to lunge for her, she feinted to one side and ran in the other direction. She didn't fool one of them and he plowed straight for Jimmi, knocking her into the wall. Her shoulder slammed into a painting pretty hard and it fell from its mounting, crashing on the marble floor. I heard the frame crack. The painting diverted the guards long enough for Jimmi to reach a door at the far end of the hall and disappear. That was the last I saw of Jimmi Veneer for a long time. I shot out the door on the opposite side of the room, pushing my way through people in the entryway. I made it outside, ran down the steps, and broke across Constitution Avenue, cutting up 6th Street to lose myself in the rush-hour crowd.

I expected to see her laughing to herself at the bar when I walked into the Fallopian, but she wasn't there. I paced the length of the bar for a while, but then I couldn't take it any longer. I went into the bathroom and jacked off, leaning against one of the stall doors. It was better than nothing. I waited for two hours, dialing her number over and over. She never answered.

I called in sick again the next day. Still no word from Jimmi. Around noon, Maude called to tell me that some dyke lawyer had stopped by the Fallopian, taking up a collection for Jimmi. She was in jail, charged with about a million counts of assaulting a police officer, resisting arrest, destruction of property, having sex at the National Gallery, and being drunk and disorderly. I told Maude that Jimmi wasn't drunk, she just had a few drinks in her system. She ignored me. Maude said the guards finally cornered her at the museum and handcuffed her until the police came. When they went to take off the cuffs, she hauled off swinging at the cops, kicking and biting, anything to get away. A judge set Jimmi's bail at fifty thousand dollars, because of the assault charges and the messed-up painting. Nobody had the money to spring her, and her trial wasn't for another month. Things didn't look so good.

I moped around my apartment all day. I tried to play bass, but I couldn't concentrate. Besides, how could there be a band when its leader was stuck behind bars? Around six the phone rang. It was a collect call from Jimmi. I accepted. She didn't have much time to talk, but she wanted to ask me a favor. Anything, I said. I told her I was sorry that she got caught, thanked her for keeping the guards off me. "Forget about it," Jimmi said. "You can make up for it by bringing me a couple notebooks and some pens. So I can finish my article." I agreed and she gave me the details about visiting hours for the upcoming weekend. Before she hung up, she said, "I don't regret it, you know. You did something for me."

Right then I knew Jimmi Veneer would never let me touch her again. I hung up the phone and opened my cigarette case. Empty, except for Jimmi's cigarette stub. I lit up the butt. It still tasted pretty decent. Smoking, I decided not to visit Jimmi. I was nobody's chore girl, not even Jimmi's. Sure, I'd send her the notebooks, maybe even give them to ole Ginger to deliver. I laughed. She'd get a kick out of that. I also decided that I wouldn't read Jimmi's article when it came out, either. I didn't really want to see what we did together pared down, laid out on paper like that. All dressed up with big words and fancy theories. But no guts. The memory was enough for me. I smoked Jimmi Veneer's cigarette right down to the nub.

Gems

Susan Rosenberg

"Jo, Jo," she said, "you have to go now. The rest of this is mine, I don't want you to come any further." How could I possibly let this woman go? I took her face in my hands. I put my lips to hers, felt the rush of her heat, and rocked back and forth. Then I slowly kissed her eyelids, her forehead, around her face, her lips, her neck. Slowly, lingering on each spot, wishing I could memorize every cell. "I want to come with you." I whispered. "No, not now, you can't," she said, as the wind swallowed her words. She mouthed "I love you" and pushed me away. I hesitantly obeyed like a chastened child. When I turned to look back, my beautiful woman, my Lily was gone.

I shuddered, and in some deep inner region of the body normally untouched, a terrible stabbing ripped my heart. The smell of cement filtered into my head and the salty sea of my dream was replaced by the concrete cinder blocks of my cell. I couldn't surface, didn't want to wake up. My heart was pinned to the bed, my limbs immobilized. I struggled into full consciousness. God, I hated my cell. I hated every bit of the tomblike cage. Lil. Lil. I couldn't bear the wrenching pain if this was how it was going to be for the rest of my life.

I knew that Lilith had died while I was dreaming. No one had to tell me; she'd come in the night to say good-bye. I wanted to strangle something, tear it apart, I wanted to run back onto the dark beach of my dream and pull her out of the water she'd so quickly and calmly walked into. And if I couldn't pull her out I wanted to dive head first and swim right after her.

Someone else was present during my lover's passage into death; she was in the prison infirmary. I'd only left to lie down for an hour. I was so angry that I was not there. Later, after I got to the hospital, they told me she opened her eyes and seemed to stretch and mouth the word "yes." Then she stopped breathing. There was nothing left to revive. She'd wasted.

The silence was intense, and strange since the prison is always noisy, even in the infirmary. I wanted to believe I could feel her presence as I stood over her. I wanted the calm to filter into me and quiet the terrible pounding. Wanda, Lily's inmate buddy, had shushed everyone out of the room to give me time alone. Wanda knew better than anyone that Lily had saved me and loved me like nothing else, and Wanda felt as I did that we had not been able to give much in return. We couldn't save Lily. Her death from AIDS was an anomaly to her spirit. It was like watching an oncoming bus driving in the middle of the road, knowing that you were standing in the road and couldn't get out of the way. I had to touch her one more time, I had to take her in my arms, brush my face against her dreads, whisper to her. Her lips looked sculpted and full. I wanted to kiss them but I didn't. My sadness stopped me. There wasn't a point to it really. I turned to go. My glance took in Lily's altar, her statue of Buddha and her meditation beads. The beads looked like polished stone though I knew they were wood. I walked to the table next to her bed and picked up the smooth and worn mahogany beads and fingered them, trying with all my attention to feel what she felt in them. I put them on her hands. Turning on my heel, I walked to the door. Wanda, a big buxom

Black woman, formerly a nurse, threw her arms around me, and with tears streaming down her face said, "Take that Buddha with you. Her mother won't appreciate it. Now, don't go hiding, I'll be seeing you! Right?" I stumbled out of the room, stuffing the carving into my jacket.

As I wandered aimlessly I had flashes of her. In the beginning we'd talked about finding love for the first time when you're already older and how it's different from youthful love. I'd said it fills a void that you already have adapted to, even made friends with. Lack of love can be something you adjust to as a lifelong state of affairs. The "lonely companion" was what I'd named mine. And then you fall in love, and it's so unexpected it shakes you to the core, throws you overboard. At least it did me. I had tried to explain this to Lily but she told me to shut up, love is love and philosophy ruins it. And she buried her lips in my neck and started laughing.

She laughed a lot. Her enthusiasm about even mundane things always startled me. We'd eaten the same pie at some meal a hundred times before and she'd still swallow it with relish as though she'd never tasted it before, treating it as a rare and delicate morsel. I would simply watch in amazement.

As I walked around the prison I couldn't catch my breath. I had millions of thoughts and my mind was a total blank at the same time. For months I'd told myself I was prepared for her death. At one point it got so bad that she finally screamed at me, "Don't bury me before I'm gone." She hadn't applied for compassionate release because she wanted to be with me till the end. Her mama took it as her final and ultimate act of betrayal. Lily said, "I love them, but you're my family too and it makes no difference where I die, I just want you there." I didn't argue. We pretended she'd last long enough for me to get out, and then she'd go home.

The days merged into each other. I put one foot in front of the other. Wanda found me and we talked. I accepted everyone's condolences. It was so strange, because inside I was completely shattered. It had to show, and when I looked in the mirror I saw that it did; I looked stricken and old. But everything just continued, the wheels of prison life didn't miss a turn. I tried to keep the routine, but it wasn't the same. I did my laundry but no one else's, I shopped but didn't buy anything. I kept looking for Lily. I tried to be casual, almost covert, using my peripheral vision, so no one would know what I was doing, looking, searching for my friend. Every time I saw someone with dreads, I looked twice and the pounding in my veins rose with each stolen glance. Despite all our preparations and discussions, I couldn't see my way clear. I tried to think of all the things she'd told me to do. One day I woke up panic—I couldn't see her face, couldn't conjure it out of memory.

Later I found a pressed flower and a note in an old shirt pocket I'd stuffed into the back of my locker. I didn't open it. I needed to save it. It was a communication from beyond, it seemed, and I felt it was the last time Lily would ever speak to me. I carried it around a long time, sticking my hands in my pants pocket and fingering it. When I felt it was time, I went to the tree in the yard. Lily and I had loved that tree. We'd spent hours under it, sitting and watching the prison life around us. Other times we'd been a thousand miles away, playing with dreams. I heard us laughing, but as I looked at the tree now, so barren, it seemed withered and I couldn't remember why it had called to us.

I sat down under the tree, but I wanted to lie down on rocks by the sea. I wanted to feel the jagged edges of those cold stones pierce my flesh. I wanted the stones to sing to me and carry me away in search of Lily. Really I wanted to die. I couldn't find my way out of all this sadness. I had not thought about dying as much as this ever before. And it wasn't even about being in prison, because what had been so wonderful about loving Lily was that we had managed to transcend our situation. Sitting there, I realized that we'd done prison, not the other way around. I hesitantly took the neatly folded note and shook out the petal. In my hand it was translucent. It was from a yellow tulip. Lily was always finding flowers and plants and saving bits and pieces of them. When I saw the neat little script I started to shake. The petal, the note, her bracelet, a cowry shell, her Buddha carving were her legacy to me. The tears finally flew out of me. I heard this horrible cry wrenching out around me, and didn't recognize it as my own scream. I stopped, pulled myself together. It took all my strength. The note read:

> *Jo—don't be crying. You blew my mind. Not to mention my body. You made me feel all right with all my different selves. Being Black, being Buddhist, loving a white woman, living and dying with AIDS. What you did for me, now do for yourself. Besides, I'll see you in the next trip. Okay? And remember to laugh whenever they wax the floors. My beautiful long-limbed darling, so elegant. (Still wish I could be described that way, yes, vain even in death. Ha.)*

I shook the tears out of my eyes. Sex, I hadn't been thinking about sex. But sex was part of this. And the floor waxing—our cover. Sex had been important from the beginning. Lily had loved my body, and it was mutual. Even after she told me the results and in a moment of terror said, "Now it's over, now you'll leave me, I'm repulsive," never for a second did I think she wasn't beautiful. I like to think if we'd been in the free world our sex together would have broken records in different kinds of pleasures. But in here we'd done pretty good, even after the HIV. I've thought a lot about this HIV stuff. Lily and I had the '90s conversation before we ever made love. I'd had it before, she never. We felt safe. Later I understood that Lily was not in touch with all this. But only later.

We fought about my getting tested. It was our first fight. My view was I didn't want to know, and I wasn't that worried about it anyway. I thought if I was infected it would make it harder for Lily, that she'd blame herself. When she started to get sick and didn't respond to the drug therapy, I focused all my energy on her and didn't give a damn about my own state. But after the umpteenth go-around she convinced me that if we knew she hadn't infected me she would fell better. We went together to get the results. When we walked in the doctor didn't tell her to get out. She simply said, "Negative." Lily grabbed me and kissed me right there, forgetting all her fears. The doctor didn't look. We flew out of the infirmary. "Doctor Rowen must be gay, don't you think?" Lily said. "Maybe," I said "Or maybe she's a rare thing around here, a human being."

Throughout Lily's sickness I never stopped wanting her. Lily's sexual self was as wondrous as anything else about her. As I sat on the hill and reread her note I realized how selfish I'd been about refusing to get tested for so long. The most explosive lovemaking we had was the time Lily thought she'd infected me. Remembering the floor waxing, I smiled. Just like she'd written. I remembered:

"I want to see your whole body," I said, "I want our bodies next to each other, every single inch of them. I'm exhausted from all this fifteen-minute sex, kiss and run, orgasm by minutes. I can't stand it."

"I know," she said. "But you know I'm just uptight. It's not my lack of passion. I don't want to go to the hole for it." Lily frowned.

"Let's get someone to watch for us, someone we trust, just for one hour, I want one solid hour."

"I don't trust anyone, let's do it in your block." Lily sighed. She was tired of this conversation.

"Where's my stout-hearted lover? Come on." I said laughing, making it easier. We thought and thought, and we finally figured a way.

I knew we had an hour, not more. The steel door closed with a clang and I put a paper over the window. Then I put a can at the foot of the door and tilted it at an angle so it would fall over if the door was opened. While I was making my safety preparations,

Lily was standing with her back to me, looking out the window. Her shoulders were hunched and the tension oozed out of her. I put my hand on her neck. "Baby, it's okay, we're cool. Here, I'll hang a blanket." I wanted to kiss her, and lick her, eat her till my tongue fell out. I wanted hours, but our minutes were ticking. "Baby, come here." Lily seemed to focus, breathe, she pulled off her shirt and moved to me. Her arms were around me and her tongue was in my throat. Eyes open, she blew her breath into me. Her tongue was my old friend, as she moved it around my mouth. My hands moved over her breasts and under her arms. The curve of her waist and the flowing hips jumped at my touch. Her nipples darkened. My shirt came off and our chests pressed into each other, warmth flowing between us. My wetness turned into a flood. She looked at me and her black eyes crinkled up. "Okay you take off your clothes," she said. My pants were off in a flash. I heaved hers down to her ankles and she stepped out of them. She stepped back and stared. She ran her hands up and down my body, slowly, touching, feeling. She pulled my nipples. "You're better naked, so very elegant." We laughed. I didn't feel elegant—more like a wet dog. "And you're a siren," I said. We'd been lovers for months, and this was the first time we were naked together. "Let me lick you, let me lick you and watch you at the same time," I said. I laid her down on the bed and spread her thighs. Her skin color, so different from mine sucked my vision into her. On my knees I began to explore and see even deeper colors. Her vagina was the most splendid one I'd ever seen, red, tight, smooth, and with each stroke she shuddered. My tongue flicked around the rim, and then toward her clit, which started to grow. Her nails were on my scalp. I lost myself in her cunt as her cum came down. I licked and pulled and her hips started moving. Tongue up, hips up, tongue down, hips down, and up and down, and then we had a rhythm and she started moaning and her breasts grew in my hands, as I pulled her clit with my whole mouth and rubbed her breasts, her face in deep concentration, and my heat enlarged with clit throbbing as she got closer and her rocking and moaning grew. I felt her orgasm at the root of my tongue and I stopped. Lily shuddered and looked at me as I came up from between her legs with her juices dripping all over me. I was soaked up to my forehead. If I could have put my head into her cunt I would have. If I could have crawled into her vagina and into her womb I would have. "Jo, don't stop, not now," she pleaded. "Lily, hold it, hold it, and then it's more intense. I won't leave you." "I can't, Jo, fuck me, I want you to fuck me, come on, fuck me." I bit her nipples hard, one then the other, as my fingers went to my own cunt to find the moisture. My fingers slid up to her legs and found their way into her. Her lips were spread and her clitoris was open; out and full, my hand went up, and she sucked it in. The walls circled my fingers. It was a fine fit. "I've never told you this, but I like it hard, baby, do me hard," she whispered. And then I was on top of her, kissing her neck, face, breasts. My hand had a life of its own plunging in and out. And then Lily started to buck and rock. "Harder Jo, harder."

"Oh yes, you like it hard, me too, I like to give it hard, anything you want," I screamed into her ear. "Let me fuck you, let me fuck you till you split in two, let me fuck you here, and let me fuck you in your ass, baby. Your beautiful round ass. I've wanted to fuck you there since the moment I saw you." And then she gasped a scream so as not to scream and draw a tip and came and came and came. With ragged breaths I looked at my watch. Thirty-five minutes left. The wax on the floor outside our cell, which was our ploy, would be dry; now it was just hardening. Lily was breathing deeply, her eyes closed. The dampness had reached her dreads. We were slick, and where sweat and cum and saliva began or ended didn't matter. "I went away, far away to somewhere I've never been," she said, grabbing me around the neck, pulling me on top of her.

I ran my finger down her behind into the crack. I squeezed her bottom. Her beautiful bottom, with the little folds of flesh where her ass ended and her thighs began. Her weight was right there in her ass and legs. My fingers went to her ass and circled it slowly, teasing, touching, brushing her, moving between her clit and her ass. She looked at me with those almond eyes, dreads spread out on the pillow. Her blackness struck me all over again, She was beautiful. "What time is it?" she asked. She was stalling me, I knew.

"We have a half hour, it's okay."

"I don't know about this, this ass thing, Jo."

"Baby you'll like it, you'll see." I got on my knees, split open her legs, and put my tongue on her lips. My whole mouth covered her and I sucked her as hard as I could, my tongue flashed to her ass and I licked all over her. I wanted her ass, but her tension was speaking to me. She shook her head. "I can't do it."

"Please, I'll go slow, you'll see there's nothing like coming from two places at once. You'll see, trust me." And she loved it, and I loved it. And the next thing I knew we weren't on the bed but on the floor, both of us naked, glistening and fucking beyond belief.

The clock gave us five minutes. We unstuck ourselves. Lily was laughing; her energy had a marvelous quality. "I'm speechless," she said "I'm wowed."

"You look insane; you know we cannot go out like this. We reek of sex." I got a washcloth and wet it and rubbed her face, and then mine, and then I took it and rubbed between her legs.

"Imagine if we were free, imagine, Jo."

"I have, Lily, believe me I have."

"This is serious, I have something serious to say, I trust you, Jo." I knew her to be telling me the truth. I was happy.

I said, "Lily, you know I never say these words, they are hard to say, you know. I love you."

"This is different, altogether different," she said. I knew she wanted to ask me things, and I would have explained as best I could, but we had to go. "I forgot where I was, that has never happened to me before." I nodded, and I pushed open the cell door and stuck my head out. I saw Lena at the end of the hall. She was pushing a buffer. "Is it dry? Can I walk on it?" Lena shook her head and said, "Jo, you're so out of it. I haven't even started." Lily started laughing and poking me.

I blinked, and for a breath she was in front of me. Standing over me, her eyes shining. She was blowing me away again. Lilith was the love of my past life certainly, and my future love as well. There was no denying it. To me our loving had been like a huge boulder flinging itself down the mountain, cutting through all that was in its path. And when the enormous rock hit bottom it unearthed ancient fossils never before seen in the light, and on the way down the stones that were pulverized later turned to gems. Lilith was my gem in an otherwise rough field.

there

Cynthia Greenberg

dark. what i imagine. a blackness that is all light and no sound. a blackness i can't move or see through. a blackness that is you. in the dark where we go, where you will take me, i will be taken. i will be had. i will be whole. you will come like a shadow swallowing the night. all hesitation. fear. when and where. you decide. that is the press of this. you. will. deciding. fancy is the treacherous thing. what it includes. who is to say. where. struggle and pleasure the same. what is the divide. it will be dark. it will be you. it will be heavy. it will be hard. i will stay. i will be still. where will you take me. what will you be.

here is the rub: why should it matter. what should it mean. my body leans. i am clear. dragons are not always to be slain. you and your hands. the rough want of need. it is more than measure. you hold more than full.

there will be lightning. there will be shame. there will be you. skin. limb. change. texture is not about cloth. choosing is not about time.

On Wheels
Sacchi Green

Suli strained her dark head away into the stinging snow. My grip
was steady on her cold, slim body, which could bear no touch,
even mine, yet scorched me with the need for hers.

She clutched the door key like a talisman. I held her above the
thigh-high drifts until the cabin door swung open; a gust of snow
made it through before I kicked the door shut, but then peace
enveloped us.

I stood catching my breath in the stillness. My arms must have
tightened; Suli did her best not to struggle, but panic edged her
husky voice.

"My wheels! Katje, please, my wheels!" I knew by her blank
gaze that she was groping toward that damned contraption. It
should have been beyond the range of her implant, but I wouldn't
have bet that the chair's control panel wasn't responding even
now, casting a green glow on the swirling snow around the van.

That wheelchair meant more to her than any human. It was no
use saying I could carry her anywhere in the cabin, anywhere in
the world! No use—disaster!—to tell her how much I wanted to
carry her, to feel her arms around my neck, her head against my

shoulder, her soft hair pressed against my face instead of straining away. My breasts ached and my nipples tautened, and I swore silently.

"Wheels. Right." An inner storm still ripped away my breath. I nudged the light switch with my shoulder, grateful that the electricity hadn't failed—yet—and got her to the couch, her shoulders writhing so in her panic to be free that it was all I could do to keep from dumping her.

It was no use complaining. We'd been through it all before. "Get your wet coat off, and then I'll shovel a path and bring in the chair." I ignited the kindling laid ready in the stove and pretended not to watch her wrestle with the bulky parka.

She got it mostly off, and I eased it away without actually touching her. When I tossed a blanket over her legs she clutched at it and tried not to let me see her shiver.

"Shoveling will take so long."

"Shall I just wade through the snow with the damned thing over my head?"

She seemed oblivious to my bitterness. "No! Don't carry it! If you stumbled in the snow…" She'd rather I dropped her than the wheelchair.

It was no comfort that she seemed to think I *could* carry a two-hundred-pound wheelchair that far. I wasn't all that sure myself, considering the snow, but six-feet-two of what my former boss used to call "busty blonde Valkyrie" has its advantages if kept in working order. If only Suli appreciated some of its other advantages!

I did have to half-carry, half-drag Suli's wheels. The snow kept drifting across the path faster than I could keep it cleared. I left the chair to warm by the stove while I brought in the rest of our gear. By my final trek Suli, of course, had summoned her wheels to her side.

I could tell the effort had hurt. Using the remote-control implant was often painful, especially when she was tired, but she was determined to master it and advance to more complex controls.

The wheelchair was a high-tech affair that went beyond state-of-the-art into experimental territory. The large wheels could still be turned manually, or driven by a joystick-controlled motor, but there was another set of controls that responded to impulses transmitted by a tiny implant in Suli's brain. Besides being able to propel the chair, she could manipulate segmented leg rests for physical therapy and electrical currents for muscle stimulation. She didn't need me for much any more.

If she got adept enough at controlling these functions mentally she'd move on to the next level—when it was perfected. She might, they said, with the help of brain implants and quasi-robotic braces, be able to walk again. But no one believed she would ever regain true feeling below the waist.

She bent her head when she saw me coming. I wondered if it was to hide her strain, or to commune with the machine in privacy behind the long, silken curtain of her hair.

Either way, I was wrenched by a hot surge of rage. Jealous of a metal-and-transistor contraption, for Chrissake! And just because she leaned on it, and let her hair brush over its surface instead of whispering across my hungry skin. And because she struggled so to master the therapy she used to accept from me.

What shook me most was the revelation of how bad a case I had. And how hopeless.

"Come on, I'll help you into the chair, and then we'll fix some supper. I'm ravenous." But not for food alone.

She put her hands on both chair arms so that she could support her upper body herself. Then I swung the rest, the part she couldn't feel, into position, and she gave a twist and ended up seated.

One of these days I'd find that she'd made it all the way into the chair on her own, using the remarkable strength she was developing in her slim arms and shoulders. Her courage was maddening...and supremely, intensely arousing. However seductive her tender mouth and satin-smooth skin, it was the steel beneath that held me and wouldn't let me go.

She followed me into the kitchen. She was wearier than I'd realized; the green light was dark, but she wasn't rolling manually either. Tonight she gripped the joystick, usually reserved for long distances on campus, and let the motor propel her.

Even hunger couldn't block out my irrational resentment of her grip on the thickly padded stick. It wasn't as though I had any corresponding organ for her to grip, after all…and thoughts in that direction could only drive me deeper into frustration.

Suli's family had been glad to hire me. She was ready to return to law school, but not ready to concede that she needed a personal care attendant. She could just about steel herself to let me give her what physical help she had to have. Even beyond that, I knew that she felt some genuine comradeship with me, and that, insofar as she could admit to needing anyone, she knew she needed me.

But not, God help me, the way I needed her.

I shoved back my chair and stood up. Suli usually cleared the table herself, but now she just sat gazing dreamily at her hands as they moved across the arms and controls of the wheelchair in leisurely, sensuous strokes.

I watched as she lightly traced the wheel rims and then the spokes and then, just barely reaching, the hubs. The green light and the smaller blue and amber ones flickered on and off as she caressed them with her mind.

If she'd been trying to drive me insane she could hardly have done a better job.

Then she started to massage the leather sheathing on the joystick. I had rigged it like that myself, padding and covering the cold metal to keep her hand from cramping, exaggerating the size and phallic shape out of some perverse sense of irony. I was being punished for it now. When she began to tease its tip with her thumb in tiny, deliberate circles I kicked my chair over and didn't bother to right it.

"I'm going down to the cellar for more wood."

Suli didn't even look up.

When I got back she was rolling along very slowly, no hands, her face intent. I straightened my fallen chair and moved a few things to clear a circuit in one kitchen door and out the other. But she seemed content just to roll a few feet forward and back, over and over.

"The wind's getting worse," I commented. "I'll be surprised if we don't lose electricity. Maybe I'll stay downstairs tonight to keep the fire going."

Her eyes still held that dreamy look, but at least she heard me. "I like to hear the wind," she murmured. "I can feel it vibrating through the house."

The house felt solid enough to me, but I didn't think that was what she meant. She was in a strange, fey mood. I sank onto the couch and waited for more of it to be revealed.

"Sometimes I almost think I can feel certain vibrations," she went on, her tone even lower and huskier than before, "deep down where I shouldn't be able to feel anything at all." She stared down into her lap. "The wind...the motor when my mind's plugged in...even...sometimes...your voice."

My insides clenched, and I had trouble breathing. *Her* voice seemed to slide inside me and touch some deep and hungry place. *Does she have any idea what she's doing? Or where she's leading me?*

"Read to me, Katje," she whispered, "read poetry to me. I want to feel your voice."

I wasn't sure I still had a voice, but I didn't need any book. The verses I had yearned, had never dared, to say to her were already sweet and heavy on my tongue.

" 'The Song of Songs,' " I murmured, " 'which is Solomon's.' "

She looked up, directly into my eyes. She did know. And she knew what was coming.

The words flowed from somewhere ancient and compelling. I missed some verses, repeated others, mixed King James and Revised Standard versions, but certain phrases resonated through my body in a thrill of longing.

" 'O that you would kiss me with the kisses of your mouth! For your love is better than wine, your anointing oils are fragrant, your name is oil poured out....'

" 'Behold, thou art fair, my love...thine eyes are doves.... Thou hast doves' eyes between thy locks.... Thy two breasts are like two fawns, twins of a gazelle, that feed among the lilies.... Thy navel is a rounded bowl, that never lacks mixed wine.... I am my beloved's and my beloved is mine; she feedeth among the lilies.'

" 'You have ravished my heart, my sister, my bride...honey and milk are under your tongue.... A garden locked is my sister, my bride, a garden locked, a fountain sealed.... I adjure you, by the gazelles or the hinds of the field, that you stir not up nor awaken love until it please....'

" 'Make haste, my beloved, and be like a gazelle...upon the mountains of spices.'"

I was on my knees beside her, my hands clenched on the arms of her chair. She made an effort not to shrink away.

"Suli, Suli, tell me what you want! Don't just...I can't stand..." I took a deep breath and leaned back, struggling to give her space. "If you'd just try to let me touch you, just a little...so gently...so feather-soft you wouldn't be sure my hand was really there..." I tried to stop, but the words kept coming. "Let me show you! So softly, lightly, that your flesh melts with sweetness, throbs against my hand, longs for more and more. You can feel that, I can make you feel that."

The chair rolled slowly backward. I let go.

"I want to, Katje." Her words were more breath than voice. "I want to feel you, but..." She raised a hand as I leaned forward, and the wheels carried her another few feet away.

"I keep wondering, dreaming, what it would be like, to feel what you feel. Don't they say it's all in the mind, anyway?" Her fragmentary smile held a hint of self-mockery. "Couldn't you…tell me what it feels like, and maybe I could feel something too."

A surge of anger mixed with hot tension. I stood up and began to unbutton my shirt. It was feeling painfully tight anyway. "So just how does this fantasy of yours go?" My voice was as hard as my nipples.

"I want you to…to be doing it here, on my wheels, while I'm on the couch, plugged in, feeling the chair feeling you. Am I making any sense?"

"No, but what the hell!"

Firelight flickered over us, hollowing out a warm, private cave rimmed with shadows. Outside, wind and snow wrapped the cabin in chaos. There was a surreal feeling to it all that made anything seem possible.

My shirt was open; without another word I bent and unbuttoned hers. She shrank away, but this time I ignored it. I picked her up, and in spite of her struggles pressed my mouth into the satiny hollow of her throat that had been making me crazy for months. Then I dumped her on the couch.

"Just feeding among the lilies. If I can give, you can give a little too." The flash of anger felt good.

Then I looked at the damned wheelchair, and the anger nearly overwhelmed me. It was just a medium, I told myself, a conduit. If she thought she could feel me through it, maybe she would. Too bad it didn't work both ways.

I couldn't do it sitting; my legs were too long for the chair. I knelt on the seat as I shrugged off my shirt and unclasped the front hook of my bra. My tingling breasts, already straining against confinement, burst free.

I tossed the clothes aside and ran my hands lightly over my aching breasts and down my belly to the waistband of my jeans. I decided not to take them off yet. As wet as I already was, it was going to get a whole lot worse.

Suli's eyes were dark and deep. "Talk to me," she said. "Tell me how it feels."

"It feels," I said, "like you're trying to drive me insane. How about you?"

"Warm," she said. "Hot. Maybe it's the fire." She slipped her shirt off; her small firm breasts didn't need support.

" 'Two fawns,' " I whispered, " 'twins of a gazelle, that feed among the lilies.' "

Her eyes were on my great, swelling breasts. " 'Mountains of spices...' "

"You could taste...oh, God, I *want* you to taste, want it so much...damn, I can't tell you how much I want you to taste!"

I cupped the taut flesh, offering it to her like fruit, but she just said, with a catch in her voice, "*Tell* me about it, tell me how it feels! All of it!"

I could see my reflection in the window behind her. The chair back came about to my navel; above it my shoulders and arms were pale, my sun-browned hands contrasting with the dark pink of engorged nipples and the white surge of breasts as full and firm and thrusting as they had ever been. I raised my arms to loosen my hair from its long braid. Wheat-blonde strands spilled over my shoulders, stroked across my sensitized skin, and I yearned for it to be Suli's dark hair coiling over my flesh as she bent to nuzzle me.

Even as I watched, the chair turned under me so that I faced Suli in semiprofile, and the glowing green light signaled that she was in control. If I could just feel a connection, too.

I swung one leg over the arm of the chair. The armrest was cool at first against my heat; I tried to keep from rubbing my pulsing crotch along it. Not yet, not yet...My hands still moved on my breasts, the waves of sensation demanding more and more. She expected me to *talk*?

"It's torture!" I closed my eyes. "Torture I can't stop! I need it...so much...but I need it to be your hands touching, stroking, making me fuller and fuller…around the soft curves to the hard tips, so lightly, lightly that I have to beg for more…I need more, more, *please*, need you to keep teasing, feather-brushing, with your fingers, your tongue…oh God, please, your tongue, I'm bursting toward your tongue, your hot mouth, my nipples straining, reaching out to be licked, to be sucked, oh, please, damnit, please, suck me, hard, harder, *harder*, bite me, *please*, suck me." Ragged moans forced their way out as my own hands did what hers wouldn't do, teased and stroked and pressed and tormented and the aching need built and built.

I was writhing against the armrest now, pangs lancing from my swollen breasts down through my liquid-hot core. I hardly noticed at first when the wheels started turning; then, when I felt the chair moving back and forth, meeting my thrusts, I looked up.

Suli's eyes were half-closed, her mouth half-open. She was stroking me with the chair, moving it with me, the expression on her face so intent it looked like pain.

"Are you all right?" I could hardly gasp out the words. "Suli, does it hurt?"

" 'It hurts so good.' " A wicked little grin quirked the corner of her mouth as she breathed the cliché. "Just tell me more, show me more." Her own small nipples were bravely erect now, and I yearned to put my mouth to them. She had to understand.

"See how hard, how swollen…" I thumbed my distended nipples as I cupped my breasts, pressed them upward, gasped as the heaviness tugged at me all the way down to my crotch. "My clit is swollen even harder, every touch here is a stab down there."

I couldn't wait any longer. I slid my hands down to the waistband of my jeans. I unzipped and tried to wriggle out of them, but my hands thrust down to find my hot, wet cleft and it was all I could do to pull them back.

I had to stand up to get my jeans and underwear all the way off. When I straddled the chair arm again the wheels began to turn, and I felt a purring vibration against my naked flesh. The colored lights flickered as I slid back and forth across them. I tried again to talk.

"I feel it, feel you, but I need more! I need your hands, your mouth, your tongue reaching inside." I raised up and my own hand pressed and probed, finding the deep hungry places but only driving them wilder and wilder.

"Damnit, Suli, it's torture! I can't get all the way! I can't do it by myself, you've got to help me, touch me, help me get there, *please*, you're getting me crazier and crazier."

I arched back…and something moved, pressed, against my buttocks. It moved again, and I knew what it was, but I hadn't dreamed that she could control it.

"Katje…" Her face was tense and her hands were clenched. "Please, Katje, do it on wheels!"

My cunt was screaming to be filled, almost drowning out the thought that she was still fixated on the machine, not me. Then she said, "Let me do it to you like this, Katje, feel it with you, please…please…"

Suli was begging me. Suli never begged.

I raised myself tentatively over the joystick. The leather sheath was firm and thick, the padded rod beneath it hard. I needed hard, *needed* hard. I moved against the tip, slicking it with my own juices, then moved more, not sure how much I could hold.

The rod jerked. I gave up thought entirely, let myself sink onto the pulsating firmness, and clamped my thighs against the chair arm as currents from the electrical stimulators tingled through me. I let Suli fill me, fuck me, as the wheels carried me across the floor and I rose and fell against the maddening pressure, danced with it, arched into it like a figure-skating partner. I dug one hand hard into my breasts and pressed the other tight against my mound, and screams whipped past my ears as my clitoris leapt and surged and went off at last like a gong.

I was wracked with the glorious reverberations. Only after endless seconds did they subside enough for me to hear Suli's voice.

"Katje, please, are you all right? Katje…"

"Yes…don't stop…more…if I can just get my breath…" But the green light seemed to pulse into me, flooding deeper and deeper inside, building a demand that couldn't wait. I moved again on the joystick, and that mechanical cock that Suli's hand had clutched, that her mind clutched now, moved deep inside me as my cunt throbbed and clenched and spasmed and the pounding waves of orgasm swept me to total release.

Very gradually, through shuddering sobs, I realized that Suli was sobbing too.

"Suli…" I saw where her hands were and dismounted so fast it hurt.

"Katje…I'm wet…I'm so slippery and wet."

I moved toward her…nothing could have kept me from her—

She reached out to me—*reached out!*—and I stumbled to my knees before her. Her hands were soft and strong as she raised my arms and drew them around her waist. I laid my head in her lap.

She held on to me this time as I lifted her and set her in the chair. I knelt again before her, and as she leaned her head against mine her dark hair swung forward around us both; and at last, in the shelter of that soft, sweet curtain, I touched her.

Remote Control
Skian McGuire

It didn't exactly require split-second timing, but I was nervous, anyway. Weegee stood me on the sidewalk for one last look, oblivious to the gawking passersby. When she reached for my crotch to adjust the bulge in my pants one last time, I slapped her hands away. She threw me a look of hurt surprise. I shot my cuff and glanced pointedly at my borrowed wristwatch.

She got the hint.

The receptionist at the front desk was one of us, but Elena's secretary would be electrified by curiosity and disgust if she knew a woman in male drag was going to spend an hour in her boss's office. The troublesome twit was being sent on an errand at this very moment; we had just watched her leave. I had ten minutes to get into the building, up the elevator and through the corridors to get to Elena's office. Ten minutes was plenty of time, but like I said, I was nervous.

Even though I'd often been called "sir" at McDonald's, I didn't think I made a very convincing man. At least I was tall enough. Weegee had to stand on a milk crate to trim my hair into the ideal configuration, which included shaving it back slightly at the temples, much to my dismay. But I had to hand it to her: she thought of everything. I'm not the only one who thinks Weegee is a genius, either. Her clients call her an electronics wizard. I call her an electronics leprechaun. Height is my only advantage over her. Weegee is just a shade over five feet, but height is the only advantage most of the world has over her. I keep telling her that we big people sometimes get a little peeved to have somebody who looks like a parakeet run intellectual circles around us. She just looks at me with that wild glint in her eye, and I know she's thinking up another crazy scheme to rope me into. Like this one.

Oh, Elena, the beautiful, successful Elena. Weegee was devoting herself to fulfilling Elena's every fantasy. I don't know how many of Elena's other desires Weegee had managed to satisfy on her own, but in this particular instance, height was definitely a problem. While Weegee could easily pass for a twelve-year-old boy, twelve-year-old boys are seldom seen striding through the corridors of Brentnor, Brentnor, Grant, Green, and Williams in three-piece suits. As Weegee pointed out to me, a three-piece suit was part of the fantasy. If she could not fit the bill herself, she generously allowed that I was the next-best candidate, equipped with electronic devices that Weegee had lovingly created and would, in fact, operate from a distance. She would be waiting in the upper parking deck of the building across the street, where she could manipulate her dials and buttons from the privacy of her lipstick-red Miata. Weegee is nothing if not a control freak. A remote-control freak.

With one last tug at my vest, I was on my way. The receptionist made a low wolf whistle when I came up to her desk, and I had to grin in spite of my case of nerves. Maybe I ought to stop and get her phone number? Maybe on the way out. I made it through the halls with only one chance encounter; the young fellow was so engrossed in the papers he was reading that he didn't even look up as we passed. I heaved a sigh of relief when I turned the last corner and spotted Elena's nameplate.

As she and Weegee had planned, her office was not locked. I stepped in and closed the door quietly, turning the bolt behind me. She was standing in front of her desk with her back toward me, palms on the desktop, leaning, as she'd been instructed. I stood there for a minute, saying nothing, as I watched her. Even in a power suit and business pumps, even from behind, you could tell that she was a good-looking woman. I was looking forward to seeing more than just some shapely calves.

I cleared my throat. Elena jumped; I would have thought the tension in her shoulders could not have been wound any tighter.

"Take off your jacket," I told her.

She was wearing a pure white blouse of soft crepe, heavy and rich looking, with a row of buttons down the back. It clung gracefully to her well-made shoulders and tucked in at the neat waistline of her dove-gray skirt, which had a little "V" at the hem. I admired her lovely form as she trembled almost imperceptibly, waiting for my next move. Clearly, Elena was not an old hand at this sort of thing. But she was game. She laid the jacket neatly across one end of her huge desk and resumed her position without my having to tell her to.

In the silence, I could hear a faint buzzing, and Elena's head dropped as her legs squeezed just a bit closer together. Weegee's remote was working. She had cued the vibrator right on schedule. I could see Elena's shoulders rise and fall as her breathing quickened. I stepped up behind her, pressing myself and the hard bulge in my pants against her ass. Elena pressed backward, a low moan deep in her throat. I started unbuttoning her blouse, slowly, savoring the feel of the rich fabric underneath my fingers, listening to the delicate whine of the buzzer between Elena's legs.

The intercom on the desk phone hummed.

"Ms. Giardino, I'm back," it sputtered. Elena gasped but recovered herself quickly.

"Thank you, Jeanette. Would you hold all my calls for the next hour, please?"

"Certainly." There was a pause. "Oh, I'll be leaving in fifteen minutes. Should I ring them in to your office then?"

Weegee and Elena had set everything up for this day precisely because the secretary would be cutting out at four. Thank God she hadn't changed her plans.

"No, that won't be necessary, thanks. I'll take care of it later. I don't want any interruptions for an hour." Elena paused as if trying to remember if there was anything else that needed to be taken care of. The vibrator was still humming away. I guess it must have made it hard for Elena to think, and she soon gave up. "I'll see you tomorrow, then. Have a nice afternoon."

"Thanks, Ms. G. And thanks for letting me leave early."

I smiled. "You're welcome," Elena said, then pushed the voice switch to "off."

I undid the last six buttons and the blouse slipped off, pooling around her wrists and flowing down the front of the desk. Elena lifted one hand, then the other, and it fell softly to the floor. I unhooked her bra and it fell away, too. She shivered. The hum that was coming from between her legs changed pitch, and Elena's head dropped forward. She pushed her ass back against me, and suddenly I felt a faint buzzing coming from between my own legs.

Wait a minute, I thought to myself. *This wasn't part of the plan.*

The dick that Weegee had built for me was certainly a wonder toy. Its body was silicone rubber; besides an ingenious harness system, it included a knob by which it was anchored in my own cunt. At the business end, a tiny hydraulic pump hidden inside worked to force fluid into the cock, where it was imprisoned by a one-way valve, creating a hard-on much in the same way that nature did it. Except that I would get mine up by flipping a switch at the right moment; I thought that was as much technological extravagance as anyone could hope for. I didn't know the thing had a vibrator built into it, too. I wasn't sure I liked the idea, especially if Weegee was the one in the driver's seat.

My clit tingled, then throbbed. "Shit," I muttered. As if I needed any more stimulation.

Elena turned her head to try to look at me. I held myself rigid, trying to minimize the distraction. "Eyes forward," I growled through gritted teeth. She snapped her head back around and I willed myself to go on, clenching all my pubic muscles tight. I kneaded her breasts and rubbed my crotch against her ass. She moaned softly; then, abruptly, both our vibrators fell still. She made a little sound of disappointment; I heaved a sigh of relief.

I leaned back and raised her skirt.

Her ass was smooth and warm under my fingers; with her stockings held by a garter belt, I only had to slip my fingers under the strap that held her vibrator in place to feel her moist, swollen cunt lips. She was dripping wet. So was I, and what's more, my cock was getting rock hard.

I'd thought I was supposed to be the one to switch on the erection gizmo; damn that Weegee.

It was pressing hard against the front of my trousers; I could swear that the part that was anchored inside me had gotten bigger, too. The state of my excitement was getting painful, and I was beginning to understand how teen-age boys must feel.

I pulled a scarf out of my breast pocket and tied Elena's around her eyes. "Turn around and get down on your knees," I ordered, steadying her as she complied. I unzipped my fly and pulled the stiff rod free of my briefs. I was amazed at how hot it felt; I held the firm, warm shaft in my hand for a moment, feeling its weight in my palm. I stoked it and it seemed to get even harder. I put a hand behind Elena's head and pulled her face toward my crotch.

"Suck my cock, baby," I whispered hoarsely, brushing her lips with the head of it. Her lips parted and she hesitated; I tugged on her hair, rocking my hips. She opened her lips wider and took my cock into her mouth.

That's when the buzzing started again. I bit back a curse. Damn that Weegee, anyway. Didn't she think I was having a good enough time without her help?

I looked down at the beauty working my love-stick. Above the silky blindfold, her brow was wrinkled in concentration. Was she having the same difficulty I was, staving off orgasm until the job was done? I watched her swirl her tongue around, then close her lips on the head, her cheeks hollowing as she sucked it into her mouth all the way down to the balls. Then she drew back on the shaft, and the pull of her mouth pressed the dildo's anchor hard against my clit. I groaned.

Now Elena knew a trick that worked. All at once she rammed my cock down her throat and drew back on it, slow and hard. Then she did it again. And again. Ah, Jesus!

I grabbed the sides of her head to stop her while I caught my breath.

The buzzing stopped. Thank God for small favors. I heaved a sigh of relief and gave all my attention to Elena, whose yeomanly effort was bound to pay off, sooner rather than later. She was doing such a good job of cocksucking, I was finding it hard to believe, as Weegee had told me, that Elena was a virgin dyke, untouched by the hands or other body parts of any man. That was why she wanted to play out this fantasy. I guess I had to credit Weegee with all the on-the-job training her girlfriend must have gotten in this art: oh, Weegee, you dog. I imagined her panting and drooling from her lookout across the way. It didn't seem, however, that she would to be able to see all that much of this spectacle. Even if her binoculars were good ones, Elena's desk stood between us and the window. I imagined my friend gnashing her teeth in frustration and smiled. I couldn't see the look on her face at this distance, but still! My breath rasped and my cunt throbbed in time with Elena's mouth working up and down, up and down, on my ramrod-hard dick. I couldn't help but take a peek in Weegee's direction.

Elena stiffened and her mouth went slack; she tried to pull back. I grabbed her head and thought fast.

"Fuck! I want to fuck you, baby. Are you trying to make me

shoot my load before I'm good and ready, bitch?" She relaxed and I pushed her away. I made a quick sprint to the window, my tool bobbing in front of me. Thank God I hadn't unbuttoned my trousers and let them drop to my ankles. I yanked the cord on the vertical blinds just as the cop raised his elbows. It took another moment to locate the rod that turned the slats closed, but by then I figured we were safe. Besides, what could he do? It was Weegee who was in big trouble now; I'd worry about that later.

I swiped my sleeve across my sweating face and tried to get my heart rate back to normal. It wouldn't do to spook Elena. Still shaking, I shrugged out of the suit jacket and placed it on the back of her desk chair. That was better. I loosened my tie and unbuttoned my collar; now I was ready. I took a deep breath and stepped around the desk, fumbling a packet out of my vest pocket as I went.

"Open your mouth," I told her and slipped the little circle between her lips.

Elena knew how it was done. Obviously feeling a little bolder now, she steadied herself with her hands on my thighs as, with her lips and tongue, she worked the rubber onto my dick. I squirmed a little, feeling the tug in my cunt. My mouth was dry.

"Good enough, baby," I rasped. "Now stand up here and bend over that desk."

I leaned over her to slip my hands beneath the hem of her skirt and felt my breath come back hot against my face from the smooth cleft of her back. I closed my eyes, willing myself to slow down. With what I hoped was tantalizing languor, I skimmed my palms up to her hips until my hooked thumbs brought the skirt to rest in folds above her waist. The buzzer wasn't buzzing now. My hands lingered, tracing the lacy edge of her garter belt while my dick nudged the soft flesh of her thigh. The straps of the vibrator came over the garters—probably Elena had put it on after she'd arrived at work. That's when she'd taken her panties off, I guessed. Would an up-and-coming corporate lawyer ride the El without underwear? I smothered a laugh. In the trance of climax endlessly deferred, my mind was wandering. I forced it back to the matter at hand.

Now my hand rose between her legs, sticky with sweat and cunt juice. I heard a low moan as I parted her lips, and when I flicked her clit with one finger, she jerked involuntarily and pressed her cunt against my hand.

With a shaky hand, I guided the head of my dick into her furrow. I could hear Elena's breath coming faster and faster. Sliding it from side to side, back and forth, spreading the slickness around until the filmy rubber was coated with it, I finally pressed the tip just barely against her hole, then stopped. I held my breath.

Elena trembled. Raising herself off her folded arms, she stretched them out across the desk and pressed her palms flat against the wood. I waited. When my other hand came down lightly on her hip, she jumped, then arched her back.

"Jesus," she groaned, "please fuck me."

I let my breath out in a rush and pressed my hips forward. Her pussy was wet and tight; I could feel the resistance as the head of my dick prodded through the opening. Her cunt gripped the shaft as I pushed in deeper, and I could feel the friction thrumming against my own clit. Groping underneath, I held the rod tight against myself for a moment as it sank to the hilt in Elena's cunt; my own pulse pounded through the hard meaty heft of it.

"Ah, Jesus," I echoed Elena. The tension in her body was gone, now: she was melting into the desktop, letting her knees go a little slack as her pussy swallowed my cock. I eased my hand out from between my legs and let my fingertips rest on the small of her back; then, ever so gently, I pulled back on the dick and began to pump.

Getting a grip on myself as best I could, I shoved in just so far, then pulled almost all the way out. Pause. Then in, just deep enough to feel Elena's cunt tighten on me, trying to pull me farther in. Then, almost all the way out again. And again. Elena locked her knees, no longer feeling quite so relaxed, I guessed. She raised up and pushed back against me, and I rammed my dick all the way home.

That was as much as I could stand. My hips took on a life of their own, thrusting my cock hard into Elena's grabbing pussy, rocking back far enough to drive it in again. Somehow, the blind-fold had come off; Elena's hair fell forward, swaying over the desk. Her fingers scrabbled against the hard surface, clutching for something to hang on to, until she reached above her head to grip the far edge. Then her cheek pressed onto the hard surface, her hair hiding her face at least as much as the cloth had.

I grabbed her hips and held on tight. With every thrust, my clit ground against the toy's anchoring base, and every withdrawal pulled the knob hard against my cunt. I wasn't going to last much longer. But it looked like Elena was galloping toward the finish line, too: she was holding herself off the desk now, meeting my thrusts. Her arms were under her face, and I guessed she was bit-ing one, from the muffled sound of "ah—ah—ah—ah" that she was making in time to my pounding. Oh, but I was close. Then, all at once, Weegee's girlfriend exploded into motion, bucking and heaving like a rodeo bronco, yelling "Oh, Jesus," at the top of her lungs. Hanging on was impossible; my dick popped out with a small sound of suction I'm sure I could've heard if it hadn't been for Elena's little prayers. I started to panic.

"Shhh," I said, "shhh." But she was quieting by then, anyway. She dropped onto the desk and raised one hand to brush the hair off her sweaty face.

"Don't worry," she told me, "these walls are soundproof."

There was a knock at the door.

Elena's head popped up. I stiffened. It was only a faint rapping noise; I wondered if we'd really heard it. Then it came again, a lit-tle louder. I bit my lip. Elena threw me a horrified look. We wait-ed; but there was only silence.

"Oh, God," she said, shaking her head, "what a stupid stunt this was. I never should have let Weegee talk…"

The telephone buzzed and the intercom light came on. I stifled a yelp. Elena's hand shot out across the desk and jabbed at the speaker button.

"Yes?"

"Ms. Giardino?" The young male voice hesitated. "Are you okay? I thought I heard…"

Elena smiled in relief.

"I'm fine, Jimmy," she told him, a little more heartily than was strictly needed. "Just doing my stress reduction exercises."

"Oh," the voice came back, then after a pause, "okay."

"*Thank* you, though, for your concern, Jimmy," Elena said brightly.

"Sure, no prob…"

She stabbed at the button and the voice was gone.

She let out a whoosh of breath. "That's Jimmy, our intern." She shook her head. "Thank God it wasn't one of the partners. Thank God…"

I was groping my still-engorged toy, trying to find the right spot to squeeze to release the valve and make the pesky hard-on go away.

"Shit," I muttered. The buzzing started again. "Oh, shit," I repeated. It was zapping a very sensitive spot.

"What?" Elena asked, twisting around to look at me. "What's wrong?"

"Damn Weegee!" I cursed. "It's vibrating again, and I can't find the…oh, God." I'd thought my urge to come had fallen by the wayside. Instead, the long-deferred climax was hitting me like a ton of bricks. I doubled over, then my knees gave out. Clenching my legs together was completely involuntary; it certainly didn't help. When I could finally spread my knees again, I tried to push the offending gizmo away from me. The buzz had become torture on my too-sensitive clit. But the trousers were in the way, the harness was too tight, and my vaginal muscles had the anchor knob in a death grip.

"Aaargh," I growled. I groped. I squeezed the thing in the spot I thought Weegee had showed me. Finally, it stopped whining, and it began to shrink, even as I watched.

"Phew." I leaned my cheek against Elena's still-naked butt. Was she giggling?

She got a grip on herself and straightened up.

"God." She pushed her skirt down. "Look," she told me, searching for her clothes, "you have to go. I'm sorry. This whole thing…I mean, it was great, but…"

"Sure. Sure," I said, trying to stuff the flabby but still fat love-pump back into my fly. "No problem," I said, unconsciously echoing the hapless Jimmy. "I'm out of here," I told her as I zipped up. I buttoned my collar and straightened my tie.

"Oh, God," she muttered as she hooked her bra and turned it around to the front. "God."

I cleared my throat, trying to think of some thing cool and suave and clever to say as a parting line. She threw me a look, as if to say, are you still here? She was pulling on the sleeves of her blouse, and I wondered how she was going to do all those buttons.

"Can I help you with that?" I finally thought to ask.

"No!" She was very emphatic. "No! Please, just…" She took a deep breath, then smiled. It was a beautiful, mischievous, appreciative smile. I could understand why Weegee was so obsessed. "I'll be fine." She walked to the door, blouse still open at the back, and held out her hand to me. I took the hint.

I leaned down, and she kissed me warmly, on the lips. So much for the illusion of anonymity.

"Thank you, Sam."

Was I blushing? I cleared my throat and turned back to the door to say something, anything, but the door closed gently and I heard the lock click.

I got all the way down to the ground floor—mercifully alone on the small elevator; there was no telling what a close bystander might smell—before I realized that I had no jacket. My brain was in a fog. Of course, my wallet was in the suit jacket; Weegee didn't want it to spoil the fall of the gabardine over my handsome, boyish behind.

I walked home. It was only twenty blocks.

I saw Weegee and Elena that very next night, when they came to the door of my apartment. I'm Weegee's only residential tenant in the building that houses her office and manufacturing plant; Elena was picking up Weegee for dinner. She had my jacket in her hand.

I thanked her as graciously as I could, considering her company. Then I dumped a little bundle in Weegee's hands.

"This is yours," I snarled, "*pal.*"

Weegee's quizzical look was priceless, as if she had no idea why I'd be pissed off at her!

For Elena's benefit, I added, "I can see why you didn't want to tell me about all those little buttons on your remote control." She'd said I'd find it boring, too technical. Ha. "You didn't want me to know you'd be buzzing me, too," I finished in an undertone. On second thought, I didn't really want to be discussing this in front of Weegee's girlfriend. But Weegee just looked puzzled.

"The dick doesn't have a buzzer," she said, shaking her head.

"It does, too!" I protested. "It got hard on its own, without me hitting the switch like you showed me, then it started vibrating. It was vibrating most of the time until you got hauled away."

At least she had the grace to look embarrassed. "Oh, that," she said. "I thought it would be more fun for you if I keyed the erection mode. It would be more like what happens to guys. You know, the penis with a mind of its own…"

"Well, okay, but making it vibrate? I mean," with as much hurt in my voice as I could muster, "that was really low."

Her brow creased. "But it didn't…" Another look of embarrassment. "Oh," she said. "I did have a little trouble with that hydraulic valve when I was testing it. It stuttered a little." She looked sheepish. "I thought I'd worked that bug out."

Stuttered! I was speechless. Elena was laughing into her hand. Weegee hefted the bag in her hand and shrugged.

"Well, hey," she said, throwing a conspiratorial look up at her beautiful companion, "back to the drawing board, huh?"

Oh, Weegee. You dog.

What Things Seem
Teresa Cooper

I went to Le Body Shoppe in the warehouse district in New Orleans when I was down there on business without Baby. The guy behind the scratched-up plastic barrier took my ten dollars without looking at me, and when he finally did I thought *uh-oh, here goes*, but he only glanced up to check my age.

"You a college boy?" he asked.

"Yeah."

"Half-price," and he gave me five back. It was damp, wrinkled; it swathed my four fingers when placed in my expectant palm.

I was given a towel, three rubbers. A key with a silver safety pin.

I glanced up at the scratchy black-and-white television set behind him showing *Jeopardy*, and then at the sign above it: "This Establishment Serves Exclusively the Male Community." I wouldn't have called it an establishment.

I waded past the requisite treadmills and step-machines. I peeled off my T-shirt in the locker room, left on my white tank top. The humidity in the room surpassed the wetness outside. A middle-aged white man bent over his shoelaces, untying and then tying them again. He glanced at me over a rounded shoulder. No eye contact. My jeans bunched around my ankles. I stepped out of them deliberately, holding my boxer briefs up with one hand, balancing myself on the bench with the other. Underwear under the briefs, stuffed with a rag.

The steamy room boasted six guys posing around the hot tub. Two in bikinis. The others wearing nothing. All of them white. One was really hot, smooth, thirtyish, a ringer for that queen Matt Damon. He nodded at me to sit next to him, dangle my calves in the tub.

"Shy," he said.

I smiled, nodded.

"Jake," he said, putting his palm in the crook of his thigh, right where his balls were collapsing into themselves. *That's a boner*, I thought, trying to suppress a laugh. Excluding videos, I hadn't seen one since high school. It was fat and shiny, sticky, clumpy. I felt like an adolescent all over again. Icky. Gross.

Wouldn't know what to do with it if I wanted to. Couldn't give myself over. Without giving an inch, I said, "I want to watch."

We went into a changing room. A guy was in there waiting, on the floor. I sat on a stool in the corner, put my hand over my crotch. Jake rested his dick atop the other guy's ass. They knew each other, no negotiations necessary. The guy on his knees pushed his ass toward Jake, pulled it back, arched his back, bowed it—anything to invite Jake to start moving, anything.

Jake pumped two loads of lube into his palm, slapped it into the guy's crack. His asshole twitched, gaping. I squeezed the muscles inside me, in spurts of two, pushed down on the rag in my crotch at my pubic bone. I watched four of Jake's fingers disappear. Then his dick, and the guy on his knees grunted, exhaling loudly.

Jake went slowly, like I would. Like I imagined I would. I tensed my ass muscles with every thrust. I closed my eyes and then it was Baby there, on her bed, still in her work clothes, skirt hiked up over her hips, pantyhose at her knees. I could smell myself, acidic sweat, yet sweet, like it comes up and hits me sometimes when I shift in my seat on the subway. Like Baby leaves on my stomach in the mornings.

Jake's tight thighs slapped into the guy's ass, and the hollow beat of it burned onto my brain. He came. I barely noticed. Pulled it out just before—more I didn't need or want to see. I got what I wanted. My ten, no, five-dollars' worth. Well worth my time. It was easy for me to say no to being next.

"You're not leaving, are you?" Jake asked me when I stood, dizzy.

I nodded. He came close, planted himself right in front of me. At that second it hit me how cocky I'd been to think I could pull this off. He kept looking at me, smiling, like they all do in the videos after coming (and I thought it was just good acting).

"Yeah, I gotta get going," I said softly, nonchalant.

"Maybe tomorrow," he said, putting both hands on my shoulders and squeezing, "you'll take off one of these." He snapped my tank-top.

When I got back to my hotel room I mounted two pillows and got off in about two minutes. Then I called Baby.

"You'll never guess where I just got back from," I said, excited, still out of breath and wet.

"Where? How was your meeting?"

"Didn't you hear what I said?"

"Yeah, where'd you go?"

"Forget it, I'll tell you when I get back in town."

Baby didn't have any time for me when I got back. A conference, two big evening meetings. On the fifth night of this I went alone to a bar downtown. I ordered an old-fashioned and saw an old friend, Jules. She asked where Baby was.

"Business as usual," I said.

"Trouble with the missus?" Jules teased, sucking on a beer. Jules had been the first to give me shit for shacking up with Baby, gave me a funeral the night before I moved my few things into her uptown apartment.

Then Jules's new girl came up, whining to play pool. Jules shrugged and looked at me apologetically, as if to say "we all fall." Her girl was cute, real cute—nice legs. That I can forgive.

Alone again, and another drink gave me the courage to turn away from the bar, peek at the girls. A few nods, more acquaintances. Probably looked like I was looking again.

She zeroed in on me the minute she came through the velvet curtains. She wore tight Levi's and an even tighter black scoop-neck bodysuit thing. Smooth skin, as Aryan-looking as Jake in New Orleans. But a girl. Just my type, just my fucking luck.

"My cousin lives in Brooklyn," she said, motioning toward the bartender. "I come into the city from Philly once a month."

"What are you having?" I asked, then repeated the order and plunked my last five dollars down on the bar.

"So 'You come here often?' is out of the question," I said, both my elbows on the bar.

"Where's that girl you're usually with?" she asked. "I remember you from the last trip."

"She's at home."

"Oh, you live together?"

"I live with *her*, her place. I don't have a place."

"My cousin's sleeping out tonight. Wanna come back with me?"

"What's your name?" I asked, stalling.

"Betty."

"What else would it be?"

"So, you game?" She looked at me so calmly, but I could tell that more than these last few minutes were riding on this. Did she know what she wasn't getting in to? Things are rarely what they seem.

"I don't have a dick," I said, knowing it'd throw her off.

But she didn't flinch. "I've got one at my cousin's."

I laughed—such a programmed response, tough yet so clearly threatened.

"Oh, or you don't want to use one, that's okay, too," she said, louder than I would've wanted her to. She said it the way Dorothy said "You're nothing but a cowardly lion." And she was right. A dare.

It wasn't Baby who'd been afraid all this time; it was me.

I went with her anyway—to prove to myself, to Baby, even to this stranger. We got off at the "D" in Park Slope. Walked up to a building where one of Baby's friends from her past lived. "You know Gigi?" I asked.

She didn't answer. She opened the door to Gigi's apartment. It was empty, but a candle was lit and Peggy Lee played softly on the stereo. She pressed her hand into mine and took me to a back room: futon on the floor, pillows, more candles, lube, a dildo, (a *dildo*), and two glasses of red wine.

"Why—" I started, but she shhsh-ed me and gestured toward the bed.

"No questions," she said, turning. "I'll be back in a sec."

I sat down on the bed, waiting. She turned the music up. The fucking thing just sat on the pillow next to me, daring me. "Step up to the plate and be a man about it."

Talking dildos? I must've been trashed. But it went on: "This reluctant butch thing can only go so far. Frankly, it's no longer endearing—just annoying."

I lunged at it, stuck it through the limp harness, dangled it at eye level. "Is that a challenge?" I asked. Just then the door opened, but it wasn't the girl anymore. It was—it was Baby!

"Baby!" I stood up. "I can explain—"

"You don't have to explain anything," she said, slipping out of her silk robe as she approached me. "Show me what you did in New Orleans."

I looked down at the lifeless tangle in my hands. "I didn't *do* anything in New Orleans."

"Then show me what you *saw*," she demanded, unbuttoning my pants. She crouched down in front of me, piling my jeans and underwear around my boots. She grabbed that thing and strapped me in, licked it, then my stomach, then between my fingers.

Baby lay down on her stomach, looked back up at me.

"Baby, you are too good to me," I said, but she didn't respond—with words.

I pumped two loads of lube into my palm and rubbed the length of the dick. It got warm. Baby arched her back, pushed her head into the pillow. I kept stroking it while Baby watched. She whined. The length of it.

I could feel warmth moving up my spine from the small of my back to the base of my neck. Like ice dripping over the length of me. *Oh my god*, I thought—and then said out loud, "I have a boner."

"You do, honey. You do what you want with it."

Oh, Baby.

Pornography for Miss X
Ilsa Jule

Part I

On a warm summer night she came into my room and declared, "I'm taking all my clothes off," and then removed her stockings. I waited a minute and said, "I thought you were taking off *all* your clothes." In one motion she raised her arms and lifted her dress over her head, then dropped it onto the floor. She pushed her underwear off in the two steps it took to reach the bed.

I watched her small white body approach me. She lay next to me, while I remained dressed, then leaned and pressed through all the layers of my clothes. I could feel the denim of my jeans and the fabric of my T-shirt against her skin. Unlike the others, she would not insist that I take off my clothes. She wouldn't speak of it, she wouldn't indicate it with her body. She never argues with my clothes. She understands butch. She knows the feel of a cool belt buckle against her stomach as part of me and enjoys it as such.

Convention wants people to believe that being close is being naked. And once in a while for me, it is. Skin meeting skin is intimacy, but fucking someone properly is about going beyond skin and beneath it too. We can both have our clothes on and fuck;

that's part of the beauty of being lesbians. Sometimes the only flesh she might feel is fingertips and lips. She can put her hands on my back and feel my spine as it lies beneath my skin; she can also feel all the sensations of who I am when I whisper in her ear and tell her to breathe through her mouth.

Her relationship to her own clothes is simple, too. She refuses to buy new ones. It's not so much that she needs to wear something that was worn by at least one other person; she just doesn't think you should pay more than one dollar for any article of clothing. She frequents the Salvation Army, Goodwill, and yard sales. I admire this discipline. Like the rest of us, she has many restrictions. I think hers are better thought out.

Her wardrobe speaks in a weary tone of its previous owners. And it is this that confuses my fingers, because the fabric is usually so soft that sometimes I forget that I'm touching it and not her skin. It is only her underwear that is in contrast to the smoothness of her skin and clothes. The silky fabric gathered around the elastic sometimes fights my hands, rubs at my wrists.

This afternoon there is no such battle.

She was lying beside me and I was feeling her skin. She removed my wallet from my back pocket and pressed its worn brown leather into her soft stomach.

She said, "I was daydreaming that it was snowing outside, that I came up your stairs and my face was cold. I wanted to take all my clothes off and lie in bed beside you so you would warm me."

I pressed the side of my face into the side of her face and was happy to hear that this winter's forecast, clear skies and temperatures in the low twenties, now included Joy beside me in bed, naked with my wallet on her bare stomach.

Part II

I once slept with a straight woman who said, "You might as well sleep with guys, you want me to do the things guys do." She couldn't have been more wrong. I didn't want her to shave her face in the morning, to stand while pissing, to take up too much room on the subway, and to think that oral sex before penetration by her penis would somehow compensate for penetration. I wanted her to know that penetration was the right way to satisfy me.

Joy and I have been seeing each other for a long time. We do not want to move in together. You've probably heard that joke, "What does a lesbian bring on the second date? A U-Haul." We spend most nights together, alternating weekends at each other's apartments. This way the whole "uptown-downtown" thing comes in very handy. We've agreed that moving in together is a form of planned obsolescence. You know you will eventually become aggravated by the person; even if you're still in love, that won't matter much if you can't stand another night in with her.

As much as we're like most lesbians, we have our differences— one that I wasn't sure she'd fancy. Neither of us is penetration-shy. In fact, we huddle with the dykes who think penetration constitutes not rough sex but rather a part of regular sex. We're a couple of dykes who feel that fingers are not a substitute for a penis. Fingers can serve in many capacities: they are great for pointing the way to new things, indispensable tools in certain areas of investigation.

We could never hear enough about penetration. "I never knew I had a pussy until you wiggled your fingers inside me"—where fingers had gone, many a pleasure was earned. But I think any lesbian worthy of a place in the Dyke March has heard enough about pussy—why bore one's lover with pussy talk? I felt it was time to contemplate that other hole. The asshole. The hole that when properly done (and none too often) yields a most exquisite sensation.

A fag friend of mine was once offended by some remark about buttfucking. I was offended by the fact that he assumed only men did it to each other. Fags have not cornered the market on anal sex, although I entrust to them all the cocksucking in the world.

As time wore on between Joy and me, I wanted her to consider the alternatives. I wondered if she had the balls for it. And bringing it up, no matter how well we could discuss anything else, was going to be tricky. You can't just talk about something like this, especially if you want it to maintain some of its charm and intimacy. Being too clinical would just strip it of the fun.

I thought a lot: When could I bring it up, over breakfast? Not likely. While commuting? Again, slightly awkward. And you can't mention it while in bed, because then it just kills the moment, and it's one of the few things that needs to have the perfect balance between an event "expected" and one that's full of surprise. This is the essence of it.

Other women I've dated longed for this pleasure; that's because they had been obsessed with my ass. This one has not been seduced by it; she is too distracted by a lot of other things I have to offer, things other lovers did not even know existed.

I'm not in a rush to get fucked that way, but I wonder how to tell her.

When I finally bring it up, it's been sent in a letter and it's still not in my words—but in references to sailors and French novelists. Somehow she starts to get the gist of it, but weeks pass before my theory (my desire and internal pleadings) becomes practice, her fingers somehow wanting to be confident enough to serve all my desires, her fingers having the confidence to overcome uncertainty and know that I will forgive any clumsiness in her attempts to please me.

Part III

She lies with her face still pressed against mine, not with cool winter skin that has just come in from the trudge along St. Mark's Place to my door. It's warm autumn skin, flushed slightly because a sweater is still just a little overdressed.

I'm not really thinking about sex. I mean, I want it and I'm sure we'll get to it, but I like to have a sloppy attitude every once in a while. She starts to chew on my mouth and runs her hand up inside my shirt and tugs at my nipples. I'm still acting remote, but she has all my attention.

I roll on top of her and get wet at the sight of her, her fingers slide inside me easily. I'm filled with anticipation. Will the talk of sailors manifest today? Now? Soon?

Before I know it, she's gnawing on my collarbone in a painful way, but I think she's enjoying it and I can endure it. I can always cross that line when something that hurts starts to feel great. Just before I scream "Stop," she does and I wonder if she heard my pleading. Can she hear my thoughts?

I notice that her palm is resting on the side of my ass. I start that internal query. It begins softly, more of a suggestion: "You can touch me there," I telepath. But she doesn't, so I wonder if, like wishes asked of a genie, mine have to be properly worded. In my mind I get literal and literate: "I'm the Captain, you're Querelle, but this time you take me and end all the years of longing. You fuck everyone who wants to be fucked exactly how they want to be fucked, but tonight you do it through me." Then I wonder if I should mention when I first tried to talk to about it. I once jokingly brought up the Dinah Shore Classic and talked about the nineteenth hole. "You know, that one that all the fags know about." I was distressed that I had to keep turning to gay male imagery.

The edge of her palm starts to move along the inside of my ass, brushing the hair, and I decide not to talk. Her fingertips brush against that pouting orifice that I hope isn't too dirty. I also hope she knows what she's doing, or this will just hurt a lot. Her fingers pressing into my asshole send through me the same sensation of being kissed for the first time. I start to reason that she's been thinking about this. She's been planning; it will be all right. She puts her head near mine and whispers, "Relax." I know that if I want this from her, and I do, then I have to. I sigh with my entire body.

She takes her right hand and puts her fingers inside her pussy,

"I'm very wet," she says, a hint of surprise in her voice. She's enjoying this as much as I am. In one motion, she returns her hand to my ass and presses her middle finger inside. I hear her gasp. I no longer have insides; they have vanished, and in their absence is a feeling of resolve.

Right now I am hers, for ever after I will have been hers, in this complete way. She glides her finger in and out. I like the sensation of her finger inside me better than when it is not. I turn into what feels like clay but looks like orange, a deep orange unlike the colors we're used to seeing flat on the printed page—I have become the color orange.

I don't come, but I go somewhere beyond that to a place I like better. She asks if she should stop, and I say yes. She lies next to me and says, "I liked that more than I thought I would. You let me into a room." She pauses, then goes on, "It's overrated as taboo, and it's understated in books. That was totally hot." She smells her finger. "This smells of the essence of sex."

I close my eyes and update my winter forecast: clear skies, temperatures in the low twenties, Joy beside me in bed, and dirty fucking.

Three of Cups
Cecilia Tan

Magda brewed me some chamomile tea with a touch of comfrey in it. I could smell it steeping from where the cup sat on the white Formica counter of her kitchenette, familiar and meant to be comforting: chamomile to help me sleep and comfrey to help clear up any bruises she might have inadvertently introduced to my flesh in the course of the evening. But tonight, as I sat with the comforter wrapped around me on her futon, watching her busy herself with spoons and saucers, I wondered if, for once, she might not ask me whether I wanted to stay up, or if I wanted to *keep* those bruises. Magda and I had been together for a year now, a year come Solstice, a year of becoming familiar to each other, a year of settling. A year when, once a week, I would come to her place and submit to her touches and tickles and her whips and paddles, and she would send me off into space, into that special bliss that we worshipping masochists know. Or she would at least try to. She carried the tea over to me and sank into the covers next to me. She was brownly naked, the black gloss of her unbound hair covering her back like a short cape. My goddess in flesh.

I took the cup and breathed the steam. It wasn't like me to be so moody after a scene. PMS, I told myself, the universal paean.

She broke the silence, not noticing my mood. "Oh, I forgot to tell you. Those fire dancers from Santa Cruz aren't going to make it to the meeting."

"Why?" In the year we'd been together I'd not only become a fixture in Magda's life, I'd also become programming chair of Leather Pagans United, her spiritual, political, and sometimes problematic family.

She shrugged and sipped her tea. "I don't know, they just said they can't, and to tell you."

"Dammit, Magda, you should have had them talk to me."

She arched her eyebrow in that High Priestess way of hers, but the way she looked at me from under her lashes suggested little-girl guilt. Magda could be a contradiction sometimes. "There wasn't anything you could do."

"I could have gotten them to reschedule, maybe, and swapped someone into their place. Jesus, Magda, the meeting's only two weeks away."

Her pouty look turned to a glare at my pronunciation of the J-word.

"I'm sorry," I said automatically. I wasn't going to have another version of our long-standing argument over swear words. She was always coming out with fake-sounding stuff like "By the goddess!" whereas my theory was, swear by using a deity you *don't* like, not one you do. When I wanted to needle her, I could make up some pretty fake-sounding stuff, too, like "Satan take my bicycle!" But not tonight. Tonight, I was annoyed already. "I'll have to come up with something else."

She crossed her ankles and leaned against the perfect white of her apartment wall. "Maybe it's time to do another mutual respect workshop."

"But last month was the relationship round table."

"I know, but I think some people could use a refresher." Her dark eyes looked into her tea.

"Like who?" I blew on my tea, trying to look nonchalant.

"Like Isa," she said, puckering her lips a tiny bit. "I've been hearing some things."

I blew on my tea some more. If I waited long enough, she'd tell me. And so she did: rumors, hearsay, gossip, and dish, which amounted to a probable suspicion that Ms. Isa, a Top who considered herself a mere second to the Supreme Goddess herself (hence her interest in a spiritual group like LPU) was coming down with a case of Top's disease. No one had come forward and accused her of being a lousy partner, but rumors did get started somehow. And seeing as how Magda felt Isa was bucking to take the High Priestess role for herself next year, she wanted to know the truth. "I can't let someone who doesn't respect her tools lead the worship," she finished. "If she doesn't respect her bottoms, she's not channeling the goddess, she's just on an ego trip."

"One way to find out," I said, setting aside my cold, full cup. "One way for sure."

If I thought it was going to be difficult, if I thought I was going to have to flirt with Isa and insinuate myself like a spy, I was wrong. After the meeting, Magda walked up to Isa and told her she wanted her to take me on for a night, a preliminary to a public worship next month. Isa said sure, she'd e-mail me about convenient dates.

That's how I came to be riding down the Pacific Coast Highway to Swanton on a Saturday afternoon. The music of my own anxiety and nerves played inside my helmet as my reflexes led me around the curves, sometimes making a little voice: come on, girl, good girl, that's the way, nice, keep on going, keep on moving, that's it, that's a girl...and whether I was talking to myself about the ride or about my destination, I wasn't sure. I had a reputation with the Leather Pagans as a bottomless bottom, a tough one who could stand up to anything. And, yeah, I had been through a lot, especially since coming to the Bay Area three years ago. But maybe having a rep was worse; maybe that meant people would go farther with me than they normally would. And tough or no, I had never outgrown that special chill of anticipation that came with a new Top, a new unknown, something new to fear.

I pulled off the highway at a tiny embankment, five parking spaces and a weather-worn picnic table. With my helmet perched solid on the sissy bar, I swung off the bike and walked to the cliff's edge. Below me, a living moon of tidepool craters glistened in the late-afternoon sun. I'd taken this road all the way down to Monterey many times; I'd seen the aquarium exhibits of anemones and hermit crabs and starfish. Here they lived as they had for thousands of years. If Mother Nature could create an organism that looked like a flower but could eat a fish, it didn't seem unlikely that she'd create a person like me.

And what was Isa? Did she have a poison sting, too?

She lived in a surprisingly suburban ranch-style house, like one you could see a dozen of in different colors along any housing development east of the Mississippi. Swanton was a mixture of run-down-looking fisherman shacks and cliff-dwelling mansions with a few odd normal houses like hers. She had converted the "family room" into a full-blown dungeon with leather-padded sawhorses, a St. Andrew's cross, and a wall covered with nasty-looking implements and bondage gear. I had a quick look at it before dinner when she gave me a tour of the house.

We sat down to eat on her back patio, where we couldn't see the ocean but we could see the sun set. She'd grilled vegetables, zucchini and red peppers and huge portabello mushrooms, mushrooms that you eat like a steak using a knife and fork, with juice dribbling down your chin. It was while digging in to one of those that she remarked "God, how I miss beef sometimes."

I kept chewing. If I couldn't chime in sympathetically, it didn't seem polite to say anything.

She raised an eyebrow at me. "Are you…vegetarian?"

She meant *aren't you*, but I shook my head. "I know, I know, I'm the sacrifice, I should have some sympathy, some kinship for the lamb. But nature, the Goddess, whoever, made me a predator, too. And I try to…stay true to that nature."

She smirked, a little teriyaki sauce in the corner of her lips. "Well, you know. I didn't give up meat for spiritual reasons. I saw one too many meat-packing documentaries and decided it was time to quit." Her tongue snaked out to catch the sauce, and there was no doubt in my mind she was as much a predator as I. Her hair was black, too, but not the wavy cloud that Magda's was—more like a smooth helmet the covered her head and neck and shone with bright bits of red in the sunlight. She could have been anything—Hispanic, Italian, Middle Eastern—but my guess was Filipina. Which got me thinking about Roman Catholicism and stuff (did she say "God" earlier?) and wanting to talk to her about becoming pagan, what road she had traveled to arrive at that choice…but whatever I might have said stayed under my tongue as she stood. I felt something change, her power come to her, the subtle shift that was the scene beginning.

"Your nature," she breathed, echoing my last words. "Your nature is to serve Her. To serve Her by serving me. To submit to Her by submitting to me. To perform with me this rite, of your own choice and will."

I felt that required an answer, but I did not know which to give. Amen, I do, yes ma'am…I nodded silently.

She went into the house and I followed her, trying to make my mind a blank, to make myself a vessel for whatever this Priestess would pour into me. But through my mind were playing a hundred other scenes, a dozen other first times with other Tops, other women I had given myself to in the name of the Goddess. There were always patterns, there were always things to be expected. So of course I was guessing. With all that equipment I wondered if she would be the type who would immobilize me, make me feel her iron grip, and then lay into me with everything she had. Give it to me both barrels, baby, I thought, my skin tingling. I can do this, I can do this, came my little voice again, the agitated music preparing me for pain. I can do this. In a basement off Divisadero I'd had my skin cut and set on fire. In an open field north of Muir Woods I'd been hung from a tree and whipped with freshly cut sticks. But usually I was tied to a bed, or secured with soft cuffs in a rack, while carefully crafted leather and wood was applied.

We stood outside the dungeon door. She faced me. "If you have anything to tell me that we haven't already discussed, tell me now."

I shook my head.

She looked for a moment like maybe there was something she wanted to tell me, but then it passed and she looked away, saying, "Take off your clothes and leave them here. Once we enter the chamber, we've begun."

I nodded. Some Tops left the bottom alone for a few minutes while they gathered their own energy, but not Isa. She turned away from me and began shedding her clothes, draping them over the back of a chair. I folded mine neatly and placed them on the floor next to the door. As I bent low to lay them down, I reminded myself one last time of my purpose for being here, to find out if Isa was…what? Safe, okay, worthy? The real thing, or not? To see if she'd respect me as an equal. Thus far she had been exemplary.

Inside the room, the fire of the red sky mixed with the flicker of the candles she lit. She indicated an open space on the vinyl padded floor, and I knelt there while my still-busy mind was cataloging details: black floor, soft on the feet but easy to wash up— Where did she get it?

The sound of her chuckle brought me back to the moment. She held a single candle and stared into it, then lifted it over her head and let the wax drip down over her small, firm breasts. Her chuckle became a throaty laugh that sounded nothing like the Isa I knew. She looked back at me, the candle burning twin images in her eyes. She knelt in front of me, waving the candle like a magic wand. The flame burned higher as it tipped, and hot white drops of wax dotted my skin. I sat still because I did not know what else to do. Unbound, uninstructed, I reminded myself it was my duty to submit.

And then she was on me, her body on top of mine, pushing me flat against the padded floor, her wax and mine pressed together, making me think of flowers in a dictionary. I hadn't realized it at first, but the instant the wax had hit me I had broken out in a sweat, and now it made my skin slick against hers. I had no idea where the candle had gone, and even though I told myself it wasn't my place to worry about it, not my responsibility, the thought remained. Her hands held my head in place and her mouth sucked at mine, and without thinking, I struggled. I was used to ritual beatings with numbers called out and the solemn gathering of energy before the piercing. This wrestling was so much more like...sex.

She reared up, hands on my shoulders, pinning me, the gleam still in her eye—not from candles but from an eager madness to devour me. This is my will, I told myself, this is my devotion, but I could not make myself sink into submission. Isa raked her claws across my cheek and I resisted, my chin up in defiance. I wanted to lie still and let her have her way. I wanted to obey, to let the Goddess ravage me if that was her will. But something in me said fight! I struggled to unseat her from me and found myself instead face down on the floor, one of her hands in my hair, one drawing lines down my back with her claws. My spine arched against that rough touch, like the tide following the moon. I tried to turn my head, but her hand held me fast. I felt her hot breath on my neck, her lips moved as she mouthed whatever incantations she wished into my skin, and then her teeth found purchase and a frisson of energy shot from the spot straight to my groin. I felt as if she had plucked a string in me, and the vibrations grew louder as I fought her, as the sensation strobed through my brain of her biting me and me bucking and her weight riding me…

Then her mouth was at my ear as my legs flailed for some leverage on the slippery floor and she spread herself over me like a blanket. "Did you wonder why you're not bound? Did you wonder what I would do?"

I didn't answer except to push harder against her. I wanted her to let go of me, to set me free. One side of me knew this was wrong, to resist like this, while the other side of me knew it could be no other way.

Her voice was loud and low in my ear, the spice of her breath surrounding me as tightly as any bonds, "Because I had to know your will. I had to know what you would let me do."

Obviously, I'll let you do anything, I wanted to say, because I haven't been able to stop you.

And then her weight was gone. I turned onto my back to find her standing above me, the windows behind her dark with night. "What will you let me do, eh, sister?" She knelt where she was and I pushed myself back a few inches out of instinct. "If you serve, you will not move. If you submit, you will not move."

There was power in the way she crawled toward me, jungle power, fierce and hungry. She crawled toward my cunt and licked her lips like a jaguar before she let her tongue snake out to sting my clit. She jabbed at it, parting the folds of my flesh with the sharp tip and sinking it hard against my nerves. I held still. I held my breath. I pressed my hands flat against the floor and let my head fall back, but I kept my legs as they were, knees bent, feet flat on the floor, spread wide for her, for Her. Her hands reached up for my nipples, rolling them in her fingers like two pepper-corns, then pulling them like pieces of taffy. I raised my head to look and found her eyes staring at me over the horizon of my mons. Waiting, waiting. Her tongue continued to jab, the sensation building to a jolt like pain, like a shock, slow but sharp, a Chinese water torture dripping acid onto my clit, moment by moment.

I had never felt a pain quite like it in my life, so bad I ground my teeth, and yet I felt a flutter in my stomach like it might make me come. Now that I had nothing to struggle against, I felt shame heating up my face. Why had I fought her? Had a year with Magda taught me nothing? How could I have failed in my devotion that way? My way is to suffer. When I go to leather bars, when I go to parties or group meetings, it's so hard to explain to some of these tops, no, I'm not a slave. I'm not a servant, only to Her. I'm not submissive, only to Her. If I obey, it is because it will lead to my suffering. If I let myself be put into bonds, it is to free me to suffer for Her. Simple, really.

The pain grew excruciating. Her tongue felt like an ice pick, stabbing the nerve cluster without mercy. But mercy was one thing I never expected. I counted the jabs to myself, grouping them in sets of ten like a weight lifter, packaging the feeling to make it manageable. I had withstood worse torture than this, and I shielded myself with that thought. The goal became to make it through, to make it to the end. How long would she go on this way?

I had lost count. My breasts were on fire, her hands grabbing at hardened wax and pinching my nipples. That little voice was there, trying to tell me to keep going, but it was fading, fading as I began to slip away, to the best place of worship of all. To that place where the mind falls aside and the body becomes the empty vessel, to that place of pure existence, pure sensation. I didn't think about it happening at the time, because if I had thought of it, it would have pulled me back to the present, back into my consciousness, and ruined it.

I let myself go, my whole body rigid but resisting nothing, my fingers clutching at a floor I no longer thought about. It happened as if to someone else, like some slow-motion movie. As my hands drew up to my chest and held her hands there while my hips bucked hard, pulling her forward and dragging my cunt across the full length of her tongue. My hands holding her hands on my breasts as my legs closed over her head and my hips shook, wringing the orgasm out over my skin, the convulsion shaking us so hard that we came apart. And then I was on her, her head on the ground and my cunt grinding into her mouth, and then covering her, my cunt against her leg, lips spread wide as I rode her, my hands raking her body and my mouth sucking at her breasts. There was wax in my mouth but it didn't feel like my mouth, there was power radiating from between my legs, and I couldn't stop myself from making myself come.

Then, suddenly, the orgasms stopped and I was staring down at my fingers, woven into the straight silk of her hair behind each ear, staring into her eyes, which no longer gleamed with hunger but sparkled with awe. She tugged gently at my hands, pulled them down to her breasts. I found myself eager to return the torture of earlier, as I twirled her nipples in my fingers and listened to her moan and cry out. My mouth to her mouth, my legs wrapped around hers, my hand sank into her pubic hair, wanting to pinch her clit, to pull it like taffy. But my finger slipped right past it and went deep into her, and suddenly I had another handle to hold her down with. Her cries became more frantic and she thrashed, but not enough to break free of me, not enough to make me think she didn't want it. My thumb on her clit, I plunged my long fingers into her and watched her hips rise to meet me. Could I do this to her for as long as she had done that thing to me?

I didn't. It seemed only a moment before she was bucking hard, her hand locked on my wrist and driving my hand in faster, her head flailing and her teeth sinking into my too-convenient shoulder as she struggled to take back from me the power I had stolen.

But I still had her on my hand, and as the orgasm subsided and my fingers could move again, I shifted my weight to keep her from sitting up, pressed my free hand against her throat, and kept my hand moving. I flicked her clit with my thumbnail and felt her cunt convulse. "I want you to come again," I heard my voice saying.

She whimpered very softly but did not say no.

I ground my thumb into her and her hips rose up, her legs shaking suddenly to give her that extra boost, and again she came. Again I kept my fingers inside her, and again I made her come. I made her come until I saw her face, and I saw that she too had gone off to that place of pureness, that place I always sought and sometimes found.

Thinking about that brought me back to myself at last. I withdrew my hands from her and sat back on my heels, receding from her like the tide from the cliff. She lay there a moment, taking deep breaths, and then she came back to herself, as well. I saw her eyes blink as she stared at the ceiling awash with candlelight.

She sat up slowly, her face impassive, and drew a shaky breath. She shifted, until she was kneeling, too, but her body continued forward until her head touched the floor in front of me. Her hands reached blindly for me and I caught them. Her shoulders shook, and I knew she was crying. She held tight to my hands, as if her tears might wash her away, and I squeezed back, helpless to do anything else other than berate myself.

What did you think you were doing? How could you let yourself go like that? I didn't understand what had just happened, and the only person I could ask was in tears.

Eventually, she wasn't. She composed herself, and even began to smile. She wiped back stray tears from her cheeks and grinned at me. "Thank you," she said.

I wasn't sure if "you're welcome" was the right thing to say at this juncture, not when I felt like an apology was on my lips. "I, uh, I didn't expect that to happen."

"No one ever does," she said, a wistful sound in her voice that reminded me I knew nothing of where she had come from. "Not many people can do that. You have a power, you know."

I shook my head. "No. That is, I *don't* know."

"Don't deny it. You felt it. I felt it. I was yours."

"Stop it." Empty words, loaded words, like guns. "That's not what I'm like. I'm not supposed to…"

Isa's eyes turned dark, confusion and disappointment registering on her face.

No. It had felt good. It felt as good as the day I had walked out of the Church, and as good as the day I had first been bound to a cross five years later, as good as the day I'd discovered as a child just what it was we weren't supposed to do with our hands in our panties, as good as the day I'd had my first orgasm from being whipped alone. But good didn't make it right. "Look, Isa, it doesn't mean anything." I pulled my knees up to my chest. "I don't know what it means."

She looked hurt. "You've taken me to a place I've never been. This is the first time I've known what it was like…"

To be the sacrifice, I thought, to be the one who gets no mercy. "I know," I said, and reached for her, cradled her head against my breast. "I know."

"I never knew I needed it this much." She was warm, and the room felt cold to me now. "I never knew that this was what I was looking for. But now I do."

I just nodded. I put her into her bed with promises I'd join her in a few minutes. When she was breathing deeply, I went back to the doorway of the dungeon and pulled on my clothes. In the driveway, I sat for a long moment on the bike, looking at the moonlit hills and wondering if I should leave. Maybe she was right; maybe I had touched something deep and important in myself, something new and vital, just as she had. Maybe I should stay and explore it more with her.

But I didn't want to see her gaze up at me with moonstruck eyes. I didn't want the responsibility of checking her for bruises and making her some tea. I wasn't ready to think that the same

Goddess who moved me to give myself up had moved me to fight and take and dominate tonight. My world was not supposed to be so complicated.

I rolled the bike to the end of the driveway before I started it. Perhaps in the morning everything would look different. But now I had a dark and unfamiliar road under me, the curves unwinding beneath the roar of the wind and the crackling of my uncertainty.

At Phoenicia
Cheryl Boyce Taylor

Your desire running over me
like a locomotive
we cook basmati rice
red bean-garlic soup

it is not enough
to get you off
my tongue
you humping my breath with fever
red as blowtorch

i rub your back
you want this all night
the moon stands up takes notice
this is a heavy night
stink with desire

in the early seasons
you sit at the window

Cheryl Boyce Taylor

count sunflowers
rising in the heat of us

—and last night
when i asked you to be here
you gave me something real
something to stand on

and i loved all the cracked
shapes of your laughter
lifting off my skin.

Tropical Storm
Robin G. White

I've always had a thing for heat. I figure, the hotter and more humid, the better. That is why I can picture us in the tropics, on a hot steamy sunny day, the sun pouring down on the white balcony outside the bedroom. I get up to take in the morning air. There are a few people milling around on the beach below: the early risers staking their claims to a little piece of sand and surf, serious tanners, I expect, who don't leave much to chance. The deep blue waves of the ocean have a rhythm and I sway to it, naked to the sun's rays.

A soft knock at the door brings me back from the mesmerizing slope of the waves hitting the beach. As I rush to cover myself before allowing entry, you step in. Dark and fresh in a crisp linen suit, you smile at me and close the door behind you. I can feel the wind blowing a cool Pacific breeze behind me.

It touches the moisture raised on my back by the sun's heat. There are no words to be spoken. I wouldn't talk if I could. Instead, my gaze meets the rich chocolate eyes that control my every moment. I can't look away. You are smiling at this knowledge.

You take a few steps forward. And I draw closer the white terry towel that barely covers my breasts and my sex. I am a little frightened, for as much as I want you, I don't know if I will submit willingly to your advances. You lift one strong right hand to my cheek and stroke it gently as you watch my eyes for my reaction. You are so gentle and you touch me like a delicate flower in full bloom. And just as I begin to yield, unfold, you pull me to the floor. In one sweeping motion, I am there beside you, exposed on the soft rug. Your kisses are passionate, hot and burning. Your tongue moves like flames scorching the inside of my mouth. I melt into you and onto you, the heat of my body rising into droplets of sweat on my breasts. You take one in hand and stroke it softly at first and then harder, with a kneading motion. My breathing becomes hard and my chest is heavy as though my entire body would cave in at another touch.

You are still dressed and I lean to undo the buttons of your jacket, but you move my hand away. You are not ready. It is me that you want, and I can feel that you intend to have me right at that moment. You mount me. I can feel the weight of your body grinding lustily at my pelvis. The fabric of your pants catches my hair occasionally and for that reason only, I want you to stop. But not really. Even the quick moment of pain when my pubic hair tugs at my flesh is exciting to me. The heat of the day and the fire of my body drench me with sweat. I am certain that I must be filled by you. I can smell the pungency of my pussy dripping with the sweet juices that you have stirred within me.

With one hand and your eyes still locked into mine, you trace the curve of my narrow waist and the full curve of my wide hips. Your hand burns the flesh of my thighs as I throw back my head and close my eyes. I relish the expectation of what I know will be a powerful moment.

With a teasing smile, you rub gently, playfully the Nubian lips at your fingertips. I embrace you, beggingly thrusting my cunt onto your hand. But you will not have it. You are enjoying the agony that you are causing. You love seeing my body writhe and wriggle. So, as you carefully seek out my most sensitive areas, you tantalize my clit, my lips, ruby red, my velvet pussy, until I near orgasm. And then you take your hand away.

I maneuver my body out from under you. You lie there, smug in the knowledge that you have me, and I want you badly. You tell me to work for it and wait for me to undress you. I do so anxiously. I so want to please you. Your taut muscles bulge from under the cool silk of the shirt that clings to your body. You arch your hips to allow me the pleasure of removing your pants.

And there, between your muscular thighs, awaits the silken pleasure, moist with beads of cum. Your grip firm and demanding, you pull my body toward you and hungrily take my mouth into your own.

I seek every centimeter of that orifice with my tongue hard and wet. I explore the origin of your hot, panting breath. And you suck me in, far in.

I begin to feel the strength of your thighs wrapping tightly around my buttocks and you flip me over on top of you. You begin again the rhythmic, grinding motion, and I succumb to it. The power of the strokes causes me to shake as we both near orgasm.

And just as I begin to feel the nearing final jolt of pleasure/pain, you thrust my face down to meet your bush-camouflaged pussy. Hungrily I lick at each sweet droplet that pours from within the fiery depths. I bury my face deep within the smoldering chasm. I can feel the thrust of your hips as you grind your dripping wet pussy onto my face. Nothing is spared this vaginal washing—not my face, chin, nose nor eyes. You shudder with such orgasmic force that I tremble. I can barely breathe. You take my face into you hands and kiss every sticky sweet centimeter.

I am delighted at having pleased you and reach down to fill what hungrily awaits my hand. You take in three fingers plunged deeply. As you ride and moan, I smile. The sound of your voice carries over the soft song of the waves beyond my balcony. I gaze into those lovely brown eyes now filled with so much joy.

And as I do, you begin to rise with me still inside. Slowly, you help me withdraw. I am bent on all fours as you mount me from behind. I feel the pressure gently at first and then harder and then faster. It is the force that one experiences when first being entered with a fist. I feel the tips of your fingers deep within me, and the width of your large brown hands demands that my lips open.

My hands claw at the edges of the rug and my head shakes almost violently as you begin to tear at the flesh of my cheeks with your teeth. You attempt to push me down with your free hand, but the strong push of your hand inside propels me forward. I cry out as I lunge toward the open door onto the balcony. I plead quietly. But every other moan and sigh gives me away. I truly am enjoying this display. I hear people below us on the beach. Through the railings I can see them in the distance. I know that too loud an outburst will give us away. So I refrain from screaming.

You whisper to me how good I am, how happy I make you. And you fuck me harder and deeper, stopping only to moisten the fingers of your left hand. You ease two into my anus and begin the stroking in-and-out motion that makes me collapse.

You urge me upward. My ass rises as though begging to be fucked, and you smile at this. I grab at the railing and hold on for support. I am dizzy with the power of your passion and I am eager to be pleased and fulfilled. Finally, I feel you behind me rising up on your knees, fingers stuffed inside. You cozy up behind my ass. I have no defense for this. I let out a shrill scream, giving us both away.

I see faces peering up at us. I hang my head in shame and as I do, I see the wry smiles of people gathering below. Someone shouts out, "Give it to her good!" And others join in. The chorus of voices grows as does my desire. You command me to lift myself up over the railing so the spectators can see my lovely face. You lift me up with hands that are inside and I lean as directed over the balcony. I brace myself in time to feel the last thrust of your hips, which enters your fingers deeper inside my soft open pussy. The heel of your hand disappears as I melt into a jelly-like mass at your feet.

I awaken to the cool breeze blowing curtains into the billowy clouds at my balcony door. I step onto the balcony to view a morning ocean rich in hues of blue and green. A golden haze rises above it, casting light on the early surfers and tanners. The sun burns a steamy hole into the morning air, and I sigh at the fragrance that wafts past my nose. It is a scent rich with gardenia, violets, and pungent sex. A bemused smile crosses my face as I think of my dream of being with you.

Water Marks
Dawn Dougherty

I have a love affair with bathing.

My cunt starts to throb the second I turn on the tap and hear the soft splash of the water against my claw-footed, porcelain tub. I draw a daily bath, sliding my body inch by inch into the piping-hot water and watching my skin turn pink before it slips beneath the bubbles. I soak for at least an hour, barely moving except to stretch my back or rest my foot on the edge, letting the water and bubbles drip down my thigh. When I'm done soaking I pull the showerhead into me and let the water vibrate over my clit until I come with the same lapping precision of ocean waves. For years I masturbated no other way, preferring a steamy, warm bath to any bed or couch. When I go to visit friends or family, the first thing I check out is how clean their tub is and what the water pressure is like.

In my bathroom I have four different kinds of bubble bath; three different types of scented bath oils; and multiple candles, loofahs, and sponges, all within arm's reach. My showerhead is a two-speed adjustable shower massager with a hose long enough to reach wherever I may be.

I know if a woman is a good match for me based purely on her feelings about bathing. I once asked a lover if she would like to take a bath with me. She crinkled her nose in disgust and said, "In water?" We lasted three weeks. Another time I had filled the tub and gotten in fully expecting my current lover to join me. She came into the bathroom, took one look at me and said, "Sorry, but I'm just not into taking baths." I had sadly resigned myself to solitary pleasures.

The first time my new lover said that she liked her women wet, I was sure she meant between their thighs. She smiled and went on to explain that what she really liked were women soaked in water. My eyes lit up.

"I really have this thing for wet women," she said. "I love women walking in the rain, washing cars, taking showers or baths. It just gets me so hot."

Did she say baths? I had to replay the last part in my head several times to make sure I wasn't hearing things. I tried to contain my euphoria as she told me about her past lovers and how they used to get in water fights and fuck afterward with water dripping off their bodies and into their cunts. She said there was nothing better than bathing a soaking wet femme with hair dripping down a curved, soft back. I was delirious.

We had been dating for only two weeks when she bought me a mouse pad decorated with big, fat water droplets. I couldn't touch my mouse without envisioning us completely drenched. Several days later she left my apartment early for work while I was still sleeping. When I awoke there was a note on my pillow that said simply, "I need you wet."

The following Sunday I drew a bath.

She was sitting on the couch reading the paper when I went into the bathroom, lit a candle, and turned on the water. I picked out a freesia-scented bubble bath and watched as it drizzled into the swirling water and started to foam. I placed a fresh bar of raspberry soap, a soft yellow bath sponge, and a white cotton washcloth on the windowsill next to the tub. The glass had already fogged over. I slipped out of my jeans and sweatshirt and put on my peach silk robe, and gave the bathroom a once-over. The room was filled with the smell of soap and candles and steam.

When I went out to the living room the paper was folded neatly next to her on the couch and she was sitting quietly with her arms crossed. She had been waiting.

I sat down on the couch next to her. "I'm going to take a bath," I said, trying to appear casual. "You can join me…" I paused, "or, if you like…you can bathe me." I was awkwardly playing with the hem of my robe.

She sighed deeply, unfolded her arms, and pressed her soft lips firmly against mine. The faint smell of coffee lingered on her mouth. "I'll take the latter of those two options." She kissed me once more and then turned my head to the side and whispered in my ear, "I was praying you would ask." A tremor started at the base of my neck and worked its way down to the tip of my toes.

"Give me a minute," I said as I got up. I could feel her eyes on my ass as I walked out of the room.

The tub had filled nearly to the top and the bubbles formed high, soft peaks. Perfect, I thought. I turned the knobs off and put one foot into the fiery water. It took me several minutes to adjust to the temperature. I lay back and momentarily hesitated while I debated leaving my hair dry (I was having a good hair day, after all). In the next instant I plunged my head into the sizzling water and came up with a mass of wet, dangling hair. I pondered how I wanted her to first see me. I leaned forward with my arms wrapped around my legs and hair hanging down my right shoulder. I sat up tall with sudsy nipples just above the water line, hair fanned out across my back. I finally settled on leaning back with one knee bent slightly above the water.

She opened the door and caught me mid-thought. My stomach did a somersault as she paused at the door and stared at me. The only sound was the water dripping slowly from the showerhead and her deep exhalation. She stood in the doorway for what seemed like an eternity, watching me.

"That is the best image I have ever seen in my entire life," she finally said.

I tried to hide my smile. She moved toward me and bent down on one knee next to the tub. She reached down and pulled me up against her. She kissed me hard on the lips as the water swooshed around us. Her hands went immediately to my hair, and our lips parted long enough for her to moan "Oh, god" softly while she buried her hands in my wet curls. She leaned back and pealed off her already wet T-shirt. She had a tiny labrys tattoo on her right shoulder. Her arms were hard and flexed effortlessly as she adjusted her kneeling position on the floor.

She settled me back into the tub and picked up a sponge. She soaked it thoroughly and released the water over my bent neck, watching the water form slick clear trails down my back and over my shoulders. The water cleared the bubbles off my body and she kissed the clear spots on the back of my neck. She soaked the sponge again and ran it across my shoulders, watching the water run over my breasts. She soaked the sponge and squeezed the water out over and over again, across my back, my shoulders, and my nipples. I was on fire watching her watching me. Both of us were soaking wet.

She picked up the raspberry soap and lathered it up in her hands. She slowly washed each and every inch of my body. Starting with my fingertips, she methodically ran her soapy hands over me until every muscle in my body ached for her. She washed my breasts in easy, soft circles while I lay against the back of the tub. She lifted each of my legs out of the water and, starting with my toes, worked her way to my inner thigh with small kneading rubs. After finishing each section she took the sponge and rinsed me off with painstaking gentleness.

When she was done washing my body she brought me to my

knees. The water ran off me as she took turns sucking on each of my nipples. My soft, wet body touched her hard, angular one and the shapes fit together like pieces in a puzzle. My arms wrapped around her neck and held tight. Water trickled down her back.

"I want to wash your hair," she whispered. I nodded and turned and sat down with my back toward her. She reached for the shampoo and then stopped.

"Um…how much of this do you use?" she stammered. I looked at her inch and a half of hair and grinned. I held her hand open and squeezed out just the right amount. Without skipping a beat she buried both of her hands deep into my hair and lathered up the long tresses. Thick soapy suds fell down my back into the water.

"God," she moaned again. She spent fifteen minutes lathering my hair as the suds fell in large clumps around us. Her forearms were covered with foam as she reached around and cupped each of my breasts with two sudsy hands, squeezed hard, and kissed my shoulder. Her nipples grazed my back as she bit me eagerly. She pushed my head down slowly and rinsed the shampoo out of my hair. My eyes were closed as the water poured over my head, and I heard her breath quicken. When she was done I flipped my head back and water splashed across the room, hitting her in the face. She laughed, gave me a kiss on the lips, and said, "You are heavenly."

I stood up and was reaching for a towel when she stopped me.

"Where are you going?" she said pushing me back. "We're not finished." I sat back hesitantly as she pulled the plug on the drain. The heat and the steam were making me light-headed, and the receding swirl of the water easily pulled my body down.

"I need you to come. Right here."

My body tensed. She placed her hand on my stomach and ran it down my belly to my legs as the water slowly drained. She pulled my legs apart and rested my shaking knees against the side of the tub. She leaned back to soak me in. Trails of bubbles and water formed on my body as the tub emptied.

She turned and reached for the showerhead and my entire body quivered. I lifted one foot and braced it on the opposite end of the tub, arching my back in anticipation. She smiled, watching me squirm. She turned the water on and ran it across her hand as she adjusted the temperature. When she was ready she ran her free hand along the inside of my thigh and gently grazed the tip of my clit with her finger. I hit the roof.

"In a minute," she said deeply, taking her hand away.

She turned the showerhead first to my feet, letting the strong current roll across my toes and around the ball of my foot. The entire bathroom was soaked, and water was dripping down her arms and chest. She worked her way methodically up my calf to my thigh, stopping to let the pressure relax every inch of my legs. I wanted to reach out and touch her slicked-back hair, but my arms were braced against the side of the tub. I could barely breathe as she slowly moved the water up my body from my thigh to my stomach to my chest. The muscles that extended from her shoulders to her neck rippled with her every move. I shut my eyes and arched my back further as the pulsating water hit my nipples. She held it there momentarily, watching the water bounce off me in tiny rivulets.

With the same slow precision, she started working her way back down my body, pausing slowly at each juncture. She finally stopped and let the pressure work its way around both my thighs. She took her left hand and placed it squarely in the middle of my chest, pushing and holding me down.

"Are you ready?" she asked. I nodded.

She adjusted her body slightly before she moved the stream to my clit. My entire body quaked as the rhythmic waves hit me. Both of my legs were now braced against the edge of the tub, which was almost empty, and my body was pressed completely back as the water rolled over me. She moved the nozzle back and forth over my entire cunt. My head spun with a hot dizziness and my body throbbed. I was barely holding on. She was saying something, softly urging me on, but all I heard was the sound of rushing water. The pressure was building up in me and my entire body tensed in anticipation.

"You are incredible," I heard her say clearly.

The sound of her voice hurled me over the edge and I came in violent waves. She held me down firmly with her hand and kept the water pressure directly on my clit. Water splashed out of the tub and poured in streams onto the bathroom floor. My body rocked back and forth for what seemed like hours, each muscle in my body releasing the built-up tension until I couldn't move.

Mild contractions were still shooting through my body when she turned the water off. She leaned against the bathroom door and ran her hand through her drenched hair. She was still wearing her jeans and boots and was soaked from head to toe.

"We are two wet girls," she smiled. I nodded silently.

I attempted to get up, but my head was spinning and I stood uneasily. She quickly grabbed my arm and steadied me. She pulled an oversized towel off the rack, wrapped it around me, and took me back to the bedroom. She valiantly tried to dry me off, but I stayed soaking wet for the rest of the day.

Q&A

Carol Rosenfeld

The wine-and-cheese segment of the meeting of the Third Thursday Networking, Social and Support Group for Professional Lesbians was well under way when I walked into the Lavender Lounge at the Triangle Inn. I had been advised that TTNSSGPL was a major cruise scene. The highlight of the evening was always "Stand and Tell," during which a microphone was passed from table to table, and each woman would stand and introduce herself. When the mike arrived at my table I made sure to spill the contents of my purse onto the floor, so I was busy putting everything back in place as the mike made its way from woman to woman.

"Hi, I'm Mindy. I own and operate Vamoose Vans. Call on us whenever you're moving in or out."

It wasn't that I didn't want the professional lesbians to see me; I just didn't want them to know that I was a bridal consultant.

Stand and Tell was followed by the networking period. I stood sipping my wine, trying to look approachable. The real estate agent, rushing toward the law firm partner in search of a country home, careened into me, splashing red wine onto my ecru silk blouse, which I had ransomed from the dry cleaner the previous weekend. A woman chose that moment to hand me her card.

"Angel Mersé, Dyke Investigator."

"So you, ah, investigate women to find out if they're dykes? There have been times when I would have paid a lot of money for that kind of information." It was the best verbal response I could come up with. I was having trouble with coherence, with remaining upright when my hormones were demanding that I lie down. With her Fra Angelico blue eyes and curly, new-penny red-blond hair that was guaranteed to drive the most congenial cherub to unheavenly envy, Angel Mersé was absolutely adorable, certifiably hot. She was also petite. I felt huge. I had torpedoes for breasts and thighs the diameter of redwood trunks that were buckling like willows in the wind. To save Angel's life, I would have to be the bottom. Lucky for both of us, that's the kind of girl I am.

Of course, it took a while for Angel and me to get to that point. It didn't happen the way it usually did in those erotic stories I was always reading. Images of rushing off with her to the nearest bathroom, booking a room at the Triangle Inn, and getting naked in her car in the parking lot flickered on my mental screen, but a more urgent matter demanded my attention. "I have to get some seltzer for this wine stain," I said.

Grabbing the nearest bottle from the refreshments table, I twisted the cap off. Seltzer splattered my hair, face, and chest. I patted my face with a napkin while Angel gently dabbed at the damned spot on my left breast, just above my bra cup. As my nipples began flaunting their presence beneath the businesslike blouse, the red that was slowly disappearing from the silk seeped into Angel's cheeks. It was embarrassing, yet I wished I was showing a little more cleavage.

"I think that should do it, " Angel said, dropping her hands and stepping back.

"Thanks."

"My home, office, and beeper numbers are on my card, in case you need help with anything else."

Most nights I fantasized about Bridget before falling asleep. But that night I pretended my hands were resting on Angel's curls while her mouth moved across my body like a planchette on a Ouija board, channeling my desire.

Angel and I began working our way through the top ten activities preferred by authors of personal ads. We went to a movie, visited a museum, attended a play and a concert. We traveled around the world via New York's ethnic restaurants, and spent a day antiquing in a scenic village on the Hudson River. Angel bought me a copy of *Winnie the Pooh* to replace the one I'd given to my elementary school library because I felt guilty about an overdue book. We discovered that we both disliked the new blue M&Ms and preferred the white icing to the chocolate on black-and-white cookies. Angel simply refused to eat the chocolate, while I ate it first and saved the best for last. And we went for walks in the park and on the beach with Betty Boop, Angel's Great Dane. At the end of each meeting, agreeing that it had been fun, we would stare at each other intently for a couple of minutes, then go our separate ways.

I was frustrated but afraid of making the first move. However, I was getting a little tired of shopping for new lingerie every time Angel made a date with me. Tonight, we'd decided to attempt a quiet evening at home. Angel proved to be a good cook. The meal she prepared was simple, but tasty—salad, roast chicken, wild rice, steamed vegetables, sorbet for dessert. After she served the coffee we settled down to watch *The Maltese Falcon*, one of Angel's favorites. Angel put the tape in and sat down in a recliner.

"There's plenty of room here on the sofa," I said.

Angel didn't take the bait. "I always sit in this chair when I watch TV."

Betty Boop jumped up and lay down next to me, with her head in my lap. I sighed.

While the tape was rewinding I started to shiver. In August. In an apartment with no air-conditioning. I tried to control it, but when my teeth began to chatter, Angel looked at me.

"Are you *cold*?"

"Nnnoooh," I said. It was hard to talk with my teeth making like the happy, tap-dancing feet in *Forty-Second Street*. "This hahapp-penns whenever I tr-try to figure out if someone is going to m-make a ppp-pass at me. I can't-ttt-take the suspense any longer. Either ttt-tell me that you just want to be friends, or kkk-kiss me."

She put me out of my misery without a word.

You might have thought I'd be preoccupied with the softness and taste of her, but the voices in my head kept buzzing, flutter-ing, zapping themselves on the light with every kiss. What if Angel wouldn't do the one thing I really needed her to do, the thing I was almost embarrassed about wanting because it was so identified with lesbians that my desire for it seemed boring and conventional. Maybe Angel was one of those women I'd read about who strapped on huge dildos and wanted them sucked. I tried to figure out why a woman would find this arousing. She wouldn't feel anything—unless it was a phenomenon like the phantom limb, but reversed. Or maybe it was a visual thing. When I came out of the closet I thought I had left fellatio far behind, and I felt a bit resentful at having it pop up again. Women's genitals were so much nicer: they were less ostentatious, and they never made you gag.

As Angel squeezed my breast my internal disc jockey turned sadistic and began playing the refrain "Girls just want to have fun," like a taunt while the great storm cloud questions rolled slowly across my consciousness: "Am I going to cry? Will I be able to come?"

I had tried talking to Bridget about the crying, once. She shrugged and said that lots of women did, if that made me feel any better, which it didn't.

"Ticklish?" Angel asked, after my shoulders scrunched up in

response to her lips nuzzling my neck.

"Yes. Sorry."

"I think we'll be more comfortable in bed." She took my hand and led me up a short flight of stairs to a loft room. Betty Boop was sprawled across the double bed.

"Betty. Off the bed."

Betty yawned.

Angel picked up a rubber toy and squeaked it. Betty sat up, then ran as Angel threw the toy down the stairs.

I slid my hands under the sleeves of Angel's T-shirt and filled them with her muscles. Then I slid them down her sides and under the cotton again, around and up to her shoulder blades, while I plucked at her upper, then lower lip, with both of mine. We sank down onto the bed and everything shifted—weight and tempo and touch. There was a desperate quality to my need for both of us to be naked. I pulled my tank top off, and Angel put her hands behind my back.

"In front," I whispered.

I had to admit that I'd had some trouble with the clasp myself. Still, it was disconcerting to see a woman with a license to carry a .44 Magnum stymied by a bra that hooked in front. Fortunately, I didn't have to face that problem, because Angel wasn't wearing a bra. Beneath the white T-shirt, her breasts formed soft sweet peaks of meringue. I brushed the tip of one with the back of my hand.

"Do you mind?" Angel said. "I'm in the middle of a highly technical operation." A moment later she was able to slip the straps off my shoulders and hold the bra in the air. "We have lift off." She dropped it on the floor by the bed and grasped the hem of her T-shirt.

I gasped and quivered.

"What?" said Angel, arms above her head, breasts exposed, the neck of the T-shirt stretching over the tip of her nose.

"Betty's licking my toes," I whispered. We both watched her for a moment.

"Would you like me to do that to you?" Angel asked.

I considered this. Perhaps if I'd had a pedicure, and was fresh from the bath, wearing that magenta silk robe I'd admired earlier in the week. "Actually," I said, wiggling my toes to dry them off, "I'd rather you lick something else."

Angel's eyes were the blue beginning of a flame. With her flushed cheeks and coppery hair, she was a creature of fire, an underworld goddess come to take me on a dark, heated journey. "The back of your knee?" she asked.

"An intriguing possibility, but not precisely what I had in mind."

"Your inner thigh?"

"I'd prefer that you bite that. But you're heading in the right direction."

Angel lay down on top of me, light in weight, but solidly muscled. As our kisses became longer and deeper, our breathing shorter and more ragged, Angel began moaning, "B...B...B..."

That's one of the problems with having a name like mine—Bambi doesn't exactly fit into a Great Moments in the Heat of Passion scenario.

"B.D.," Angel sighed.

I held my breath while Angel's mouth moved up my inner thigh. As she lapped and circled and thrust I offered up an inarticulate chant. But some part of my brain remained on guard duty. Was I making too much noise? Taking too long? I was afraid I might break if she kept on going. "Don't stop," I gasped, clutching at the sheet with my hands. I wanted to be on overload, my clit so charged that it would black out my brain like New York City in the summer of '77. But when it did, it was less of a shattering than a slow sinking back into the here and now. I turned away from Angel, curled into myself, and wept. When the worst of it had passed, Angel smoothed my hair. I sniffled and headed for the bathroom and a tissue. It wasn't the crying that was so bad, it was blowing my nose afterward.

From the doorway, I looked at Angel on the bed. Her patch of blonde pubic hair fascinated me, and I lay down between her legs for a closer look. Her hair was straighter, sparser, silkier than mine. I rubbed my face against her like a cat marking its territory, then turned back to lick her clean, alternating long slow strokes with quick flicks. With Angel's every moan I became more predatory. When she pulled my head away, I lifted myself up and over. And then I, who had never been able to work a hula hoop, found my hips in orbit as I pressed myself to her.

With Angel curled behind me, her arm draped across my stomach, I listened to the nocturnal city sounds of the occasional car or subway passing and remembered Jean, my only woman before Angel. "You should make love with lots of women," she'd told me, and it wasn't so much an endorsement of promiscuity as an acknowledgment of pleasure taken and given; a kind of blessing. While my skin cooled and the scent of sex still lingered, I pictured myself lying on soft cool grass, entwined with an amazon Bridget, then spread-eagled beneath the gaze of an imperturbable Maxine. But they were remote figures on my fantasy stage; it was a delightfully mortal Angel whose breasts caressed my back with every breath. I was starting to doze when a new sound intruded. The snoring was impossible to ignore. I sighed, wondering if I'd ever get to sleep.

"It's not me," Angel mumbled. "It's the dog."

I placed my hand over Angel's to hold her to me, and closed my eyes.

Me and Mrs. Jones
Donna Allegra

Usually when a woman says she is bisexual I nod politely and walk quickly away. But as Paige's hair rises like birds' wings streaking across the sky, rules for alternate-side-of-the-street parking are suspended.

She's finally done away with her wet T-shirt and is down to a dance bra. Studying her is a pleasant pastime and I pore over her exposed body. Even her pimples fascinate me. Shadows of perspiration outline her behind, which is fashionably accentuated by the ridge of Calvin Klein underpants that peeks above her sweatpants.

This crush is just a pastime. Paige is married and was raised south of Jimmy Carter. She may be living in New York City now, but I am too much of a colored girl to trust my affections to southern hospitality.

Alison's teaching voice interrupts my reverie: "Girls, do we want to see the men dance in their own group?"

My face wrinkles with irritation as a chorus of hoots rises around the room. Some are mock, most are eager.

The seven men in dance class assemble at the center of the studio surrounded by a circle of enthusiastic women. I try to keep my exasperation from showing. I've heard at least four of these men call each other "girlfriend."

Alison directs with a Marilyn Monroe breathiness, "Okay, the third group is men only. Work it, fellas; ladies are watching."

Paige catches me cutting my eyes and rolls her own with a grin. I snort sour at the testosterone on parade; she stands amused.

Paige and I are in the same rehearsal group. After the first rehearsal with Claude, Paige archly tells Alison, "I'm not worried about remembering all those steps. Avon is a Virgo. She retains everything."

"I don't retain anything except water," Alison says glumly, then attempts to drawl, "Paige? Up north, we don't go 'round calling people anal-retentive."

"Don't take it like that," Paige protests. "I'm not putting Avon down. If my tits weren't already screwed in place, I'd probably wear them on my earlobes. Avon just always gets sequences and the fiddly fidgety moves right."

"Okay, I'm anal-retentive. And I'm a kick your ass for talking about how I can't let go of anything." I put on a menacing look.

Paige doesn't buy my wolf ticket and purrs, "Avon, honey. You have allure. You take awkward choreography and give it a flow that smoothes the quirky parts."

Alison nods in agreement. I feel flattered but self-conscious. Embarrassment prompts me to say, "Do you want to work together on the choreography sometime, Paige?"

"Now there's an offer. Can I pay you in plastic or will my first-born child do?"

It makes me nervous that Paige—I know this sounds conceited, but she wasn't the only one—could see a quality in my dancing that made her notice. I wished I knew what it was so I could make sure I kept that quality in place. I craved attention. If I couldn't hold a lover, as Tamara made clear, I wanted to at least attract other women.

Paige and I start meeting evenings in one of the empty studios at Twinkle Toes. She is the office manager so we don't need to ask for permission.

"I'm glad Claude wants us to choreograph a section," Paige says as we settle into work. "Now how are we going to get this jazz funk ballet up and running, Avon?"

I propose we choreograph as a game: "I'll make up a movement and then you add to it." We trade steps back and forth, working out kinks along the way.

I come up with a show-off movement that takes me down to the floor for my next eight beats of choreography and Paige says, "I don't want to try the floor work just yet. I've got too much at stake teaching ballet to pre-pubes to risk an injury."

I do the floor and Paige, the standing version. Sweat films us both and I catch whiffs of her body scent from my ground position. I wonder how I can get more of her smell without appearing like a dog sniffing.

As Paige writes notes on what we've created, I look over her shoulder, inhaling the delicious flesh of her bare limbs. She probably has no idea how much I am cruising her.

Over the next few weeks, conversations at our private rehearsals somehow become intimate. When we are next together in dance class, I feel I have a buddy. Paige's active friendship—a hug before class and touches during—make us appear as lovers in my mind. But I also like that she is married. I can remain safe from the messy entanglements that always arrive with my sexual attractions.

In rehearsal, I feel Paige's liquid eyes float across me, her pupils like a bull's-eye wherever she sets her mark.

Claude has twelve dancers, four to a unit. Mark, a man I ordinarily like, doesn't merit all the oohs and giggles Alison is giving him. Off the beat with the hips, he mangles the hand ephemera, but Alison cheers, "Go Mark!" as he messes up Claude's choreography. On the funk riffs, he follows me like mad and gets too much into my space. I cast him a jaundiced eye.

Claude has us split into our three smaller units and Alison says, "Mark, you lead us."

"Listen," I say to my group. "We all know most of the choreography, why doesn't each of us take a section to be responsible for?"

"Oh, but Mark looks so good doing anything. He should lead," Alison coos.

"Avon's on the money," Mark counters. "Avon, you should take the funk. I'm having orgasms watching the body you've put on Claude's footwork. We can each choose a part to be responsible for." He speaks as if this were his idea.

"Oh, but Mark, we want you to lead," Alison sulks.

After a few more "Oh, but Mark's from Alison, Paige says, "Alison, just for shits and giggles, let's try Avon's notion."

The interlude burns me. If I were a man, Alison would show a lot more respect. Even when she teaches class, Alison pretends not to notice when I work my ass off. All I get are some covert looks, not even half the response Mark gets simply for being male. Fucking men get everything and don't have to lift a finger to have it handed to them.

I feel my hand yanked. Even though I realize Mark is attempting to turn me, I shove away, "Hey, back up."

"Avon, I was taking you as my partner." His face flushes.

"Well, try asking first," I say, angry and embarrassed at my distaste.

"Dance with me, Mark," Alison says. He twirls her and his eyes whimper kicked-puppy glances my way.

I stay pissed throughout group rehearsal, brood during the break. Paige startles me with an offer of a sip from her bottle of Evian. "You know, Avon, lesbians aren't the only ones who appreciate women. You know what excites me? Strong gals who won't make men out to be gods. I'm inspired when females don't put up with their arrogance or suffer male foolishness."

By now I know Paige is not a nicey-nice southern belle—she was more likely the hellcat who'd left town on the back of some boy's motorcycle. But I am surprised that she doesn't think male privilege a thing of the past. Which is what Alison seems to believe. Fucking idiot with no sense of history. Or just plain idiot.

Paige mistakes my sour expression for skepticism. I soften when, with a wry smile, she declaims, "Men are never frigid. Only women. Men may be impotent, which is embarrassing, but women are considered mean and selfish. He may be distant, but she's unloving. And a woman who wants her own satisfaction is a nymphomaniac."

She pauses. "Wayne doesn't exactly call me a slut, but that's the spirit of what my dear husband believes. And if he doesn't stop this born-again man-of-the-house kick and mind his manners, he may end up as my was-band."

We each drink from her water bottle. After a lull, Paige says, "Wayne knows I have affairs, Avon. He doesn't like it, but he wants me around so he lumps it."

"Really? I've been operating my whole adult life around the premise that if I have sex with someone, we put a picket fence around it and live happily ever after."

Paige snorts, "It hasn't worked that way for me. I'm a big enough girl to get mad about not getting sex the way I like it. Wayne needs me to fondle my breasts and talk about the times I was with a woman. I'm tired of his charades. Believing that stuff got me married in the first place."

I raise a suspicious eybrow to question and Paige says, "I grew up in Charlottesville, Virginia. Charlottesville is located about two hundred years behind the rest of the country. I was expected to get a boyfriend, get a respectable job, get married, beget two kids."

I nod, feeling kinship with Paige. As I look at her peach cleavage, the breasts plumped close together, sex-feeling spreads like water spilled on my pants. I try to absorb the desire with the thought that she's probably "bi-curious," but I can't summon my contempt for that breed of women. Instead, something in me whimpers against the thought of sneering Paige away.

"We sure have heck of conversations when we rehearse, lady," Paige says.

"Yeah, I thought dancers were just disgruntled jocks." On impulse I tell her, "I don't really want to date anyone. I just want to know that I'm attractive to women."

"But Avon, you're beautiful," Paige protests.

Twice more during the course of rehearsal, she tells me, "You're so beautiful." As I stand behind Paige on the floor I take a different look at myself in the mirror. I wear an aqua-green T-shirt that's a good color for me. My dancing hits the pocket every time. Maybe it's my premenstrual state—somehow I blossom before the blood comes down.

I hope we can keep this mutual admiration going and not get messy about it. I want a friend for the long haul.

The New York City performances at The Mill, where other dance people make up the bulk of our audience, go fine. Tonight is our first out-of-town gig. I wonder how we'll be received as I stare dumbly at a computer-printed sign on the college dormitory door.

The philosophy at Twinkle Toes keeps teachers and students on a first-name basis. I frown at the sign's unfamiliar rendering of my name, "A. Hicks," paired with "A. Jones."

Shit. Dollars-to-donuts that I'm stuck rooming with "A." for Alison for this upstate New York show. Now I know there'll be no rest for the weary in the little town of Bethlehem. No telling when—or if—Alison will go out for drinks and I can have peace and quiet.

I hear footsteps and turn to see Paige lugging her satchel. Her glad smile sweetens my disposition.

"Who're you with?" she asks, looking at room doors for her number.

"Alison," I say dismally.

"Hmmm. I can't find my quarters. The ruffian downstairs said room 308."

"That's my room, but it's me and A. Jones."

"Why that's you and me, Avon Hicks."

"But 'Paige' isn't spelled with an 'A'—not at the beginning…" I babble.

"My full and proper title is Anne Paige Cameron, and technically, that's Cameron-Jones. If you will be so kind as to make just a little room, I will assume my rightful position as your roommate for the weekend."

After the evening's performance, Alison, Mark, and some others talk about where they'll go to eat and have drinks on this upstate campus.

"I skipped breakfast and lunch. I'm being so good these days," Alison enthuses.

"All I want to eat is sleep," I say to no one in particular. I'm so wiped, a quiet dinner alone will suit me to a tee.

"I knew you'd have some reason not to hang out. You're such a prude, Avon. You should let me show you how to have fun." An undercurrent in Mark's voice laps too close for comfort.

"Fun? What's that?" I say to play off his remark. Boys and girls in mating games is not my idea of a good time. I catch Paige staring and shrug, "I don't have such good social skills."

"Hasn't been my experience." She gives me a curious look and leaves with the others.

I've been biting the inside of my mouth mistakenly throughout the entire meal, hoping Paige won't return any time soon. I nearly choke when the door opens and she turns on her bedside lamp.

"So who was at this fête?" I ask, not caring but making an effort to converse.

"The usual suspects and an assortment of musical nuts." Paige surveys my bowl of broccoli and mung bean sprouts, the plate flecked with brown rice, the miso soup in a cup.

"Goodness gracious me, Avon. I've discovered your secret. I thought you never ate."

I swallow with difficulty, feeling as if she'd walked in on me masturbating. "Two meals a day. I just like to do it out of the public eye."

"I know what you mean. Eating a decent meal is harder than starving." Paige flops on her bed with a sigh.

I look up in surprise. "You too, huh?"

"You're a dancer, right? Maybe any woman in America?" She deliberately stands in profile before the room mirror and sucks in her lovely stomach. "Plus, you forget," she scolds. "I'm a southern belle. I have an added imperative to look picture perfect."

I relax a notch. Paige wasn't an anorexic who took an hour to eat a bran muffin, but I hadn't sensed in her any particular energy about food or not-food.

"Should I leave you alone or can I just turn my back?" she asks.

"Hey, you live here as much as I do," I try to sound sincere.

"I think I will leave and let you eat in peace. Maybe I'll go to the campus square and look at the locals, bite the dogs..." She pauses, then adds pensively, "or the rats and squirrels—whichever come along first."

She reaches to turn off her lamp, whose shade swirls like a skirt blown by the wind.

"Bon appétit, Avon." Paige's tone feels like a kiss to my forehead after being tucked into a comforter, my head on plumped pillows.

The next day, we have dinner in our room. We start talking about the performance and Paige gushes, "You were so hot on stage! From the way the men were looking at you I don't know if you'll be the sex fantasy of the season or cited in the court papers as probable cause for divorce."

By degrees, I feel unsure. I don't know if Paige is working me or what. Flattery is the best drug in town to catch a girl's attention and the best aphrodisiac to get her juiced.

Nerves spur me to say, "Wanna hear something shocking, Paige? Sex doesn't interest me. I wouldn't mind lesbian bed death if my lover was committed to me. I don't know how to fuck someone and then go on my merry way. I'd never be a candidate for sluthood. My autobiography could be titled *The Love Life of a Spinster*. I'm just not sexually motivated. I want to settle into a steady relationship without trauma-drama."

Paige's arched eyebrows became matching slivers of moon. "Are you sure you're a lesbian, Avon? My reliable sources say that major drama is a required course for advanced lesbianism." Paige grins that slow smile of hers and looks at me from eyes in a kaleidoscope of brown, yellow, green.

"Avon, we should have sex."

I wince in alarm. It's one thing to harbor a wish, but Paige's interest in things sexual outdistances mine. She'll expect me to take the lead and know it all. But recreational sex isn't my game. Sex as a means for connection, depth, quality energy, fine and groovy, but I'd starve in whoredom.

"I don't want to be a straight woman's dildo, Paige." To soften it I add, "I'm sexually incompetent. I do what I can in bed, but if you're out for erotic thrills, you'd better look elsewhere, Mrs. Cameron-Jones. What I really want is someone to love me."

"Okay, be like that: the next time you need a hand with something? I'm a tell you to use the other one," Paige laughs at my dismay. "And mama does love you, honey."

Relieved that she isn't mad that I balked, I wonder what she means.

Paige motions me to toss over her cigarettes, "Since we've just done sex," and pats the place by her pillow. "Sit here, so you'll be downwind of Marlboro country."

She does look alluring exhaling a filmy stream of gray. I sit and

Paige's voice conveys both frustration and argument. "What is lesbian? What does bisexual mean? Those labels make no sense. I've had women lovers and men lovers. And what's that say about me? I like to think I'm omnisexual."

I'd deliberately let pass all her previous mentions of having "been with women." Now I am ready to ask if she is using the plural for just one taste. I hope she is not going to tell me that her first boyfriends were Black. Lord, don't let her be another white person who's into chocolate.

I have a lot of feeling stirring me, so I start carefully, "The word *lesbian* means a lot if you are and the whole world says you should be with men. It meant plenty to the boys at school who called me lesbian names, shoved and pushed me when no one could see them pick on me." Paige nods, her face alive with the sympathy I'd come to love in her.

" 'Lesbian' means something out of science fiction to the straight men looking at porn flicks to get their sagging dicks up. They love to watch two women have sex and then have a man come on the scene to make a conquest of a 'lesbian.' " At this, she cackles. The sound of her laughter has gotten good to me.

But I don't leave off where we agree. " 'Lesbian' also means something different to women who sleep with women and maybe with men, but don't want people calling them dykes in the old-fashioned mean and nasty way that people who aren't lesbians say 'dyke.' These women huff they're bi or het—not 'lesbian,' Paige."

I wish I smoked so I could take a drag and exhale a stream for emphasis. Paige's face twitches to remain neutral and I push myself to say, "So don't give me that, 'I don't want to be boxed in with a label' bit. The name means plenty to the other bisexual women who think *bisexual* is a dirty word and will say that they are lesbian to have a cooler image. Maybe they somehow identify with lesbians, but they also want to have sexual relationships with men. Then they commit to a man and casually say to their dyke friends, 'I'm seeing men now.' The word means plenty," I end firmly.

Paige's eyebrows furrow and her eyes look at the dull green bed-spread. I don't want those eyes to go blank and close up on me; still, I can't leave off: "Omnisexual—what's that mean? Small animals like goats, pigs, deer? Aren't they hard to catch?"

She is quiet and I anguish over unzipping bitterness I didn't know I had in me.

"Touché, Avon. I've been with women and I married a man because I needed to be married. I wanted my family's blessing and the neighbors' approval."

I feel my face close and she sees the look, but she doesn't turn her eyes away.

"You're a new breed, Avon. You can live in the light and love who you want to and say to hell with the ones who can't handle it. Once upon a time I couldn't even conceive of that. You're beautiful and strong and brave. I don't believe in forever. We might manage a long time together or maybe just tonight."

My face trembles with a wordless, troubled expression.

She looks even more intensely at me, "You can tell me 'no' and keep your pure-dyke honor. But you want to sleep with me, Avon, I been smelling you for weeks."

Paige is not begging and her eyes plead like someone who has enough to need nothing. I'm the one found out in my hiding place. Desire pulses in me. I argue with myself to ride it out: hormones have no yearnings for higher values; they're one-track-minded endorphins; amoral sluts, each and every one.

Paige leans across the bed to kiss me. Her lips probe with a question and my tongue presses back to answer.

I feel her smile welcome me to position myself on top. Butch for life. Somehow pleased with myself in this, I unbutton her blouse and take off my T-shirt. I pull off her pants and press myself against her long line of thigh to slow dance while we kiss. I let my fingers tickle around her pussy fat until her reassuring sighs and encouraging leg-spread urges my hand to travel around the mouth of her pussy. The delta between her thighs fast becomes slick with girl ooze.

I feel my way into Paige by her sonar. I don't know how my hand feels inside her. I've never been penetrated and don't want to be. I touch her inner flesh and listen for feedback—a symphony of sighs.

The gush of her pussy feels like okra. I'm not sure what I am doing in there and don't have a direct sense of what makes her feel good other than her lovely moans. Her gorgeous sounds are music that give me direction.

I spread my fingers gradually and let Paige be the conductor for this symphony. I orchestrate my movements to keep her sounding pleasured—until I start to tease. Then I hold back my hand before finally giving in to push up and over the ridge inside her pussy as Paige's voice cries out. This is the song of sex, and God it's sweet to give a woman this pleasure.

It's work to sex a femme, but Paige's response gives me joy. I feel important and butch. Then I feel mute with wonder to see her in the throes of orgasm. Her face contorts like hand-blown molten glass—delicate, transparent, exquisite.

Her body erupts in unfolding layers. Her desire to be fucked draws out the best in me. I feel privileged to participate in a miracle as the peaks of sexual feeling lead this woman seemingly off the planet.

We cuddle and lie still. I lightly caress her ear and the side of her face. She gives off little sighs like bubbles blown from a plastic holder that drift on puffs of wind.

"That was lovely sex, Avon. You have great hands."

I feel amazed and proud—because I'd had no idea I did so well.

"You carry a lot of sexual energy in your hands and hips." Her voice sounds so wistful that I want to promise her something, anything, for reassurance.

Relaxed, we settle into sleep around 1:30 A.M. At 8:00, I'm wide awake and conscious of Paige in the bed. I feel protective and butchy because she still slumbers and I am newly awakened.

Three days later in Alison's advanced class, Paige and I end up adjacent to each other to perform the choreography. Paige improvises and puts her hand on my shoulder, linking us for the ending of the dance combination.

The next weekend, we both make our excuses not to hang out with the company after the show.

On the terrace of our room, watching the wide-awake stars, I lay my head in Paige's lap and she does not object. She wants me to be the butch and take the lead.

I have a shiver of fear that she will turn on me the next morning and run tearful to sob at her husband's dickside. As if she could read my mind, Paige says, "I'm not thinking about comparing this with fucking anybody else."

She strokes my locks, examining the dreads and smiling with a question she can't put words to. I marvel at her fascination with my hair. For centuries African-American women have been ashamed of our hair's texture and possibility. I'd never thought it could be mysterious to someone else.

Caucasian hair is all too familiar to me; I have seen the styles, textures and coloring of white people on every magazine cover, TV set, billboard, and movie screen since I was knee-high. I let Paige explore and feel a world of patience for whatever she might ask about my hair or say about the contrasts of our colors. Scent, taste, texture—those skin sensations hadn't been tried by race and condemned, but color presents a field in which to marvel.

Tonight will be my turn at the receiving end of sex. I've already cautioned myself that sure, Paige had been interested in having me fuck her. Maybe she'd be happy to string me along and take, but not give in return; then probably carp and complain to boot.

"What are you holding back, Avon?"

"I'm trying to keep my heart protected and at the same time keep it open, Paige."

"When I was about three thousand words old…" As I try to lift my head in wonder to see what story she is about to tell, she leans over and kisses me, her tongue making it clear this is no time for any back talk.

I feel drunk on her mouth juice. Her perfume weighs heavier than the scent of honeydew, and somehow I taste a tongueful of peach.

We go back into the room and I am hard-pressed to remain present during my turn in sex. I have to resist going into one of my love fantasies in which Paige is my happily-ever-after.

Her mouth eats me out like a pubis-friendly mower. I feel myself molt into a siren piercing the night—the sound close at hand, gradually decreasing in intensity, then somehow far away and gone. I want to stay with this feeling of desperate sweetness.

When her tongue stabs and suckles my breasts, I hump up her thigh, feeling like a cavalier taken by a femme mount. I don't know what Paige feels in her mind any more than I know what she thinks at the center between her legs, but right now I feel wanted and would keep this treasure forever mine.

I keep her body pulled close with the scented darkness lulled back to silence and cradle the secrets of the stars.

El Tigre

Catherine Lundoff

"I have but recently arrived in this new land, sent from my home
in disgrace for believing the seductive words of a young noble.
Now my child and I will both pay the price: she raised as a bastard
in the convent, and I sent to this cursed place. I am to be the new
'companion' (a term that I believe to be synonymous with 'maid')
to a Doña Fernanda, a widow and distant cousin of mine. It is
hoped by my cousins in Spain, the only family I possess, that here
in Mexico far from my disgrace, I will find a suitable marriage. I
hate them all."

Closing my diary, I find my gaze drawn to the window and the
courtyard below. Dimly lit archways open onto a dusty open patio
with a tiny central fountain circled by small orange trees, a sad
replica of the great palaces of the Moors in my beloved homeland.
I lean on the edge of the window, inhaling the warm evening air
in great breaths as I try not to weep.

A noise below causes me to pull back into the shadows. In the
dusk, I see a cloaked figure emerge from one of the archways and
walk swiftly toward the stables. Surely it is some servant of the
elusive Doña Fernanda, whom I have yet to meet in my two days

here. A servant on an errand, yes, that's it; thus, I try to dismiss my curiosity. But my gaze follows the figure as he emerges leading a black horse, mounts, and rides rapidly from the courtyard. What errand could call for sending a man out onto the dirt roads outside of Veracruz, just as night falls?

I ponder this question as I draw the shutters closed. There are many such thoughts for me to mull over, first and foremost concerning the purpose of serving as a "companion" to a woman I have not seen. At least my room is plain and comfortable, though far from luxurious. The bed, with its carved wooden posts, seems large enough for two, and there is a strange and beautiful woven cloth draped over the wardrobe that holds my attention each time I approach it.

I bow my head for the prayers that do not come before the image of Santa María, which rests on a carved wooden shelf. Then, placing my rosary before her statue, I read the Bible in the wide bed until I fall asleep, one of the few things that I can thank the nuns for teaching me. I wake with a gasp many hours later, my nightdress open at the throat, shivering in the night breezes from the open window. Surely I closed that, I think, as I dash across the room to shut it.

It is only when I return to the large, soft bed that I remember my dream. I saw a woman wearing the clothing of a man(!), standing over my bed and gazing down at me. She was tall and lean, wearing a long black cloak. Her high cheekbones and long black hair marked her as mestiza, one whom my countrymen see as "tainted" with the blood of the unfortunate *indios* of this land. She was beautiful and even in my memory, I was drawn to her. Drawn to her, perhaps, more strongly than to the young lord whose words brought me here.

I found that I wanted to taste her lips, as thoughts that had been carefully suppressed in the convent returned. I remembered my strange feelings for Sister Teresa, the strongest and most comely of the nuns, and my desire for her touch, even her punishments.

Here was another one to awaken that desire I thought long dead.

My awareness shifted as her hand brushed my hair from my face in this dream of mine, the most vivid I have had in some time. As she touched me, I found my lips caressing her hands. I blush somewhat to think of it, but only a little, for I am a fallen woman at only eighteen summers, not some convent innocent who has never known carnal desires.

I drew her onto the bed, reaching out to pull her lips to mine for a kiss. Even though it was only a dream, I felt the heat rush through me at the imagined touch of her lips. She showered my neck with kisses as she unfastened the top of my nightdress to expose my shoulders and neck. In this dream, I knew that I would give her anything she wanted, though I should burn in flames for eternity. I felt her teeth at my shoulder; then a dreamy lassitude overtook me and I fell into a deep sleep.

Having remembered, I lie awake until the first birdsong drives me from my bed to gaze out the window. My hands go to my shoulder and looking down, I can see a strange mark where I was untouched the night before. I shiver superstitiously and cross myself, more from habit than belief, for the *iglesia* never did aught for me but tell me that women who bore bastards were doomed in the hereafter. Nevertheless, I fear this unknown mark as I fear the heat that she awoke. I try to pray, but find that my thoughts will turn only to the night before and to my daughter.

The tears come, unwanted, when I think upon my little one and know that I will never see her again. That thought pains me more than the realization that I am alone and unprotected in a new land, with strange marks upon my shoulder. I hastily wipe my eyes as one of the servants enters silently to tell me that the Doña will see me after I have eaten my evening meal, then exits swiftly.

It strikes me as odd that all of the Doña's servants are so very quiet, so sullen, so quick to disappear. Most are old women, with craggy, unsmiling faces, garbed always in black, much like this one. Perhaps the Doña's household is still in mourning. What must this woman be like to rule such a house of sorrow? My curiosity consumes me and the day passes slowly until my dinner arrives. I eat the odd mixture of rice and beans quickly and put on my most respectable dress, the finest of the plain black serge dresses that my cousins let me take when I departed. I wear it without adornment in deference to the house, then I defiantly fasten my black lace mantilla about my head and shoulders. The lace was my mother's, the last bit of luxury I was able to hide from the voracious hands of my cousins; I will not have the Doña think I have no pride. I turn to follow the servant to meet my new mistress.

I am escorted to a room at the back of the house, one without windows in the dried clay that they call "adobe." The single candle barely illuminates the colorful carpet, the heavy wood furnishings, and the room's only other occupant. She is heavily veiled, wearing a black silk dress trimmed with lace, and seated in a ornately carved wooden chair. I cannot not see her face as I make the appropriate curtsey, and so I study her curiously in a manner that many have found impertinent. Somehow, I sense that she finds it amusing. "So," Doña Fernanda's deep voice fills the room, "you are sent to me from our shared cousins in Spain, and I am to feed you, house you, and find a match for you." I nod miserably. "And what will you do for me?" I know now that she is laughing at me.

Indignantly, I raise my head. "I can read and write, as well as play the harpsichord and other instruments. I'm sure my lady will find my abilities to be quite satisfactory."

"Good." That voice behind the veils purrs at me, and I feel a rise of that same heat that I felt last night and once again this morning. I gasp in horror and glance down quickly in hopes of covering my confusion. "I am ill much of the time, which forces me to rest during the day as it is much too hot for me. I would like to see you in the evenings, at which time you can entertain me. Once I get to know you better, we'll see about a match for you.

Meanwhile, I suggest frequent baths to keep off the heat. The climate differs greatly from Spain." She rises to press my hand gently. I am dismissed, thinking as I leave that she does not seem much like an invalid.

Several days and interminable nights pass in which I am not sent for to be companionable, or otherwise. I read on the patio, attempt to gossip with the servants, and wonder if my dream will return. The servants are not forthcoming about our mistress, saying only that the Viceroy granted her permission to keep her husband's lands after his death and not to remarry, highly unusual in this land where wealthy widows are courted assiduously. I wonder how she did it, and whether I will be foisted on one of her unsuccessful suitors. I long for more details about this woman who weighs so on my mind.

While I learn little about the mysterious Doña, they do tell me about another local enigma: a strange masked man, known as "El Tigre," who has been paying nightly visits to some of the notoriously brutal landowners in the region. It is said that they are much kinder to the *indios* and peasants who work their land after such visits. As I have heard something of unchecked abuses, this news gladdens my heart. Perhaps he will rescue me from my boredom and disgrace, along with his other good deeds. Or, I dare to dream in my most secret depths, *she* will return.

To fill my days, I take advantage of the Doña's small library, where I read many interesting and surprising works. Among the most interesting things is the mere existence of a library. Ordinarily, a wealthy woman in my country would possess only the Bible, and she would be fortunate to be able to read that. The Doña must have been brought up by the nuns as well, I think, or else blessed with a remarkable parent. One of the works that holds my attention has the forces of darkness as its topic. I read about demons and succubi, about creatures who steal infants, and about those who seduce men in their sleep. I cannot help but wonder if my dream lady is one of them, but I can find no reference to such a female demon visiting a mortal woman.

I also begin to bathe in the sunken pool, as I've been advised. One night, as I lie soaking in my thin, white shift, I hear someone enter. Thinking it to be the quiet housemaid, Consuelo, with more hot water, I murmur "*Gracias.*" The chuckle that answers is certainly not Consuelo's, and my startled eyes open to find the Doña kneeling next to the pool. Immediately I am torn between wanting her to find me irresistible and wanting to conceal my body, made very visible by the wet shift. Years of convent training make me draw myself up, instinctively covering myself with my hands. As I sit up, she tilts my head back, and lifting her veil, presses her lips to mine. My wet arm slides from over my breasts and goes around her neck of its own accord, as though I were possessed, as perhaps I am. I feel her hand move down to cup my breast and to caress it. The nuns' distant voices shriek warnings as my flesh burns at her touch, and I respond, racing far beyond their reach.

My delighted gasp is permission enough for her, and she pulls me onto the towels next to the pool. I am amazed at her strength. In the dim light, I cannot see her face very well, but her kisses tell me that she is the woman from my dream. I draw back in amazement to study her cold, fierce beauty. "I have dreamt of you…" I whisper.

"No dream, little one. I could not keep from your charms. I have known that I must have you since I first saw your portrait and heard your tale. But you must know that I am not like you. Even our cousins would not have deliberately delivered you into the power of a demon." Demon? I study her avidly, my heart racing, knowing I must seem wild-eyed with terror.

"I am not mortal, *dulce*. I will live forever, surviving on the blood of others. The warm light of the sun is death to me, so I must sleep during the days and move about only in the dark. I have been this way for many years, after my husband's bite brought me over." She pauses distastefully on the word "husband."

"I knew nothing of what he was about, having been a convent-bred innocent, much like you, *amor*. He fed off me until I became as I am now. I learned enough to hasten his end in revenge for making me a monster, and to savor the joys of a woman's body from one of his erstwhile loves. Now, I find that I am lonely, and long for the warmth of a mortal lover. But I will not deceive you as I was deceived." She turns to me, eyes glowing, "Will you share my bed, knowing what I am and what I can do?"

My hand strays to my neck, to the marks she left in my dream vision, now made stark and real. "I must draw deeper than that, *amor*, draining you close to dry before you become as I am. If I terrify you, you have only to speak and I will find you a husband. I am nothing if not honorable." She smiles a sad, twisted smile. I reach out to that sorrow. What are we both but women with naught except each other? I draw her hand back to my bosom.

Her hands are on the strings of my shift, and I am lost in the soft touch of her lips, her tongue, as she kisses my neck. Soon my shift is down around my waist and her mouth is on my breast. I feel my back bend as her tongue strokes over my breasts. My hands scramble at the fastenings on the back of her dress; I want her to be as vulnerable as I am. She evades me, sliding the wet shift lower as she lays me down on the towels.

She licks her way along my legs, and I am filled with a desperate sense of desire and panic. What is she doing to me? Her tongue reaches the space between my legs and I scream with delight, with horror, as she sends flames through me. Truly I am damned now, I think, but if this is hell, heaven can be no better. I am swept along by the strokes of her tongue until all my muscles bend at once and I must cry out. She licks her way back up to my mouth and I see that her eyes are even larger and darker than before. I pull her to me, but not before I notice how long and sharp her teeth are, and I gasp in terror, marveling that I had not noticed them before. Torn between fear and lust, I hold her off me for a moment. "Do you mean to kill me?" I manage to ask.

"I mean to possess you completely." Her eyes mesmerize me and I fall into them, not caring if she drains me dry or if such desires will cast me from the church forever. I feel her teeth graze my neck, and I bend my head back so she can reach me, can drink my blood, though it means my life. Her teeth sink in and I feel some pain, then a joyous lethargy as I slip into a deep sleep.

I awake tired, but gloriously happy. If this is what it means to be a "companion," then I shall regret only the loss of my daughter. I do realize that it will not do for the servants to see her love bites, and I wrap a silken cloth around my throat. Once again, some days pass before I see her again. The others, particularly Consuelo, who has served her lady for a long time, warn me not to disturb her. Do I want to be as she is? I cannot answer this question, and so I am in a fever of impatience, barely sleeping or eating for dreaming of her, yet torn with fear, for I am not ready to die.

As I stand near the window on the second night, I see the cloaked figure once again leaving the house. One glance and I know it is she, so strong and purposeful is her stride. With nary a thought as to why she would ride at night, I run downstairs in my shift with only a silk shawl over me. I reach the patio just as she leads the horse from the stables. "Take me with you!" I gasp.

"I cannot, my love." I see that she is dressed in men's garb, wearing a sword and a mask, and I realize who El Tigre must be. I plant myself before her, and without a second thought, I tear my shift open at the neck in the hope that my offer will be enough, for I know that men hunt for El Tigre and I fear for her as much as I want her.

She growls and her arms encircle me, lips pressed so hard against mine that they ache. "I must feed elsewhere lest I kill you. When I feed from the landowners, I can terrify them into treating the peasants better," she whispers into my ear as she kisses it, her hands running over my body under the shawl, in spite of her words.

"I'll guard your horse and wait for you," I whisper. "Please. I don't want any more nights without you."

She studies me for a long moment, eyes midnight pools that I drown in, her long, lithe body graceful and powerful. Finally, with a dry laugh, she swings onto the horse, pulling me up before her and wrapping the cloak around us both. "Very well, *dulce*. I would be pleased to savor your charms before this evening's less pleasant task." Her arms encircle me while her hands rip the shift further until one of her hands cups my breast. I arch my head backward onto her shoulder, gasping as the heat fills me.

The horse takes us where it will, until I look around to realize that it has come to a stop and we are in an old cemetery, some distance from her hacienda. Tall trees surround the stones marking the graves of the dead. It is a strange sight, lit only by the moon. Some of the stones lie at odd angles as though the dead themselves had shifted them; I shiver at the thought. "Does this spot frighten you, *amor*? I feel a special kinship to it, and it is undisturbed by those who seek El Tigre. I will take you home if it is too much," she murmurs in my ear.

Something about this place of the dead draws me as well, despite my terror. Suddenly I find that I desire her touch here, with the eyes of the ghosts on us. "I fear nothing while I am with you, *mi amor*," I whisper in a voice scarcely my own, as I place my hand on hers and hold it to my breast.

She pulls her hand away, leaps from the saddle, then lifts me down to the ground. As I touch her waist, I feel the coil of a long whip at her belt. Without thinking, even as she unclasps her cloak to lay it on a long, flat gravestone, I pull the braided leather from her belt. My eyes close as I think back to the convent, the many beatings that I received from Sister Teresa, the look on her face as the leather hit my skin and the way her hands felt as she touched me afterward. I did many things earn those beatings and that touch. Perhaps...I turned to Fernanda, holding the whip out. "I was very wicked to follow you the way I did," I whisper.

Her sharp teeth flash in the moonlight. "Oh, I must remember to thank our cousins for such a wicked companion as they have found me. I have longed for a lover who would indulge all my desires of her own free will." The whip snakes along the ground as she turns me to face a standing stone. She shreds the shift from me and forces my legs farther apart with her knee. I am not so much breathing as I am panting, like a dog, but I do not care. Nor do I feel the cold, even as her first stroke pushes me forward so that my breasts touch the icy stone. My head hangs over the stone as I embrace it, the whip snaps along my back, the burning of my skin and the burning in my belly becoming as one. My cries fill the night.

Five strokes and I can barely stand. I feel her stand behind me and run the handle of the whip up my legs. My moans and whimpers are beyond any restraint that I feel capable of exercising. I feel her lick the small amount of blood that she has drawn off my back as the whip handle slides farther. She bends me farther over the stone and slips it inside me. As she begins to thrust, my knees buckle and she has to hold me against her as she pushes the whip in and out of me. This is what I dreamed that Sister Teresa would do, and I am crying, begging for more, begging for I know not what, until my whole body can take no more and only her strong arms are holding me upright.

She picks me up and puts me on her cloak, her teeth finding my neck. I manage to unfasten her shirt to touch her breasts as she feeds. She pulls her bloody teeth from my neck as I wrap my legs around her waist. "I must feed elsewhere tonight, *querida mía*. I do not altogether trust myself with you." Dragging herself away, she wraps the cloak around me. "Wait here. I'll return within the hour. Sleep." At her last word, I slip into a great abyss, imagining that I see a great gray wolf running from the cemetery and down the road.

When I awake, I am in my own bed. I wonder if I have dreamt it all until I feel the stripes on my back. For a brief moment, I am afraid that I have gone too far, that she will kill me in her passion. The thought fills me with only a vague apprehension, something that puzzles me. Does my life mean so little to me that losing it is nothing? Or do I trust her, a creature of the night, not even mortal, so much that I will place my life in her hands?

I contemplate how little I know of her, of her life and what she is. I think back also on what my life had to offer before her: disgrace, at best a joyless marriage, at worst a life of dependency upon more-fortunate relatives. As I have only my daughter in all the world that I care about other than her, and I cannot have my little one back, I make my decision to throw in my lot with Doña Fernanda. With the matter settled for the moment, I rest, saving myself up for my beloved.

Some nights later, I am called to play the harpsichord for Fernanda and some guests from the surrounding haciendas. She sends word of this by Consuelo, who brings a note as well, which says, "*Querida*, I desire your help in entertaining some of my kinswomen. Much will be asked of you tonight. If you wish to please me, leave off your heavy undergarments when you come to me. Trust me and remember that I have some control over both myself and others." I dress in an agony of apprehension and anticipation.

When I enter the room, I see four women, two of whom are kin to Fernanda in some manner that I only dimly comprehend; the two others are mortal. They are all older than I and wear the plain, simple garments of spinsters living on their family's largesse. Yet, I am drawn to their power and grace. These are not the sullen, broken women I am accustomed to seeing in wealthy households, but instead are like the abbess of the convent, both comfortable in their strength and somehow otherworldly.

We dine and the others study me almost as assiduously as I examine them. An exchange of pleasantries reveals that, as I had suspected, the others are all *dueñas* and companions, unmarried women and widows. The evening meal of oddly flavored chicken and rice passes quickly. Once we have finished, Fernanda dismisses the servants and bolts the doors securely. Smiling mysteriously, she ushers me to the harpsichord.

After I play, which I find makes me more homesick than I expected, Fernanda draws near and gently strokes my hair. "You look sad, *dulce*. What is it?"

With little regard for the others, who are tactfully engrossed in their own conversation, it tumbles from my mouth: "I love you, but I miss my daughter."

"Where is she?" Fernanda asks, as though she had always known about her. Perhaps our cousins had told her.

"In the convent of Santa María near Madrid," I offer in a rush.

"We will see what can be done. Now, would you like to help me entertain our guests?"

My heart fills with hope as I gaze up at her. "Anything you want of me, you are welcome to take, even my life."

"I don't want to take your life, but I desire you, your passion, your beauty. I want my friends to see the beauty of your body and your surrender as well," she whispers.

"Oh, yes!" I find the words pouring from my mouth, any thought of propriety swiftly forgotten. She sits beside me on the bench, her hands unlacing my bodice. I hear a gasp from one of the other ladies as Fernanda bares my breast, then bends to take it into her mouth. My arms encircle her neck, frantic moans arising from me as I slip beyond self-control. The thought of the other women watching makes me burn hotter with desire, rather than the shame that I should feel.

I gaze back at them to see one of the women pull another to the floor before her, turning her so she can watch us, and sliding her hand into the other's bodice. I see the second one's look as the questing hand finds her breast and she moans as she meets my eyes. My beloved's hands pull my dress from me, leaving me in my light shift to face the women across the room. The woman caressing the other's breasts pulls a sharp dagger from the table and slices the second woman's dress from her with nary a scratch. My breath quickens as I watch.

As Fernanda undresses me, she reveals to the others that I am suffering from the curse of Eve. Pulling the rag from between my legs, she growls deep in her throat, and the others draw near, pulled to my blood. Swiftly, Fernanda kneels between my legs and begins to lick me ferociously. Her two kinswomen hover nearby, their companions forgotten for the moment. The thrill of fear only makes me burn the hotter. They could tear me limb from limb at this moment and I could do nothing to stop them. Fernanda lifts her head to gaze at me, eyes burning and mouth bloody. "Share," hisses one of the other women.

She favors them with a sharp-toothed smile. "Are you afraid, little one?" she asks, looking at me. I nod, too overcome to speak. "Do you want them anyway?" I nod again and she moves to hold me as another takes her place. The two human women stand watching and touching each other, too overcome to resist the sight of my pleasure. The fierce tongue drives me harder and harder until I cry out as my body arches out of control. The third moves to take her place as the second lady returns to the two companions. I hear their moans mixed with my own. My hands grasp her hair as she feeds. Fernanda's fingers tighten on my breast as she kisses me, her tongue inside my mouth. Once again I am transported, crying out into Fernanda's mouth as that insistent tongue strokes and slides inside me and against me. The other woman sits up panting, my blood on her fangs.

She watches me for a moment more, then bows to Fernanda and moves to join the others. One of the human women has pinned the arms of the other, now stripped of her dress, while one of Fernanda's kin caresses and kisses her. She begs and moans, arching her back and opening her legs to express her desire, but the kissing and biting continues. The sight makes my breath catch in my throat and I reach for my beloved. Her fingers slide inside me. Her other hand turns my face toward the women as one of them pulls a leather belt from her dress and begins to lightly smack the bared legs and back of the woman now kneeling before her. I squirm against Fernanda and she pinches my breasts hard.

"You're very wicked to want another, my sweet," she growls in my ear.

She pulls me from the bench and across the room in a single movement. I am pushed to my knees, my face between the legs of the woman I have just seen whipped. "Lick!" Fernanda's order cannot be denied, and I taste another woman for the first time. The belt's sharp smack distracts me for a moment, only to have the woman catch my head and pull my face back into her. "I'll stop if you don't please her." This threat is unneeded, serving only to inspire me further. As the sting of the belt warms me, I move my hand up to part her with my fingers and push inside as Fernanda did to me. Her fierce cries of joy warm me until I beg for my loved one's touch, her hands, even her teeth.

As the other woman holds me in her arms, kissing me fiercely, I feel Fernanda's tongue begin to follow the welts made by the belt. She laps the blood from my thighs like a cat as I crouch over the woman on the floor, passionately returning her kisses. I see Fernanda's hand go to the table and take something from it. Her finger pushes into me. I spasm with pleasure, moving my legs farther apart for whatever she wishes. Her finger moves and I push against it, feeling a new sensation of pain and pleasure. A second finger joins the first and I begin to rock backward against her hand. Then she pulls them out, heedless of my disappointed cry, and pushes something hard inside me. It fills me farther than I thought possible, and all thought of anything except the rush of heat that fills me is gone from my mind.

Her finger enters my other opening and I enter a world of pleasure that I never imagined before. My moans and cries are pulled from my throat as I surrender all control to her, my demon lover. She possesses me utterly until I collapse upon the woman under me, whose hands touch and fondle me the whole while.

Fernanda's hand roughly catches my hair, bending my head back as her teeth sink into my neck. "Make me yours," I whisper.

"You already are," she whispers back as I fall away into unconsciousness.

When I recover my strength some days later, I find that she has booked my passage on a ship to Spain, as well as providing an armed escort to guard my virtue. I carry documents authorizing the adoption of my daughter by some relatives of the Viceroy. They will keep her nearby, and I can at least see her grow up, though I cannot keep her myself because I am not married. Still, it is more than I dared hoped for. As I stand on the ship's deck, I think on my parting with Fernanda.

"Will you make me like you when I return?" I asked, filled at once with trepidation and desire.

"Do you want to live forever?" she responded, eyes blazing.

"With you," I answered from my heart.

"Perhaps when you return, El Tigre will require some assistance. We will have to see if you are worthy."

"Let me prove it to you," I whispered, stepping closer.

"When you come back…" her finger passed gently along my cheek, and she vanished with a swirl of her cloak, leaving me on the dock where I first came to this land. I have only my thoughts of her to warm me on the cold shipboard nights. Those and her mark upon my neck, which stays strangely hot to my touch…

Unfinished Tattoo
Gerry Gomez Pearlberg

It was three A.M. and I was sound asleep when the doorbell rang. The candles in my room had almost melted down. It was dangerous, I knew, to doze in a room full of burning candles, but there seemed no other condition under which to wait for her.

She wore eyeshadow and lipstick. A brown leather jacket. In her hand, a large paper bag. For the moment it took me to unhook the front gate, she lingered on the threshold of my stoop, part of her still belonging to the street, where desires linger unfulfilled, and part of her almost within my grasp. I relished the moment of that transition, of locking the door behind her, pocketing the key, and turning to kiss the evening, that other world, from her lips.

When she came in, my dog knew exactly what it meant. He greeted her briefly, then scampered up the stairs to wait for us at the foot of the bed. He knew where we were headed and that we always went directly there.

In my room she said, "I have a request." She asked me to cut her clothing off with my knife, the one with the iridescent white pearl handle. It had once belonged to a famous star, a very famous star, a singer; I won't say her name because you wouldn't believe me anyway. The blade was blunt, so it took a while to slice away her dress, her slip, her fishnet stockings. It was more like sawing than slicing, which gave things a refreshing, amateurish tinge. I pressed my blue-jeaned knee against her mound. The slow, insistent sound of slashing cloth was like rain hitting the window: suspenseful and energizing but also somewhat sad. We were enraptured with the leisurely near-violence of it.

When all her clothing lay in tatters on the floor, only the delicate gold chain with the sacred heart of Jesus adorned her body. That, and the half-finished tattoo on her inner thigh. It was a tattoo she had started—a small blue serpent—but had given up on when the pain of the needle's repeated penetrations became too great. Something to do with accumulation of pressure, she said. Her thigh bore the coiled tail of a rattlesnake, half realized, whose front portion appeared to have slithered into her very flesh, or been absorbed by it, or simply slipped into a realm beyond that of skin and bone. I was fascinated with this unfinished tattoo. It meant the world to me.

Back then, I thought she was so beautiful. Now, eons later, though we no longer speak, I still do. I don't exactly want her again; what I want is even more improbable: to revisit that night with her, to remain in it as if it were a room. I want the sound of her satin slip rending apart while her blue lipsticked lips spread wide. For her to say to me again, "My mouth is a sex organ." For the glint of candlelight, a knife blade, her dark, dark eyes, the ninth orgasm, and the sacred heart of Christ, that glorious, damaged metaphor. For rain the way it used to be when water was still free. For those first roiling sensations of love in spite of all the evidence—hard and soft—against it.

In her nakedness, she eagerly undressed me. Everything but my belt fell to the floor: that she kept close at hand. Nude and kneeling, we held each other for a long time, breathing not speaking, our pubic hair sparking.

Finally, she opened the paper bag she'd brought with her from the Metropolis. A rectangular Styrofoam container lay inside. She opened it like a jewelry box, and the candlelight glancing against the assortment of sushi seemed nearly divine. It transformed the deep red tuna into slabs of velveteen, soft steps to an ultimately unattainable altar. It illuminated the ginger slices like shards of stained glass the color of pink dogwood blossoms. It made the wasabi gleam like club moss, and the scaly black-green nori almost translucent, at once stiff and yielding, a half-snake coiled in its den.

"Where I come from," she whispered, "when a woman is attracted to someone, she feeds them with her fingers."

She lifted a piece of yellowfin sushi, rubbed it lightly against the wasabi bulge, dipped it in the small plastic cup of soy sauce, and put it to my lips. We went on like that all night, fucking and feeding each other and playing with my belt, and with the chopsticks, experimenting with the wasabi's steamy insinuations on mucous membranes. The room smelled like ginger, horseradish, salt—mouthwatering and clean.

In the morning I awoke to gelatinous fish roe in the sheets. I looked for her, but she was gone. Something to do with the accumulation of pressure, I suppose.

I still come upon remnants of roe from time to time when cleaning behind my bed. They have somehow retained their rubylike sheen, though desiccated now, weightless, and harder.

from *The Blue Place*
Nicola Griffith

There used to be several distinct kinds of gym. When I was growing up, school gyms—in whatever country—were sunlit and silent, the air dead and dusty with the scents of climbing ropes, ancient pommel horses sweat-soaked and bare on the handles, and a thin, greasy overlay of plimsoll rubber scraped off on the wooden floor during countless skiddings and bumpy landings. All very genteel and closed off. Working gyms in the city were meatier, more burly, with dim overhead lights, chalk dust, laboring fans, and metal everywhere: clanking nautilus, ringing free weights, clinking dog tags. Male sweat and Ben-Gay. Hoarse huff-huff of pumping, the occasional burst of loud boy conversation: the game, the fight, the conquest. Dojos, on the other hand, were defined more by body sounds: the slap of open hands on arms, thud of bare feet on kick bags, the heavy, almost soundless impact of a rolling fall...and the voices, karate kiais like the cry of a stooping hawk, the very particular half-swallowed *hut-hut*, like a gun with a sound suppresser, of a whole school of people going through their katas, the endless, rhythmic susurrus of breath as half a dozen students meditate in zazen.

The precinct gym in City Hall East was less than a year old: beautiful sprung wood floor, whispering air conditioning, full spectrum lighting. I took off my shoes, stood in the middle of the floor, and closed my eyes: soft hiss of air conditioning, faraway rumble of East Ponce traffic, slow turning thump of my heart. I breathed deeply, in and in until my belly swelled with air, out again through my nose, in, out, letting my hands rise a little with each inhalation. Then I stretched up, and up further, held it, came down, palms to the floor. Held it, held it, and on the outbreath bent my elbows further.

I moved through my routine automatically, stretching tendons and ligaments and muscles, and after twenty minutes I was as flexible as a whip.

There are only four schools of Shuto Kai karate outside Japan. I had learned it in England, on Tuesday evenings and Sunday mornings in an old community center whose concrete floors were always still sticky with spilled beer and cigarette ash from the event the night before. I had studied with five men under the instruction of a truck driver with a sturdy Yorkshire accent and a real love of the art. He taught me the way of the empty hand. I would kneel in zazen on that unheated concrete floor in the middle of winter and extend my arms. He would lay a heavy pole across my wrists, and the battle would begin, the battle of breath and pain and will. The first five minutes were easy, the next ten just about bearable, the next thirty a nightmare. Sweat would roll down my neck, and Ian's voice would boom from the walls and rattle the children's drawings pinned there. "Breathe through the pain! Breathe! With me, in and *out*. In and *out*." And my shoulder muscles, which had already taken me through two hundred push ups and an hour of sparring, would burn dully, then sharply, then with pain bigger than the world. And the only way through it was the breath. In and out. Falter and you are lost.

And after forty or fifty minutes, the endorphins kick in and the childish drawings on the wall assume a crystalline edge, the colors deepen and bloom, and my face relaxes utterly. All there is is a tide of breath, sweeping up and down the beach of my body, until each cell is as distinct as a grain of mica and I feel washed clean. I sometimes wondered what would happen if I just...stayed there; whether the endorphin high would burn itself into my cells permanently and for the rest of my life I would smile gently around the edges, even when I was breaking someone's legs. But then Ian would take the pole away, shout, and we would be running around and around the hall. Twenty minutes. Two or three miles, usually. Then we would do a kata.

Katas are choreographed series of fight moves against one or more imaginary opponents. Done well, they are a meditation and a dance. They range from the most simple, railway-straight line moves against only one opponent where you use nothing but punches, to the flying, whirling battle-an-army dance of the Basai Dai. You don't learn the Basai Dai until you get your black belt.

The first few months I studied, the katas were my reward, the fluid dance, the grace, the hot whistling power of punching tight air, of using my whole body. It was only after my blue belt, the second kyu, that I learned that the real reward of learning Shuto Kai was understanding my will. I learned that pain is only pain: a message. You can choose to ignore the message. Your body can do a great deal more than it wants you to know.

And so, although for all practical purposes Shuto Kai is not a particularly good martial art, I still dance its katas.

I did the fourth, which has all those difficult kicks, and the Basai Dai. My breathing was as smooth as cream, my blood oxygenated and rich. I was probably smiling.

I moved on from karate to kung fu, a Wing Chun form, the Siu Nim Tao, or Simple Idea. I was on the second round of pak sao, the slapping hand, when the door opened. Even with my eyes closed I would have known who it was. Her scent was a little more pronounced today, even though her hair was dry. I nodded very briefly but did not stop. Ding jem. Huen sao. She started stretching. Bill jee. Moot sao, the whipping hand. She was wearing black spandex pants and an emerald body sheath. I concentrated on the form.

When I took the last slow breath and released it, she straightened. "First form?"

"Yes."

"Want to chi sao?" It was a challenge.

"Take off your shoes."

"My shoes?"

"I value my feet."

That angered her. It was meant to. Always take the advantage. I extended my right leg, and my right arm, elbow down and in, wrist level with my sternum, fingers parallel to the floor. She did the same. The backs of our wrists touched. Well-shaped nails, no wedding ring. Her skin was dense and fine grained, taut over smooth muscle, and her bones slender. She looked the sort of woman who has studied ballet for twelve years. Her eyes were blue, the deep blue of still-wet-from-the-dye denim, with lighter flecks near pupils tight with concentration. Her hair was in a French twist. A French twist for the gym.

Chi sao means sticky hand. The wrists stay touching. All moves are in slow motion. It's a game of chess using balance.

I moved my hand forward, the first inch of what could have become huen sao, the circling hand, but she stepped smoothly to the side and, without even moving her arm, countered. But the counter of course became her own move, which was to keep stepping, trying to lead my arm away from the center of my body and leave me unbalanced. So far, all beginner's moves. Her baked-biscuit skin slid back and forth over her collarbone. As the pace intensified, I wondered how women got those tans. The color was delicate, never too heavy, never too light, and they had it in February and November yet they never seemed to use tanning salons. Their eyebrows always arched perfectly and their hair was never out of place.

Who are you? Blank concentration for a reply.

She was good: well balanced, smooth, knowledgeable about the connections between feet and belly, wrist and elbow and shoulder. She centered well and breathed unhurriedly.

I wanted information and stepped back, signaling a pause. "Sern chi sao?"

She merely nodded and extended both arms. Double sticky hands.

We moved faster this time, our legs bent lower, circling around the gym in jong tao, a deadly waltz. A woman's center of gravity is generally about two inches below her navel, just where the belly rounds. No matter how fast you travel across the floor, that point should move in parallel. I was taller than her, but having one's center of gravity higher is a disadvantage, so I moved in a lower stance. We were both sweating lightly now, and our breath came faster. Her skin felt marvelously alive beneath mine. We moved back and forth, and my belly warmed, and I knew hers warmed, too, as we revolved around the gym and each other, a planet and its satellite turning about the sun.

Time to let her know which was which, to show her I didn't much appreciate having my wallet stolen at the scene of an arson and murder. I moved more strongly, breathed in great long gushes, as though my breath alone would move her aside. Her body sheath was dark under the arms. My belly burned hotter. She began to move just a little out of balance. I made a slow biu tze, the shooting fingers, up toward her eyes, with my left hand, and a going under hand with my right. Being out of balance, even so slightly, meant she had to either let me through or speed up to regain the advantage. To speed up meant it would become almost a sparring session.

She sped up.

Differences in skill become more apparent with speed. I harried her round and round the gym, in no hurry, enjoying testing her. She began to spar in earnest. She snapped a punch at my head, which I palmed away easily enough, then launched into a series of battle punches, hoping to drive me off balance. I centered then stepped right through her with a double circling hand—and in my head, for a split second, moved over both her wrists and dumped her on the floor—but in actuality let the moment pass.

She felt it, felt the moment when I could have thrust the heat of my belly against hers and taken it all, and now the whole character of our sparring changed. I led, she followed. It became a dance, teacher and pupil. I would ask, she would answer.

When we came to a halt, wrists still touching, in the center of that beautiful gym, her face was as smooth as butter. We bowed to each other. I waited.

"Can I buy you coffee?"

Losing the Artifice
Shoshie Tornberg

If you cut a careful, clear line all the way around the purply green skin of an avocado, and if you nudge your finger into just the right, soft place on its skin, its convex breast will pop concave and whole in your hand. If the season and the sunlight through the blind slats of the window are just so, you will hold, in your world-weary palm, the tenderest green morsel you will ever taste.

The thing about BJ was that she could charm you like it was art. She knew how to make a woman melt like—well, like every good lesbian is supposed to make a woman melt—like ripe fruit in a hot mouth. But every poet meets with an ineffable moment, an unexpected poem in the world that her formulaic skills cannot pen. Like pungent, wordless ecstasy that demands only abandon.

She thought she knew her lines for a while. Cliché as you thought it was, you blushed delightedly in all your baby dyke splendor when she sent you a rose wrapped in plastic from her DJ booth in the dyke bar. When you thanked her loudly from the booth entrance, pulsing with dance music, she kissed you on the cheek and told you that one beautiful flower deserves another. What do you do when a woman gives you an old, old line, and you

know it is old, and yet, you really believe her? What do you do
when this same woman, so butch your heart skips, asks you for
your number at the end of the night?

What do you do when she calls you, and you go out for coffee
after her shift spinning at 2:00 A.M., and you realize you cannot
let this one get away? What do you do?

The sex was distant and strangely surreal. One-sided. Were you
really a dyke if you didn't fuck back? Well, it did not matter. And
neither did her strange and frightening insinuations about leather.
And whips and chains. Or whatever. You had always dismissively
rolled your eyes. Until you knew you were also rolling your eyes
at her. You shifted uncomfortably and brushed these thoughts
away. You were leaving tomorrow for the long summer, going
safely eleven hundred miles away. Boston.

And you did leave. To come out to your parents one weighted
afternoon in June after planting impatiens in the garden with your
mother. (Years later, you still help her do this, and you wonder
why she chooses flowers that need replanting each year). Your
parents did not take the news all that well or take it fully at all that
day—like impatiens refusing their rich soil before the year is
through.

So what did you do? What did you do in this town with no
friends and a sister who thought dating girls was weird and something you'd better never tell her friends? You called BJ all the way
in London, Ontario, and nursed breathless against the soft flesh
of her deep voice that said all the right words. You kissed the rush
of her breath-heat traveling such a long distance. You danced a
savory, meandering journey with your tongue along the imagined
and remembered contours of her flesh made real in her voice. And
one delicious night, when your parents were out of town, the
phone rang at 2:30, and she fucked you perfectly with a vocal performance whose finale exhausted you through resonating, tearful
orgasm.

You were making two thousand dollars as a camp counselor that summer. Not much would be left over when you finished paying your phone bills.

You were talking to her one afternoon on the phone about nothing, when she unexpectedly offered herself, ad-libbing her lines away from the script, "How would it be if I came to Boston for Pride?" Your first Pride March. A hotel room in the city. Sex. Maybe love. And S/M. Shit! This was not just a phone game. You squirmed. "Sure. That would be great!" you lied.

The truth was that she had described her take on S/M to you. It was a piece of real people's lives you had never known. She said it was about power and trust, not abuse. And you had felt what you thought she had meant in your one-sided night together in the flesh. And you didn't like it much. You didn't understand it. And even aside from this new way of looking at power, you felt you were being cheap with yourself in her bed. You took sex, because you could. It was available, and you were still young enough to believe it might never come again. But she was a different kind of lover now. Before, you had seen, over coffee, in her eyes, the ways that your unassuming youth had disarmed her artfulness. But now, you had also seen pieces of her spirit. And her sadness. She had touched you with her voice.

You told her all this before she bought an eleven-hundred-mile bus ticket. The bad parts, too. Yes, even the parts that may have made her want to stay in Canada. She was surprised. She did not feel that it had been one-sided. Her stony past, she said, had not melted so much in so long. The sculptor's tools breaking. The stuff of the air not clearing space as it should. The obelisk or statue chiseled awry, evading the artist's planned vision.

Now she could show you Pride, and you could show her your beautiful, crazy, historic city. Because at least you had told her. Neither of you had an answer, but you had told her.

You met her at the bus station; wild, hungry kisses fell out of you and all over her. You were the perfect dyke virgin, with every rainbow, parade color bouncing you with delight and giggles. And she loved you in your delicious youth. And you felt your youth and her love. An ineffable poem you would later try to pluck from the summer city world, but would not be able to.

You spent Pride night together at an Avenger party, where you clung to each other and to beer you did not finish. It was a hipper-than-thou sea of black-and-silver clad lesbians. Not knowing anyone and bored, you both went back to your Brookline guesthouse to put your tired, prided girl-selves to sleep.

She undressed you with choreographed fingers, her artistry resuming. Your Doc Martens and their tangle of laces. Your baseball cap, set asymmetrically with a single, carefully-chosen Pride button. Your standard-issue tank top and suitably faded cut-offs. The Pride rings she had bought for you. The boxer briefs she had asked you to wear, because she thought you were so sexy in them. A costume designer's lesbian vision: it was now tossed into an artless pile on the floor.

You lay sleepy on your stomach. BJ poured heating massage oil (furtively smuggled across the Canadian border) onto her hands. She began to rub that tense part of you, that tight handle of flesh between your neck and shoulder, where you carried everything heavy. Her fingers sashayed slowly under the spiky shelves of your shoulder blades, along your strong, resting whip of a spine that could undulate your whole self into an explosion of dance. You moaned quietly while her hot, oiled palms moved along your naked sides, grazing and then dancing away from the edges of your breasts, spilling from beneath your warming body, from behind a growing nest of musky underarm hair. She kneaded the flesh by your hips and the backs of your woman-thighs. Propping yourself onto your elbows, your back to her still, you breathed her name audibly. BJ. The pen name she had given herself.

At that moment, with one BJ hand on the back of your thigh, one by your hip and a delectable moistness between your legs, the steady, quiet rhythm of that room froze and then shifted. She had drawn an even, steady line right through you. You dipped your head low and turned to face her with all the child in your eyes. The slow curving inside-out of an avocado-skin cup. Starting in your center, a breathy, unexpected note birthed new into the world: "BJ. Would you fuck me? Please." You meant from behind. You meant on all fours. You meant screaming and cursing and flailing wild and rabid. You meant hard. So it hurt. You meant, top me. Please, please top me.

But you didn't say any of this. Just a plaintive "BJ. Fuck me. Please." The bed fell away, and when it did, it tugged her top's heart down with it like a weight. The collapse pulled her head into an involuntary nod. Yes. You did not need to say anything more; you could see in her wide eyes that some poems didn't need to get spoken into the world in order to be.

She placed a sure and reverent left hand on your shoulder, as if resting her thumb into just the right spot on your skin to peel it back; to turn you more fully inside-out. With the fingertips of her right hand, she stroked your slick labia, your beating clit. When her fingers were wet, and she was sure of the throbbing flesh of you, she entered you, your hungry, wet cunt clasping around her full fingers. She fucked you with those fingers, reaching to the edges of your very mind. She held your ferocious, writhing body beautifully down, lest you claw her perfect, untouchable skin in ravenous hunger.

She had opened you. Your charged, pink flesh, steaming and wet. A sticky, peeled avocado in the sun.

All these years later, its sweet, salt taste has stayed in your mouth. Leaving you craving it. Again and again.

The Letter

from *The Leather Daddy and the Femme*
Carol Queen

As Demetrius packed his bags for a short trip to New York, he called me over to his place. Jack lounged on Demetrius's bed, still careful how he arranged his body because of his recent piercing. "Hey, doll," he said when I entered.

"Hey, Jack. Hi, Demetrius. What's up?"

"I've thought of an entirely new adventure to keep you occupied while I'm out of town and Jack's dick's in a splint, that's what's up," said Demetrius. "Now that we've taken this much responsibility for your social calendar, we can't just be leaving you idle for days at a time. Lord knows what you'd go dragging home."

"I'll be good!" I said. "You don't have to keep me occupied, either, unless you want to."

"Oh, darlin', this is a big 'want to.' Here." Demetrius held out an envelope.

"Demetrius, this is addressed to Georgia Strong!"

"Yes, and that's Mistress Georgia Strong, to you, upstart, unless she tells you to call her something different."

"Yeah, like 'Mommy,'" said Jack. "Or 'Sir.'"

Obviously the guys had decided to send me on a joyride, and

they couldn't have picked a hotter, scarier, or more alluring one.

"So dear, tomorrow at noon you're going to show up at the address on the envelope. Wear very upscale girl drag, please, and give Georgia the letter. She'll let you know what you are to do next."

I managed a nod, though my mind and cunt both burned, and tucked the letter safely into my jacket.

"Don't wear that ratty fucking thing," said Jack.

"Of course not," I said.

"Oh, and Randy? Remember every last teeny tiny detail. Jack and I will be looking forward to hearing all about it after you come crawling home."

"I'd go with you just to watch," said Jack, "but I have a feeling you should go alone. So it can just be—what do you call it?— 'women's space.'"

Noon the next day found me downtown at the Hotel Nikko. When I asked for Georgia Strong at the front desk they phoned up to make sure I could be admitted, then sent me to the penthouse. Hands shaking even though I tried to control them, I rang the bell.

Ariel answered. This did not surprise me, for I had seen neither hide nor hair of her at home since the party, and I'd already figured she'd run away from home to join Georgia. Given her long and checkered career, where else could she run to? The night streets of the Tenderloin were twice as exciting as the circus, and the costumes were almost as good. It would take something even more exciting than that to get Ariel's attention, and Georgia was obviously it.

Georgia had her elegantly tricked out in one of those very feminine lady-CEO power suits. Expensive pumps I'd never seen her wear caressed her feet with supple Italian leather. So they'd gone shopping already. Perhaps this was going to be serious.

"Hi, baby," she whispered. "So you found your way over."

"Yeah, the generals posted me here. How does this work? Do I give you the letter to deliver, or what?"

"Actually, I think you should present it to her yourself." Oh, right. My plum-colored silk suit rustled in the silence, and I fought harder to control my trembling as Ariel gestured me in.

Georgia sat at a simple table near a window. She had a deluxe executive day-minder in front of her, and a phone. At my approach she rose. "Dear Miranda, hello."

"Good afternoon, Mistress Strong," I managed, heart fluttering. "Demetrius sent me to deliver this, with his regards."

"Thank you." She took the clean cream-colored envelope, which I'd been very careful not to soil or wrinkle, and opened it. While she read it I glanced around the gorgeous Japanese-style room, which gleamed with polished teak and rosewood. Stylized ikebana arrangements sported one flower each, and part of the room was screened from view by a series of rice-paper panes. Suddenly I felt far from San Francisco—even, in spite of Ariel's presence, far from my old life.

Georgia smiled as she put down the letter. "Miranda, do you know what this says?"

"No, Mistress Strong."

"Demetrius and Jack have been so kind as to give you to me for a negotiable period of time. Tell me, when do you next have responsibilities? A job to report to, for instance?"

"Monday morning, Mistress Strong." It was Saturday now. "And if I needed to, I could perhaps call in...I have leave accrued..."

"The old 'Boss, I'm all tied up at the moment' routine? We don't operate that way around here. But thank you for your flexibility."

In fact, I had quite a bit of leave accrued. I wondered if I should just call in now and say I'd be in a bit late...say, two weeks late. But that's just my inner pig talking, I reminded myself. Did I really want to lock myself up for two weeks with Georgia Strong?

Seating herself again, Georgia had had to sweep her long, gleaming hair back to keep from sitting on it. She evoked such feelings of loyalty, almost reverence—at least, from the people in my tribe. Today, for me, her gender seemed a null, a promise, a projection screen; neither masculine nor feminine, or perhaps both at once—but no less erotically powerful or compelling for the confusion I felt when I looked at her. Yes, locking myself up with her seemed like the best idea ever. This must be how Ariel had felt when Georgia took a shine to her: it felt like having a new lease on life. Not that I needed one, given how busy Jack and Demetrius had been keeping me, but the plain fact remained: somebody like Georgia Strong walked through your life only once.

"Miranda," she said. "Clothes off, please. You can hand them to Ariel."

I stripped. Ariel appeared at my side to take the silk suit. Being without clothes felt natural to me, but next to Ariel in her CEO drag and Georgia, who also wore power clothes, I felt very naked indeed. With every stitch draped over Ariel's outstretched arm, I suddenly remembered my posture and stood up very straight. Muscles tight, shoulders back, my breasts stood out. A crazy thought followed: my nipples were a few inches closer to Georgia than the rest of me.

"Thank you, Miranda. Now if you'll excuse me for a bit, I have some work to finish up before I can give you my full attention; please get on that window seat to my right, so I can look at you. Stand, please. Legs spread. You needn't hold yourself rigidly— stay relaxed and you'll be able to stand longer. If I have you only for forty-five hours, I certainly will require your endurance."

I obeyed, climbing into the recessed window. It had enough room for me to stand with my legs spread, as she had instructed, and San Francisco could look up my ass. Perched many stories in the air, I felt myself get wetter and wetter, glad that it was daylight and anyone who cared to look up would have something to see.

Georgia made a few calls and took some notes. She seemed to be moving fast on establishing her San Francisco office, and more than once she conferred with Ariel. After nearly an hour she looked up at me—my platform put me a little above her, like a sculpture on a pedestal, the better to be examined when Georgia desired—and told me to turn around. Now, with my back to her, I could see out, see tiny cars driving and tiny people scurrying below, could imagine I saw one or two stop and stare up for moments at a time.

"You do seem to take to this," said Georgia at last. "That tells me a good deal about you, Miranda. Step down now, please." When I obeyed, she said, "Now kneel back on the seat cushion, facing the window. Legs spread as wide as you can get them. Good."

I could not see her and did not dare look behind me, but I heard fabric rustle as she removed some article of clothing. Seconds later I felt her hands on me, taking hold of my ass cheeks, spreading them, and then a cold, wet dribble of lube. I braced myself as well as I could on the padded ledge. No sooner had I clutched the edges of the cushion than I felt the tip of her dildo at the mouth of my asshole. Its push in, steady and inexorable, felt like heaven—or just a little bigger. Her hands on my hips pulled me back even as she thrust in.

Georgia's cock soon eclipsed any other reality. She used it to make people hers, I dimly realized, to prove her possession and sustain it. She used it to please herself, too, for her thrusts were so hard and fast that they had to be turning her on, maybe bringing her to orgasm. Unlike the men I had been fucking, she stayed virtually silent, all still fury and control. Soon she had me pressed up all the way against the window, tits against the cold glass (which felt wonderful on my still-tender nipple piercings), hands clawing it uselessly for a hold. She caught hold of my shoulders and used the leverage to fuck me down hard, harder and faster, onto her cock. I screamed, swore, begged, prayed—not for mercy, but for her to drive me all the way out of my mind this way, for her to drive herself as deep into me as she could get. In her possession of my ass with the cool devil-prick dildo I was the one who'd lose control, not Georgia.

Georgia was tall, easily six-one. She had more strength than any woman I'd ever known. She picked me up from the ledge, impaled on her cock, one arm around my waist and one around my shoulders, lifting me away from the window. She turned, holding me this way, and sat on the ledge where I'd just knelt, me on her lap now, her cock still buried deep in my guts, keeping me pinned against her. My feet could just reach the floor. Ariel sat in the chair she had vacated, watching, a new Ariel I didn't quite know. Her eyes on me made me feel very, very exposed.

"Fuck this cock with your ass. Fuck it as hard as it just fucked you," Georgia ordered. I had to struggle to keep my balance. I fucked until my thighs were aching and sweat streamed into my eyes. My clit felt huge, untouched this whole time. Her cool orders isolated me, an effect that was just the opposite of what I felt when Jack devoured me with his dominance, and I fucked more and more wildly to try to reach her.

"Ariel," said Georgia, "come over here. I want you to spit on your hand and work this girl's clit until she can't stay on her feet any more."

Ariel did exactly as she was told. She had worked my clit a thousand times, but this time it felt different from any other time we'd made love. Maybe because this time we weren't making love: we were making something for Georgia.

I lay in a sweaty, fucked-out heap on the floor. Georgia looked down, not quite disapprovingly. "Miranda, you'll have to be able to take much more than that. You're a little bit spoiled, I fear. Two daddies." I looked up at her fuzzily, knowing I'd have to pull myself together if I didn't want to get thrown looking like this into the Nikko elevator, emerging in the marble lobby like something the cat dragged in. Besides, I couldn't bear the idea that I might displease her, that she might turn her back on me.

I managed to get to my knees. I'd been fucking with the big boys lately, but she was a tornado. "What can I do to please you, Mistress Strong?" I finally whispered.

"Hmm, draw us all a bath, I think," she said, and indicated a shoji-screen door. Behind it I found a room-sized Japanese bath. I fumbled in its low light for a minute, figuring out where the taps were; I even found a screened cabinet full of towels, and I laid out three. She had said, "Draw us all a bath."

Out in the main room, Ariel had removed her fancy CEO dress and now busied herself helping Georgia disrobe. What Demetrius had never seen emerged before me: Georgia Strong, all six-feet-plus of her, slender but every bit of her muscled. The muscles ran and rippled under her skin like a wild cat's, elegant, powerful. Her small breasts hugged her chest, their softer planes not detracting from the effect of strength. While Ariel hung up her suit, Georgia knotted her long hair onto her head and secured it with a pair of ebony chopsticks.

The hot water of the bath relaxed me, started to clear my head, and again I tried to imagine what Georgia might want me to do. She allowed me to sponge her and Ariel, laving their bodies, which left me hungry to put my hands on her—but that seemed impertinent.

"Ariel, sweet beauty, how would you like to arrange for a meal?" Georgia said at last. "Call it up from downstairs, if you like. I don't expect we'll want to go out any time soon." Ariel left the bath and complied; I could hear her as she called room service. Georgia turned to me. "That really left me feeling very unfinished. Miranda, come take care of that, please."

I couldn't quite believe what I thought she meant. Georgia sat on the edge of the tub, fine long legs spread. "Right here, Miranda," she said. "You understood me the first time." And she gestured to her sex, her mound trimmed short, her clit protruding a little, the vulva lips a dusky plum almost the color of my silk suit and looking just that silky. Kneeling to her, I moved my mouth toward her; when I got close she took me by the cheeks and put me exactly where she wanted me.

I'm sure I've made it plain that I love sucking cock, but nothing could ever compare to the feeling of her pussy filling my mouth succulently, her clit connecting electrically with my upper lip, her cunt ripe and juicy for my tongue to lap, soft where my teeth gently came together, asshole just below it all, and wouldn't you know my tongue found that too, wanting to give her everything just as she had taken everything from me—and wanting too to make a connection with her she couldn't deny, couldn't stay aloof from. She kept her hands on my face, guided me as I licked and sucked, burrowed and nibbled, slicked my face with her salty arousal. Her comes were quiet but obvious, all tight muscles and spasming release. I went at her until she stopped me, wanting to give her as much pleasure as she would take. I did not touch myself, though I suppose I might have, and I did not try to enter her with my fingers—if she had wanted that from me I knew she would tell me to do it. The greatest liberty I took, putting my tongue in her ass, filled my cunt with peppery heat, as I worked myself into her tightness as deeply as I could. By the time she lifted my face away, having had enough, more was slick than just my cheeks. I had to wash again, though I had been in the water all along.

Ariel had set out enough sashimi and rolled sushi to feed an army, but I hadn't counted on my own hunger after that workout. We all feasted. Georgia fed both of us from her own plate, dipping the pink fish into wasabi and burning us with it. This did exactly nothing to ease my cunt's burning.

Evening fell, darkening the windows, spangling our view from the high penthouse with city lights. Georgia instructed Ariel to roll a futon into a bolster shape. She ordered me to lie over it. She bound my hands and fastened my ankles to a spreader bar, one of the most lewd of S/M devices. This position both exposed and immobilized me, and I did not know whether to expect blows, the softness of a tongue, a hand in my ass, or another of Georgia's furious sodomizings. I did not dare try to peek behind me to see what might be coming, and she left me there for what seemed like a very long time, waiting, feeling her and Ariel's eyes on my spread-open holes.

There followed the whipping of my life, which I got for no reason except that Georgia wanted to do it. She started with her hands, spanking my ass hot and pink. It made me desperate for her hands or mouth on my clit, but she did not care, of course, what I was desperate for. Twenty minutes into it she put a butt plug into my ass, which made the spanks' sting transmute into pure sexual sensation. She left the plug in, moving next to a paddle, which thudded against me like a new way to get fucked. I knew the rain of blows had begun to mark me, I felt red welts raise, and I lost track of the border between pain and pleasure.

"Ariel, fuck her for me," Georgia said after one particularly heavy thwack had made my asshole tighten down hard and my back arch. So Georgia took a rest from hitting me while Ariel's clever, familiar hands moved in, one wiggling the plug enough to send waves of sensation through me, the other burrowing into my cunt, first two fingers, then three. She brought me to the edge of a big come, but she stopped immediately when Georgia said, "That's enough." My old lover had become something for Georgia to torment me with, and I wondered in a rush of panic and pain whether she did not want to touch me herself.

More blows from the paddle. Each strike sent red waves of deeply erotic pain through me. Just as I verged on losing it to the intensity of the blows, they stopped. Next, Georgia pulled the butt plug out and used my ass again, even more ferociously now that I was spread out and shackled to the spreader bar, ass in the air, nowhere to go, nothing to do but take it. She had not given me a safe word, either. After every few deep, pounding strokes of her cock—she was still slamming into me without making a sound herself, though by now I sobbed and screamed—she slapped my ass hard, then grabbed the reddened, sensitized flesh of my ass cheeks to spread me farther for her, I think just so she could more easily see the pornographic vision of my asshole spread so wide and filled so full of her. Georgia, I dimly realized, got a kind of intellectual pleasure out of this that equaled or even exceeded her pleasure in the body. She did it and watched it simultaneously. And I found there was a parallel pleasure for me, knowing that I was the one she chose to use. I began to hope I would not come, so that I could stay suspended on the intimate tight wire of need she had forced me out upon.

After sodomizing me she repositioned the butt plug and hit my ass again, with several repeated blows that fell on both cheeks simultaneously. Then she told Ariel to resume fucking my cunt. More fingers this time, and I felt her stretch me wide, wider, as Georgia watched and oversaw. I silently begged her to keep her eyes on my cunt, keep watching how much I wanted what she let me receive, how much I would take for her pleasure.

Ariel added more lube and worked her hand in deeper. The whole hand—of course she would go for the whole hand. She stretched my cunt unbearably wide; her hand was big, as big as Jack's. I tried to fight my own panic with deep, slow breaths. I wanted to show Georgia and Ariel that I could take it. "Don't let off, Ariel, keep pushing," Georgia commanded, and I begged them please, please to take me, to use me, to make me, make me take it, make me fucking take more, more.

At the widest point of Ariel's big hand, when I thought I would scream aloud with the intensity, Georgia started working my ass with the paddle again, with hard, rhythmic blows that promised not to stop until my cunt was satisfactorily full. My yells sounded oddly quiet in the big room, and Ariel's hand took an eternity to slip inside, but they had made me take it. When her fist finally filled my cunt, I floated high above myself.

Now Georgia dealt me blows while standing in front of me, her cunt in my face, my mouth sucking her like a kitten sticks to its mother, her spanks still raining on me from the opposite direction so she wouldn't interfere with Ariel's entry. And Ariel worked her fist inside me, every subtle motion feeling huge, every cell of me bound and spread and used according to Georgia Strong's wishes. Even through crying, screaming climaxes, I felt peaceful, cared for—for they had given me what I begged for, had made me take what I could not—and I felt so very sexy. If a creature like Georgia wanted to watch her cock pound my asshole, watch lube froth up around the tender rim from the force of her fuck, then every bit of me must be beautiful, desirable. I could not have been happier— unless she had turned around and let my tongue go for her ass.

Leash
Michele Serchuk

Amanda and I were sitting in my living room after karate one morning, reading erotica, feeling each other out. Not literally. We were talking about bondage, the excitement of the forbidden. Fine in theory, but when she asked me if I liked being dominant or submissive, I froze. Couldn't say the words, didn't know her well enough, choked on shame and pride. I got out some words about power play, the erotic tension built into switching roles and the transfer and exchange of power. All true, but I didn't own anything directly. We went on to safer topics.

Sunday afternoon, a few weeks later. Amanda sashays up the stairs, her libido reaching the fifth floor while her feet are still on three. She wanders about, losing clothing matter-of-factly. Well, yeah, it's not like we've never changed together before. Forbidden fruit, dancing sprite turns naked around the room. Shows dark against white walls, cocoa sleek, fuzzy and wild. She's happier without clothing, wants you to see her body. I know the feeling.

"Look what I brought," she says. Amanda brings toys. A leash and collar, black leather strip twirling out of her woven pouch.

She stands sassy in the middle of the white floor, showing me what she's brought to play with. "I have another one at home with spikes, but I didn't want to get too intense, you know?"

"Oh yeah, right. Cool. A leash." And what the hell am I going to do with a leash? What's proper leash protocol? I don't want to say this is new to me, appear unsure of myself. Death before embarrassment, you know. My first impulse is always to act cool, a bad habit I'm trying to break. From inside my cool I'm trying to think, to gather myself. I'm more than a little intrigued, but something about this still makes me feel squirmy.

So, what is it about this leash thing? It's this object-thing and I want to conceal it, deny it. I don't want to deal with its existence. Much more than any silk scarf or bathrobe sash tied tightly around my wrists, this object embodies my fascination and lust for power play, those words, *dominance* and *submission*. Object of ridicule, subject of snickering jokes about pathetic degenerates, shame I didn't think I owned. I feel lurking vestiges of someone else's puritan values and a flash of political indignation. Scarves are garments until the moment they become bondage, but that leash and collar has no other purpose. I want to touch it. I want to hide.

That object in Amanda's hands is confession, and I am remembering my grade-school jump rope made of stretchy, orange rubber tubing with white handles. I am remembering the thrill I got tying my ankles together in my dark bedroom at night when no one was watching. I was too young to know that heat flash as sex but old enough to know it was "bad," to know better than to tell anyone, ever. I'm thinking of all those spankings my Barbie Dolls got. I'm thinking I don't want to think about this now. I just want her to kiss me.

Turning to find her, I move into her arms. We begin exploring each other, steamy and soft. Who is she, I wonder, and how can I please her? I've forgotten the collar, lost in her skin, in her curves. Something in her lies sleeping and I want to wake it up, see her on fire, feel her passion. I glide over her, inhale sweet spice, taste salt.

Amanda makes whimpering, cooing noises as I slip fingers into her, feel her inner walls suck me inside. My fingers explore, feel the hard dimple of her womb as I push in deeper. I feel her slick and warm against my thigh as she rides me, fingers between my legs, stroking me. I float, riding lazy waves of sex-thrill.

I have forgotten her toy. She hasn't. It's in her hands again and I refuse to say "Hey, wait, I'm a leash virgin." She gives it to me. Oh no, what the hell do I do with this now? Nice girls don't play with leashes, and feminists don't tie people up, especially not other women. Funny, I don't recall these thoughts ever being so loud when I've played this way with a man. I don't know if it's the leash/scarf thing or a gender thing; my hormones are racing and I'm not even certain right now why I'm doing this, but I can't back down and, truthfully, I can't resist the challenge.

I hold her down and slip the collar around her neck, moving her body forcefully, feeling her size and my strength. My robe is by the bed and I slip the sash out of the loops, grab her hands, and bind her wrists. Her pleasure is obvious to me, incites me to give her more, her movements and noises showing me the way to be this person, to dominate her. She squirms as I run the leash down between her breasts, between her legs, and yank it hard, up her back. Pinning her to the hard futon, I pull the leather tight. I wonder how the sharp tugs on the collar must feel and imagine the deliciousness of being trapped. Her ass twitches back and forth as she rubs herself against the leash, and I tentatively spank her a few times with the looped handle. It makes loud, satisfying, slapping noises. I do it again, more forcefully this time, and watch, fascinated, as she twitches harder.

I am whispering to her, nibbling on her, watching her get hotter and hotter. My hands run over her body, moving her as it pleases me, catching her head, pulling her in to kiss her, spreading her thighs to expose her clit. I want to make her come.

Remembering how she liked being penetrated, I begin to fuck her, not exploring like before but pushing, thrusting, filling her. Her response is immediate and fierce. She cries out and gives herself to me, wet and open. I have four fingers in her, see her juices shiny on my knuckles. Her moans come wilder and louder as she rubs herself back and forth over that black leather leash, swallowing half my hand, as she comes.

We sit up laughing and I untie her hands. I'm beginning to surface, not sure where I've been, not even sure if I'm back yet. But she's not done, she remembers my words about role reversal and power play needing to go both ways. That leash and collar is in her hands again and her imp eyes are fixed on me. "Your turn," she says.

Big mouth. Amanda is reaching for my neck. I feel politics and pride screaming in my stomach as a heat wave engulfs my cunt. I can't move. No, I don't want to move. But I want to struggle; I feel our near-equal strength as we wrestle, knowing she has to win. She has me, slips the collar around my throat, jerking my head back by my hair. It feels dangerous and forbidden. She tightens the collar almost past the point of comfort; blood pulses at my temples as I feel its rough pressure at my throat. I move over to give myself air, relaxing my guard; she has me, pulls me where she wants me, flat on my back. She wants my hands; I see the sash and hold out my wrists even as I pretend to fight. She ties them so tightly that the only way to keep it from hurting is to bend my elbows with my arms stretched out and over my head. I have never felt so helpless. Slowly I recognize that there is nothing I can do, that she has to please me now. I lie there, wrists aching, and luxuriate in the realization that I am hers and the pleasure now is mine. She has a dildo in her hand as she moves in over me. *I'm your captive*, I think, *do me*.

Amanda's eyes sparkle. Her hand twists in my hair as her gaze travels over my body. My breathing sounds ragged in my ears; I am waiting for what comes next. I feel her body pinning me down and the heat of her thigh against my crotch. Nothing comes next. I am waiting. Amanda is staring at me.

"You like this, don't you?" she asks. Her voice is soft, low, and in complete control. I buck upward and grind against her hip in response. "That's not an answer. Tell me. I'm waiting." I can't speak. I am choking from deep inside. The words are stuck in my chest somewhere and I cannot say anything. I wonder what I had been thinking of when I started flirting with her that morning on my sofa. I remember starting off feeling so daring; I don't think I had believed this would actually happen.

Amanda tugs on the leash and my mind bounces back into the present. There is no place to hide. I can't move my head to escape her hot, brown stare, so I close my eyes. I am conscious of myself inside my body and of each passing second. The moment becomes very long and I silently beg her to resolve it for me.

"I won't be the fall guy for you, girl. You'll say it. Watch." Amanda gets up and leads me to the window, keeping the leash short and tight. We look out over the roofs, onto streets bustling with Sunday, Chinatown commerce. "Who are you afraid of? Them? You afraid of what they'd say? Or is it your friends, hmm? Afraid they wouldn't approve of your politics?" Amanda is stroking my hair. I feel her warm breath in my ear as she whispers to me. She hasn't let go of the leash. It's beginning to get dark and lights go on in the building across the alley. I can see my neighbors watching TV and preparing dinner. I stand naked, collared, peering through the thin curtains.

"Amanda, the neighbors...they'll see." I hear myself. I sound ridiculous. Amanda begins to laugh. She sounds delighted. She swings me around to face her; the look on her face is pure evil. She reaches over, flicks on a lamp, and yanks on the curtain. The flimsy rod falls easily out of the brackets. We stand framed in a pool of light over Canal Street. Amanda holds the leash and collar tight in her left hand as her right hand snakes around me and begins stroking my clit. Her teeth tease at my ear. My knees get weak and suddenly I don't care about my goddamned neighbors, the women at the karate school, or anyone else for that matter. I want her to fuck me and I don't care if the whole damned world knows or what anyone thinks about the way I want to be fucked.

"Make me come. I want you...to...please." I'm having trouble with words but I am speaking, after a fashion. She's laughing, loving this. Her hands are getting rougher, her teeth biting down on my neck, leaving red marks on my skin. I can see our reflection in the window and wonder who is looking up. I imagine the shoppers glancing up and noticing the glint of light off the thick, shiny collar, suddenly realizing what they are seeing. I imagine them going home hot and bothered, thinking about us later with husbands or girlfriends or maybe jerking off in the dark, alone. "I want them to see you fuck me. Fuck me." I am screaming it to her. At this rate they won't have to look up, they'll hear me.

"Stay here. Touch yourself. And don't turn around." Amanda unties my hands and kisses me, practically sucking the breath out of my mouth before she leaves. Her footsteps pad across the floor and I hear her rustling around in that bag of hers. I lean against the window frame, put one foot up on the sill, and begin to stroke myself. I can feel the leash hanging down my back, gently swaying. I feel it brush over my ass and I rub harder as I look out the window.

Amanda is suddenly back at my side grabbing at the leash and twisting my nipples. I can feel something hard and rubbery pushing at my ass. She has fastened the dildo on with a harness. A harness. Oh god, do women really use those things? I've seen one before but it was hanging on the wall at the Ye Olde Local Sex Shoppe, not on a lover. I want to see it but she won't let me turn around. She has one hand on the leash and the other across my chest as she forces me back against her. Her hips are powerful and thrust the rubber cock deep inside me. I feel myself scream as I ram into her. She staggers backward, regains her balance, then pushes me up against the window. I lean forward, holding tight to the frame. The glass feels cold on my breasts and I feel her breasts soft against my shoulder blades as she fucks me with deep, hard strokes. The sensation is deliciously perverse. Her long, sensitive fingers stroke my clit, and I feel my legs begin to shake. Heat spreads out from my belly and I can no longer stand. Her strong arms hold me up as I scream and tremble in front of that window. We fall to the floor and lie in a sweating, quivering heap. I put my head on her shoulder and let her soothe me to sleep.

It's early evening and she has gone hours ago; I am out walking in the world. I can still smell her spicy aroma rising off my body. The breeze blowing my hair across my face carries the perfume of her sweat, unchecked by Secret for Women. Her smells are so loud in my nostrils, I can't imagine that anyone talking to me doesn't notice. They don't. Each waft of scent triggers visceral memory. People see and hear me from so far away; I feel like I'm in a bubble waiting to land. My smile is full of secrets as I turn the corner for home.

Struck
Laurie Stone

I like fear. I like feeling where my skin ends when something strikes it, scratches it, tries to get underneath it. I like tension. I like the tension between what I want and what I need.

I fear I will touch too many people. My hand likes to go where it doesn't belong. I like the tension between being welcome and scaring people. It's such a thin line.

I like cruelty. Doesn't everybody? A man who has toyed with me gives a boring lecture, and I'm happy. I feel good. A woman who applauds my setbacks becomes fat as a hippo, and it's as if I'd won the lottery.

I like shoplifting. Chocolate is good, but I don't steal chocolate cake. The pieces are too big. It has to be something I can palm. I like the tension of eating.

I like the way semen smells. How would you describe it? I like being seized by a taste. I like being in a position to be corrected.

When people say they are going away, I say, "I will miss you," but I don't miss them. I miss people I want to fuck. Maybe it's only the fucking I miss, or not even the fucking but the idea of fucking. I like the tension of loving people one minute and forgetting them the next. I like fucking people I don't like. I like being wrong about the people I want to fuck. The mistake is like healthy sleep.

I like mother's milk. I like not knowing whether I'm sucking cock or tit. I like having my mouth and cunt and ass penetrated at the same time.

I like being unattached. I like being tied up. I like making the wrong impression. I like penetrating a man's mouth.

I met a woman at a party. I thought her head would explode like in a Cronenberg movie. Every word made her think about being misunderstood. She acted like her meaning was too precious to expose. I said, "It's annoying to be controlled, but it's funny. It's funny if you're not shocked."

Before my father took off his belt, he would say, "You're due for a licking." I would see a tongue on my skin. It would hurt. I like not knowing when I'll be struck.

When I'm with Oscar, I think I'm welcome when I'm scaring him. It makes me operate from inside a box. I like being loved for the wrong reasons. It makes me unsure if I should protect myself.

I like a smell that is almost sickening. I like a feeling that is almost painful. I like having the same dream. A man is on all fours, over me like a dog finding a plaything in the woods, sniffing at it gently and then licking, having friendly sex that makes me forget whether I'm in love or not, happy or not, gnawed at by doubts, losing money, giving away too much, failing at work, failing in friendship, symptomatic of diseases.

Fan is beautiful. She has clouds of hair. It's red, impossibly gleaming, waves of it cascading over her forehead, dancing around her cheekbones, flying down her shoulders. Her body is lean and statuesque. Her voice has a laugh. She holds her chin up. She likes being everyone's desire, but it is not the most important thing. Being everyone's desire shows her everyone's desire, and she does not like what she sees. I like watching people fall in love with her. She acts as if she didn't care. I think they like the whipped cream she places between herself and them. I imagine her cradled and sung to by men who can talk to cats.

A dominatrix told me she liked living out her fantasies. She said that not all women did. Some preferred to play with themselves, as if thinking about sex were not also a physical activity, as if the mind were not part of the body. She had made a living from her sexual activities. She was aroused by her work. It was her subject, too. She had nothing else instructive to say. She thought she had devoted too much of her life to sex. She had missed out on other experiences. When she named them, they were dull, like going shopping for linens at Macy's.

I like being taken from behind. I like the tension of being trusted. I like prominent veins. I like knowing everyone can tell.

I like women with space between their teeth. Anything can happen. Everything they wear looks soft, smells good. They present their bodies as a gift. They can't be shocked. They bet on the future. They carry foreign money. They attract children. Their embrace is like a silk cord. They make an impression without leaving marks.

I like scars. I like cells that don't forget. I like fighting sleep. I like the intelligence of gorillas. I like being bent over a chair. I like healing on my own.

I was riding my bike up Sixth Avenue on a balmy night, late, so there were no cars, and I was sailing in that way that makes me forget what I'm made of. I was wearing a thin jacket I wanted to shed, but I didn't want to stop. The left sleeve slipped off, but the right cuff caught on my wrist, and the next thing I knew I was sprawled on the pavement, my left hand cut, my left knee showing a trickle of blood, my left hip bruised. Most of the damage was to my left hand. I groaned whenever I squeezed the brake. I groaned so loud, I had to laugh. The hand swelled. I applied ice. I thought I'd broken a bone. I couldn't decide whether to keep the hand still or to flex it. I thought I should have X-rays, but I didn't go. Weeks passed, and it didn't heal, but in time the swelling went down, the bruises faded, the stiffness eased, the strength returned.

The hand didn't forget the injury. A place I press below the knuckle sings.

I am looking at a man I slightly know. He is obsessed with himself in such a humorous way it seems he is talking about someone else. Stray need makes him sexy. He acts as if his life depended on his attractiveness, and he seems even to know that this need fuels his sexiness; he's a type that's touching in a girlish way. But he pretends he's shy. He pretends his hands are tied. He pretends he has to be seized or drunk. It's disastrous to play his way. He doesn't want to be right about his allure. He doesn't like the tension of that responsibility.

I like feeling where my desire ends when something is beyond it. It makes me unsure if I should protect myself.

I had a lover I scared and excited, though many things had the same effect. Fear made the lover bold. Excitement made the lover shrink. The lover flattered and flirted. The lover didn't imagine my loneliness, though the lover knew I was alone. I didn't imagine the lover's anxiety, though it was detailed for me. I didn't pursue, but I rendezvoused when asked. The interest made me hopeful in a way I couldn't control. Each time the lover appeared, I was reminded there was nothing for me. I was sent a gift, the note signed with love, and then the lover disappeared. When the lover resurfaced, my anger was equivalent to the self-reproach that had been tripped. I felt I was abandoned because I was unworthy, though I knew it wasn't true.

I like pornography intended for someone else. I like a mind I can penetrate, a mind that splits itself open for me, like halves of a papaya. P. once said, "I want to eat papaya from your cunt. I want to shave your pubic hair. I want you to wear a corset." P. wanted to have sex that sounded uncomfortable but wasn't. The desire was touching in a girlish way. P. liked the scars I had acquired through accidents, liked giving me tests.

I like the footwork of boxing. I like encouragement that's like a corset. I like the discovery of irony by children.

A woman once told me she could think off. Her capacities seemed those of a mutant or a mythological beast. She could do it on the subway. She could probably do it anywhere, but I'm choosing the subway because of the vibrations. She would cross her legs and squeeze her pelvic muscles and somehow work up a cricket-like friction in her clit, or maybe friction wasn't necessary, the mind being sufficient. She would rock, or maybe not. She wasn't specific, or I don't remember. I liked the swagger in her smile.

I like women with passports that are heavily stamped. I like skin that's tattooed. I like the consequences of penetration. I like sex that's postponed. I like being on the receiving end. I like computers that talk. I like being slapped across the face. I like mixed origins.

My friend Andy fears that things can't change, but can only get worse at a faster rate. He fell in love with heroin, like a princess being awakened by a kiss. He was committed to oblivion. He bore the consequences of penetration. He liked sex that would put him to sleep. He thought of his dick as a needle. Women swarmed to his dead eyes. He liked women with nothing to lose. His curiosity was sweet. He was afraid of his ideas. He loved swallowing cunt. He didn't kill his intelligence. He treated his body cruelly. Women swarmed to his cruelty. He nursed his cruelty the way he did his drugs. Women with the power to think off found him a good fuck. He didn't feign shyness. He didn't need to be seized. He liked killing himself. He liked life. He could always express his beliefs. He found contact excruciating. His face grew skull-like. He kept the smell of cunt on his hands.

I like reversing my position. I like when honesty hurts. I like the thin line between masochism and courage. I told Sammy I believed in change, though when I gave examples it sounded like I was trying to cheer myself up. I find comfort in his size. He's too big to slam into a wall. I like separating because it hurts. I like being slowed down. I fear I will run out of patience and renewable cells. I like disliking Sammy. I like not having what I want, because it's what I need.

The Rack

Lucy Wikersham

My lover is a builder of tables, chairs, bed frames, and wooden boxes. She drafts her own designs and buys her own supplies. Sometimes, if I ask with the appropriate charm, she builds things for me. A desk for my computer, a butcher-block cutting board for my gourmet fantasies. I am lying on my back, head slightly tipped over the edge of the futon mattress, dreaming a design for her. Sprawling next to me, she traces the light covering of sweat that slowly winds its way from the hem of my short tank top to the curve just above my navel, dropping off suddenly toward the bed. I squirm slightly with the tickle.

"Make me a table," I ask, my words chopped into the fan that pounds hot air just above my head. It is an early August evening that begs for fantasy without motion.

"You already have a table." She is bored by my request. Her finger continues to drag over my skin, passing just under the waistband of my loose cotton boxer briefs. She is not going anywhere, but constantly moving. She is a tease.

"Not a table exactly, more like a platform, the kind of table you lie on when you go to the chiropractor. One that lets me lie on my stomach without squashing my face. One that lets me lie above you but not on top of you."

"So you're saying you don't like to lie on top of me?" She is offended, but not sincerely. She waits for detail. Her articulate mind is already drawing the straight pencil marks of the board edges. I see the spaces between the supports for my hips, shoulders. She is waiting to see what is not covered.

"I want you underneath me," I say, "but free to move. I want my legs to be supported, but also restrained. I want a '90s version of a medieval torture device: the sex rack."

She laughs, an internal rumble like the one a cat used to make from under the bed. Her fingers continue their patient movements around, across, gaining some momentum. "Why do you need a device?" she pouts.

I begin to describe my vision to her, my hips moving slightly with the anticipation of perfect angles created by such a feat of exotic carpentry. The empty air above my shorts is acute: nothing to push against as the heat becomes concentrated from my extremities, crawling in from my fingers, toes to flush my outer and inner lips, to the clitoral core. A padded board would press on the lowest reach of my gut, where innocuous belly meets raw sex, the final frontier of intangible star-crossed skin. "Think of it," I murmur, rubbing my hand across my ribs and slowly lower…

I am suspended just a hair-width above my lover's mouth, close enough for her to touch her tongue to where I am now aching, to push between the inner flesh, to the tiny heartbeat that burns in anticipation of a mind-blowing physical flush. My legs are held apart by spring-balanced boards, pressure-sensitive to my growing ardor. Her tongue flicks lightly and I fear now that I might actually drip on her, something one doesn't normally notice mid-fuck.

The soft, wet pressure-suction blend is almost more than I can bear, and I squeeze my thighs together, coming up against the genius of the "rack." Resistance is causing my inner muscles to clench around nothing, as I am being made to wait, torturously, for each next element of pleasure. I grind my pubic bone into the "hip board," as my lover has named the structure, with such originality, knowing that if something doesn't happen soon, I'm going to scream "Fuck me, you bitch!" so loud that she'll lose her lease.

My lover has excellent timing. Just as my fingers clench harder than I thought possible into the pillow supporting her head, she slips three fingers into me, and I instantly bear down on them, not caring if I break her hand. My legs are (magically!) allowed to slide a bit closer together, but not close enough to provide critical tension. I am so slippery that I feel as if her three fingers were nothing more than a Q-tip, and a cheap one at that. "Fuck me harder," I mutter, groaning slightly, no longer caring if I sound like an ass. I almost feel her smile on my clit, as she removes her fingers and substitutes something longer and wider, and I almost buck against it, it's so deep. It feels like three hands or her whole arm and I think *I don't give a shit what it is, I've never wanted to come so bad in my whole li*—"uh-uh-uh," the boards are creaking slightly, and I almost lose it, praying the whole damn thing doesn't collapse in a million pieces. My legs pull closer together, resistance easing as I approach the edge. Tighter, tighter, I don't think all the Kegels in the world could have prepared me for this moment—

—small nuclear fusion bomb on a direct path from her tongue—explosion of heat and pain-pleasure rushing up through my stomach, down to my kneecaps—

my head shoots forward and my fingers press through her hair to her scalp and I try to control the riding of my hips, but my brain has shut down momentarily and she is gently sucking as if to coax the last few drops of tension out until finally I press my thumb into her mouth, easing her away, and I tumble off the rack onto the bed beside it. She crawls onto the sheet next to me and slowly begins to trace my hot and weary skin with her fingertips—

"Do you really think that's necessary?" she asks, rolling onto her elbows to let the fan blow in her face.

Exhausted, I toss my discarded tank top and boxers off the bed and roll into the crevice between her triceps and her rib cage. "I guess it's just one of those weird fantasies," I muse. My hand slides over my stomach and down between my legs. "I'm going to be sore tomorrow," I complain, drifting into sleep.

Lullaby for a Knife Sharpener
Sarah Fran Wisby

Jesse. Sharpen your knives on my long bones. The first time you came by with your bag of stones, sat at my kitchen table with all the contents of my knife drawer glinting up at you, dazzling me, slices of mirror refracting your beauty as you ran the long stones along each dulled edge of metal, making it fine again, I thought about cutting up chickens. How with a good sharp knife, the gristle slides off like butter, the slippery meat opens to you as if it had waited its whole simple life for this moment.

Even after you'd finished, and laid the knives gently on a dish towel, all pointing the same way like teeth in a cared-for mouth, even after I'd paid you and you'd said "Thank you, ma'am" in a shy, self-mocking sort of way, we stayed at my kitchen table and drank half a bottle of wine. You never seemed to be in a hurry. Not that night, or any other when you'd come around. The trouble lay—and trouble is always lying coiled up someplace close by— the trouble lay in not knowing when you'd come around. And buying the toughest of meats, using my knives as often as possible, wishing them dull so I could call and ask you back only made me feel like the worst kind of woman, the kind who waits.

I never wanted to be a waiting woman; who does? But at some point I realized I had spent my whole life in anticipation, a slightly parted mouth, red and superstitious, frozen in a state of readiness. Waiting, I suppose, for a kiss to end all kisses. The big one, ominous and delicious, where you melt and melt until you disappear. But when wanting itself becomes bigger than the thing that is wanted, well. My grandpa would say, if it was a snake it woulda bit you. Meaning: everything you ever wanted could present itself on a tray with dancing girls and you wouldn't notice. You've got your eyes closed and your lips open and all that's happening is your mouth is going dry.

My mother never waited for anyone or anything, not as far as I know. She was a go-getter from the get-go. I always picture her with car keys in one hand, her pocketbook in the other, and a crazed look in her eye. Whenever I saw that look, I scrambled to do whatever it was that needed doing: getting my brother into his snowsuit, or mopping up spilled apple juice, or just getting out of the way.

The second time you came over I knew I would seduce you. I made lasagna and garlic bread, and salad with red bell peppers and artichoke hearts. I was feeling poetic in the grocery store and I put my thumb over the label so it read "choke hearts"—it seemed appropriate to my mission. I asked the neighbors to watch Otto for the night—college girls, I buy pot from them sometimes.

In the middle of dinner I took your hand and placed your first two fingers in my mouth, all the way to the back of my throat, the soft, spongy part that reminds me of a cervix. Your other hand found the wetness between my legs and I moaned, feeling the fullness of being entered in two places at once. "Oh, Annie," you said. "I had hoped, but I wasn't sure..." My hands found the curls at the back of your neck, the only place that wasn't full of hair grease, and held on.

I went back to work not too long ago, just a couple of days a week, and my first day back the other cooks were talking about some shrink they'd heard on the radio. Jeannine told us how he'd said that as soon as we become lovers with someone, as soon as we lay claim to them, we start expecting them to fill all the gaps our parents left in us, give us all the love we never had as children.

Cathy started laughing, shrieking almost, pounding the counter with a floured fist. "That's so fucked!" she wailed. "How ridiculous can you get? No wonder, God, no wonder the world is so fucked up." I kept chopping up broccoli florettes, tossing them in a metal colander so large it always reminded me of a flying saucer. I didn't think it sounded so outrageous to ask for those things from a lover. I mean, where else are you gonna get them?

Seems like my heart is always tripping over itself trying to catch up to the way the world works now. You're not allowed to own people anymore. They come and go and you're just supposed to be okay with that. I want to belong to somebody, and if they don't want me anymore they can just put me in a burlap sack with some rocks and throw me over the bridge. I'm tired of being free.

All my knives at your disposal and you had to use your own pretty little hunting knife to mark me. This was the fourth time you came by, but only the second time you fucked me. It started out silly. I giggled when you pressed the flat side against my throat and told me to unbutton my blouse. I giggled when you traced circles around my nipples with the tip. I gasped when you pressed the tip between the bones that fence in my heart.

I knew you weren't trying to leave any permanent traces, just scratches really, a lopsided heart with angel wings. It took three weeks to fade.

The first night you came by unannounced there was no booze in the house, so we drove to the Grand Union. I waited in the car watching snowflakes sizzle when they hit the windshield, watching my white breath fill the VW like ether, temperature fronts clashing in and around the car like religious armies, each trying to win over the other side.

You came out of the Grand Union the way you burst onto any scene, shoulders back, chest up high like a bulldog, shy puppy grin on your face. Then your heel caught a patch of ice and you skidded, regained your balance for a second, then pitched forward to land with the bottle of whiskey smashed under, or rather through, your hand—your left hand, the one you live by.

I ran to help you up. "I'm taking you to the emergency room," I said firmly, putting my arm around your waist as if you might have trouble walking with an injured hand, and as if I could hold you up if that were true.

"I don't have insurance," you stated, as if that would matter to me. We were already seated in the car. I revved up the engine to warm it back up. I was kinda revved up myself, excited by the prospect of being useful to you. I wondered briefly if it was fucked-up of me to take a small measure of delight in your dependence. I was pretty sure Cathy at work would think so.

"They have to take you whether or not you're insured," I told you. "Jesus, you're bleeding all over the place!"

"I'm sorry." This was said so earnestly that I wondered if you were in shock.

"Oh, Jesse. That's not what I mean. I mean it's serious. I don't care if you ruin the ripped-up seats." The only towel in the car was full of dog hair. I didn't want to give you that so I took the Indian-print scarf from around my neck and wrapped it around your hand tightly. You rocked back and forth holding it and seemed to be trying not to cry.

"Look, Annie, I'm not going to the hospital, okay? I'll figure something out. Take me home with you and I'll make some phone calls, see what I can figure out."

By the time I pulled into the driveway I knew what I was going to do. I got out my sewing kit and some unwaxed dental floss, sterilized a needle and threaded it. Got out the rubbing alcohol and the Vicodin. Got to work.

If there's anything I know, it's how to stitch things up so you can barely see the seam. Flesh isn't so different from thick upholstery fabric, the satiny kind that stretches when you sit on it, and lord knows, I'd watched doctors sew me up enough times. Made my eyes focus on the surgical needle and black plastic thread that looked like insect parts so I could tune out my mother explaining why I was so accident-prone.

Not that I didn't believe her. I believed I was prone to being in the wrong place at the wrong time, the wrong girl in the wrong skin, the wrong daughter in the wrong house. I would turn too suddenly and knock into something and that something would pound back. I would tumble into a wall, or into the hot stove, or against the edge of a paring knife. I rarely heard the words that accompanied my tumbles, for I had a thick layer of cotton that descended into my head at such times, and it kept my brain from colliding too harshly with my skull, but once I heard the words "little bitch"—they sounded squeezed out like sourness from a lemon and for a long time I heard nothing else.

Sharpen your knives on my long bones. A tender anesthetic, your hand inside me, curled as if to grasp some brass ring, some key to some faraway lock. Your eyes locked onto mine, always a contest to see if I can hold your gaze without blushing or feeling my blood surge into tears. Since the baby, a fist is the only thing that can fill me to capacity: I'm a plowed field, I'm a workhorse, I'm a petunia coming apart at the petals, I'm a sucking wound, wrapped around your wrist. Who is being bandaged here? Who is being healed?

The hundred-and-twelfth time you came over—well, to tell the truth it was only the twelfth, but it felt like so much more. I was always counting, adding articles of evidence in my head, wrapping things up for safekeeping like wineglasses in newspaper. I just wasn't sure how to measure things, what standards to use. My own obviously wouldn't do; they got me in trouble more often than not. I'd expect a field of rubies instead of gravel and blood, that skinned-knee feeling, but all over. I'd mistaken a certain blistery rawness for love too many times.

The twelfth time you came over you let me make you come. We had been smoking a little pot in the living room, tending the fire in the woodstove, and you lay back on the couch, unzipped your jeans, and said, "Come here, little girl."

I nuzzled my face into your crotch and worked my fingers past the sharp teeth of the zipper, through the cotton flap of your briefs, and your fingers found my mouth and I took them as if it were your cock and I gave the best head of my life, fucking my own face with the whole of your hand, your right hand, not the one I mended for you, although that one had almost healed, a puckered scar running between index finger and thumb. You held my hair away from my face with that hand while I fucked you stealthily with my own little fingers—that part we don't talk about, that part that is hard for you—and soon you started bucking your hips and pressing my head hard into your crotch, choking me on your cock, then letting out the softest little moan and stroking my hair and we didn't move or say anything for the longest time. Then I heard the baby crying and got up to go feed him.

Jesse. When you touched my throat it went dry. When you laid your hand flat against my chest it was as if a cellar door had opened, and I tried to suck you deep into my darkness. I wanted to swallow your flame without extinguishing it, keep it burning in my belly.

Every time you fucked me I wanted it everywhere at once. All the way down my throat like the tubes they feed you through in hospitals. So far up my pussy I could feel my uterus contracting, remembering the baby, that kind of fullness. So deep in my ass I'd start thinking about all those miles of intestine and wondering if I could digest you in reverse, shit you out through my surprised mouth. Wouldn't that be something.

All that winter, everything I felt was grand and unspeakable. Maybe because I'd been nothing but a mother for so many months, I had grown used to communicating through blood and through milk, through lullaby. I thought you knew the song I was singing. I thought I recognized your song.

To have neither you nor the pleasure of your company didn't occur to me. I thought it was up to me. If you wouldn't love me, not right away, at least I would have your presence. If it was a bit hollow, a bit vanishing at the edges, at least it was you, the huge physical fact of you. A body choosing to keep time with my body. A body intersecting with my body in the kind of pleasure that could turn a girl religious.

But you left. Your body left. It ran away to be with your mind. Eloped in the night with no attempt to warn me. I loved you. Why is it so satisfying to say that now, now that you aren't around to hear it? Now that the words are implicitly sad, parentheses around loss, two pathetic arms that hold nothing. Loved. You.

Sharpen your knives on what's left of me. I have been carved down to nothing, a skeleton of longing. You left me all wrong, turned inside-out like a pair of spent gloves. You were lifted out of me too soon, like a C-section baby, a baby who couldn't bother to be born. I woke in a fog, needle and thread in my hand, stitching myself up.

The Scrimshaw Butch

Gayla Mann

I don't fight well till I'm in a rage. As a matter of fact, I fight pretty much like a girl till someone's about killed me or scared me so bad I feel like I'm gonna die. And no one, absolutely no one, leaves her mark on me. Danne knows how I feel about that. I would die first. Well, tonight Danne had a few drinks and decided she'd waited long enough to put her mark on her "property." She tied me down, which was wonderful, but then she started in with one of Tony's blades and something in me snapped. I don't know how I did it, but I was out of those knotted ropes in about half a second.

She was my dad, then, taking something not hers. And me grown big enough to do something about that drunken bastard's huge, calloused hands. I gasped in air and squeezed out rage. Furious, she tried to force me back down.

To make an ugly story short, she saw the wrong side of these painted nails. I left and came down here to the bar while she was under the sink looking for peroxide. I needed to visit some familiar turf and cool off for a bit.

It's been about five years now that we've been sharing the same bed, my waitressing tips shoring up her drinking. I'm not usually this nasty, and she doesn't really drink all that much, but tonight the woman said the wrong thing, did the wrong thing. Nobody marks me. Nobody owns me.

But someone did, once, and the strange thing is I allowed it, even craved it, needed it. Felt shivering ecstasy in the harsh salt spray of her touch. I have an old, unframed black-and-white picture of her taped up to the fridge. I carry her knife, too, so in some small way it's like she's still with me. But she isn't. She's about as far as one body can get from another. My Tony's dead.

Danne couldn't get me to take down that picture or leave that knife at home even if she took after me with her fists. Danne's my butch, and they are how they are, and I don't especially blame her for trying to take the piece of me I hold separate even from her. I understand pride, and I understand the price of loving under someone else's shadow.

I've watched this place, this "club" they used to call a bar, change over the past twenty years, too, the younger women coming in pairs, each of them wearing lipstick and spandex. It's not something I can bring myself to understand. I am a femme. Faded now, and perhaps not so fluffy over the years as some have been, but I have loved my butches since the first time I screwed up the courage to come down here. First time, I sat near the doorway in that corner over there with Suzie and Bette, friends from high school who knew they were different from other girls. I was afraid to be seen but afraid to be ignored, too.

That was a long time ago and styles are different now, but the women are somehow the same, and the smell of stale beer and smoke. The younger butches are starting in on that James Dean look again. Even today the butches hang out over there in the darker corners skirting the pool table. It's some kind of butch thing, half in the flare of the table light, half in the mysterious dark. See the one with dark short hair flipped to one side? She just bent her head to light a smoke. Cowlick's just like Tony's.

Butches were everything I was not: aggressive, brave and strong, cigarette-smoking, pool-shooting, brawling, swaggering dykes and proud as their ducktails. In a way I loved them all, the butches I've been with over the years, but there was only one who left her mark on me.

After this particular fight with Danne I can't avoid remembering. My own special ghost is holding me tighter than a living hand ever did, curled in the hair at the back of my neck. I can pull on a draft and hear the hum of conversation over the CD player. A CD is smooth and sleek, with all the dirt, sweat, and moans cleaned right out of it. But I don't need a jukebox playing to remember Tony.

Her name was Tonya, and no one can step into her boots. I called her Tony, but just about everybody else called her the Scrimshaw Butch. Or Scrim, or just Butch. I was about twenty-five when we met, and I'd had my share of loving. But this woman held me loosely so I could float and at the same time had a net around me made of so fine a weave that if I strayed too far my body would fall to pieces.

She talked to me for three months before she ever bedded me, and when she finally took me she knew the most minute and intimate details of my life. And like everything she attempted, it was perfect. When she was with me, there was never an instant when her attention wandered.

She owned me, she's dead, and I'm still hers, even after twenty years, because most of me is dead now too. I felt the connection go when she did. The energy band that was between us since the first day we met broke into about a million fragments, but it didn't lose its shape. Like the glass they put in windshields these days, you know, it cracks up but doesn't shatter all over your face. And those bits and fragments are connecting me to her still, pulling me slowly where she wants me to be. With her. Because, like she'd say, that's the way it is.

Scrimshaw Butch. Sounds a little silly today, but she wore it like she wore her bomber jacket and sunglasses. Always, and with a whole lot more than pride. Her name, even the "Butch" part, was who she was. Tony was upper-crusty even though she looked working class. All the butches did in those days. Jeans and a work shirt, solid colors only, maybe a stripe but never flowers or prints. Leather boots, the jacket and the shades. Simple, but the cloth was always good, and she smelled clean, like laundry detergent. No matter what kind of sweating she'd been doing, if you know what I mean.

Anyway, she hung out in this dive we're sitting in now, with Danne and Cass, Gina and Rachel and Terry—women who worked in jobs guys do—and with me and the other girls, Bette and Suze and Jamie, Jackie and a couple others. Danne and Terry and Gina all worked construction when they could get away with passing as men; Cass and Rachel did dock work and sometimes painting. Tony hung out with some of the gay boys, too, and they kind of looked up to her in a weird way I never did understand. Tony was an artist, but she wasn't full of herself like most rich people.

She started out in art school but dropped out when she met Old Emmett, the scrimshaw artist. He was just an old rummy hanging out at the docks carving on stuff that looked like white chocolate, or maybe something a little harder. Like bones. One day she went right up to him, friendly but tough, with that walk she had that said she owned the dock and everything on it. Kind of a swagger without the threat. I get carried away, sometimes, remembering the simple things that made me burn.

Odd how fresh it all is after all these years. I even adopted a kid fifteen years ago who's grown and gone now. Guess that makes me really too old to be femme anymore. I don't know. Old habits die hard.

Anyway, Tony asked this ratty old guy a question. She wasn't afraid of anyone, no matter if they had red eyes or boozy breath or filthy clothes. No matter if they were bigger than she was or meaner looking. She walked right up and asked him what he was doing in that tough butch way of hers, with just a few words, only the necessary ones. And he surprised her by not saying a word in response. He gave her this "You just can eat shit and die" kind of look and turned his back on her. That pissed her off, and if it was anyone else, she probably would've decked 'em and forgotten all about it. But the scrimshaw man ate at her, like the constant lapping of the tide or the ever-present scree of gulls.

She started to hang out at the dock with her sketch pad in her shirt pocket and her pencil behind her ear. She watched him staring at the last of the riggers, the clipper done up like a museum, in its own specially fixed-up berth. She didn't get too close, didn't watch him work right off. Just stayed right on the edge of his peripheral vision, letting him get used to the scent of her.

She tailed him to the dealers where he bought his bone, and hanging just out of sight she learned what to look for: color, hardness, shapes that would take the blade. At the store she could sometimes even get away with watching as he etched a few quick lines in a piece he'd just bought. He'd cut, look close, then cut again, crosshatching heavily then lightly, then he'd grunt and rub it all over with his blue-stained thumb. He'd sell small finished pieces for food and blue dye, which he used for the deep-etched grooves. He saved the big pieces for liquor.

After a couple visits Tony got to know Marty, the shop owner. Marty told her who the old guy was. He said he didn't know how this sour old coot from New England had ever managed to wash up in Galveston, but he said Old Emmett was the greatest scrimshaw artist alive, maybe that had ever lived. Even showed her this yellowed magazine cover with the old rummy's face on it.

Before that summer was over she knew she was going to learn scrimshaw.

She hung out down to the docks every day from sunup to sundown, staying just outside of what he might notice or complain about. In the long warm days that followed, they never talked to each other, never waved or recognized each other, never even nodded their heads. But each of them knew. Day after day the shadows crawled over the dock.

One day he left a half-etched, half-weather-worn piece of whale bone out on the bench next to Marty's. I don't think it was an accident. It was one of his practice pieces that showed all the different marks you could make. Of course she learned them all, then left it back on the same bench.

I didn't worry about her out at the docks alone. We didn't have that kind of relationship. But I missed her fist in me and her teeth on me. I'd never know when to expect her, and all of a sudden she'd be there, stinging like a mud dauber, sudden, fast, sharp and sweet. Then she'd be gone before I could get my breathing back to normal, before my heart rate could slow. And the marks of her passing were on me. In her wake swirled the strange comfort of familiarity: the half-remembered pirate of innocence, the painful spark of pleasure.

On a couple of occasions that summer, when I was too bruised from our last time together, she'd lay me back in her arms and stroke the aches out of my body, touching me gently, tenderly. Then she'd talk to me about the life she'd found at the dock. She'd talk about the people, the expressions on their faces that showed the stories of how they'd lived. The way she talked, I saw images of faces etched on people like scrimshaw is etched on whalebone. She talked about the sea and its moods, and how she felt connected to the earth and to me when she felt it move. She said I was like the ocean. And she knew she was one of the old-style clippers, fast and smooth but mean as the dickens and ready to stand tall in any storm. A lot of her talk was about the talent of that old rummy living in a paperboard shack down on the dock.

She had taken to marking me early in our relationship. The butterfly touching, soft-on-soft stuff didn't get me off. Just made me feel nervous. I wanted a strong lover who would take control, give me an order, tie me down, and fuck me hard. I guess I just couldn't feel it the other way. Sometimes her strong, short-fingered, powerful hands touched me in gentle ways that scared me away from her. Sometimes I ran straight into someone else's arms, but she'd just wait for me and I always returned.

For me the marks are lessons learned, badges like in the girl scouts. My Butch striped and welted, cut and pierced me with just about any implement you could name and a lot she'd make up on the spot. She always knew just how to use something on me so it felt perfect, even if she'd never practiced. She made sure we both got our pleasure, more than enough, every time. When my mood changed fast, from hating her to wanting her to being frustrated with her to being so far up in Heaven I couldn't even see God anymore, she would just climb on and ride, using me like a stone to sharpen herself.

She turned out a lot of scrimshaw, and even took to the idea of selling her stuff to tourists. I came up with the idea, and while I thought it was all still talk, Tony and Cass piled into Terry's pickup. They bounced and jostled their way over to the lumberyard. Then of course, they were out in Cass's garage all night long, building, we womenfolk watching those sweet butch curves and bringing them beers.

Danne dubbed that little shack the "Scrimshaw Butch" and even painted its first rough sign. Danne was always a little bit in Tony's shadow, but she looked up to her like a boy looks up to his older brother. And sometimes I think the shadow of a gravestone is too hard for her to live under. Too hard for anyone.

Anyway, after I got the permit they hauled that thing down to the boardwalk and Tony was set. The business turned a fine profit in season, and in the fifth year they moved her into a permanent store with four walls, just up the beach from Marty's place. The back room was where she'd take me, tied to the boards in a million configurations, or chained to the wall, or wrists and ankles tied over a sawhorse or two. The room where she did all her scrimshaw, where all her creative energies got spent.

As I'm telling this story I remember one scene in particular because I still feel what I felt then when I play it over in my mind, and I can always do with remembering that feeling. It had been weeks—almost a month—since I'd seen her. I got a little crazy with wanting, a whole lot angry she'd left me hungry for so long, and I was only just a hair away from begging her. Somehow she always knew, and I never reached the point where I actually had to beg. I know she wanted me to, but she could never quite manage to contain herself long enough for me to break down and beg. Or maybe she was just being kind.

She called after that eternal three weeks, and the liquid melt of her voice flowed down my ear and dripped into me. My body shimmered, crushing, burning, wet, sprung from pores and pussy. She said only, "Hello," and I could only sob and grind my panties into the stool by the phone. I was tension and desire and her telephone tongue issued commands sweet as peppermint candy and terrible as a cane. She needed me. Now.

I dressed exactly as ordered, too anguished even to tease at rebellion by wearing white garters with my black silk hose. Then I hurried to the corner store and guiltily spent money on the luxury of two avocados, one large and hard for me, a ripe one for her, and a small tin of smoked oysters. The weeks of waiting, and the hard avocado I pushed in quickly in the market's tiny washroom, stretching me, had built me to such a pitch of desire that I knew that at a fingertip's touch I would come. The lips of my sex were swollen, firm and drenched, my slit open and quivering.

I walked the strip down near the docks with a quick, firm step that caused my breasts to chafe against the stiff black lace of my bra, and a fullness like a fist clenched and rolling in my pussy. I was blind to anything but the end of my journey, and the release I needed to live another day. The last block to Tony's shop was an agony of terror and anticipation. What would she do to me? Through what pains would she seek her pleasure this time? In frightened anticipation I must have closed my eyes for several steps, but somehow I was forcefully knocked over by a man walking swiftly toward me. He stumbled, then fell directly on top of me. He caught most of his weight on his hands, so all I felt was the crush of his groin and legs that pinned me down. I screamed, arching my back. Not in shock or surprise, but with an incredible, joyful release: the weight at my crotch violently pressed the fullness of the avocado inside, and the jarring impact of the fall spilled the sounds from my mouth. Eyes clenched shut, I came, humiliatingly, shuddering through every muscle of my body, right there in the middle of the pavement. I looked up, into the sea-green of Tony's eyes. A wicked chuckle rumbled deep in her throat, and she murmured, "Pardon me, Ma'am, I must not have been looking where I was going," and thrust the hardness again into my flesh as she made the pretense of getting up awkwardly. "Are you hurt?" she asked innocently, as I moaned and came again.

In the back room of the shop, pretense faded entirely, and my stern Master replaced the innocent stranger. I was still whirling at the skill with which she had built my passion, and with the precision of a craftsman, sliced the edge from my both fear and my passion. How easily she played with me. No cat with a mouse between its paws could have looked more content. This had been planned to stabilize my neediness, the fire banked to be built again, this time at her exquisite discretion.

Each perfected layer of clothing had been mussed in the fall, and I could tell by the arch of one eyebrow that the indiscretion was noted. After obeying her command to strip down to my garters, I fell to my knees, urgently kissing her boots, caressing, holding, touching the only part of her she would allow me to touch. When she pulled me up with a leather-gloved hand at the back of my neck, I knew not to dwell near her crotch. I smelled her, though. Mixed with leather, the salt and sweat and juice of her made my mouth a hungry, dripping slit, my tongue a twitching cock. I moaned, swaying on jellied knees toward and away from the scent. Her hips swayed an inch closer, an inch farther away. Then, like opposing poles of a magnet, my mouth locked to her jeans, open and chewing, drugged by her pungent musk.

"Not now." She growled, to cover the moan I know I heard. She slapped my cheek hard, twice. I said sounds that were not words and gloried in the small victory of a slave: the minute evidence of the Master's desire. The ache in my knees on the plank flooring became a baseline of pain to the rhythm of men working the pulleys on the dock, the staccato of roughly bitten nipples.

I closed my eyes when she covered them with the blindfold of buttery leather. She had worn it between her legs, so the touchable smell of leather entwined with her fragrance. My tantalized nostrils added their own riff to this ever-growing symphony of sensation. The sound of her boots echoed first off to the left; I heard the sound of a door closing, perhaps a drawer opening, the slash of a whip against a chair back. The boots walked close again, briskly, then no sound at all but the shouts of the men outside, the whistling groan of ropes in the pulleys, the slam of a crate hurled to the dock. The bare but constant lapping of wavelets against the pier.

Seconds clicked by: Where was she? My heart quickened, I clenched my back against a blow that might or might not come. Struggling to relax again, I heard a loud bootstep from the center of the room. Another person? No, it was Tony, I recognized her grunt as she expended effort in some mysterious preparation. The chains and padlocks spoke next, and no upholstery or padding on the wooden planks contained their clatter.

"Are you holding it, or did it pop out?" she spoke in a normal voice, placing the smallest length of heavy cold chain around my neck. I answered yes, I was still holding it. When she said "Good," I relaxed at the mildness of her tone. I thought perhaps there would be pleasure, first, after all. She tightened the length of chain cruelly around my neck and ordered me to push the avocado out. I bore down and moaned as it stretched, pulled, and pleasured. She caught the avocado. When she rammed it hard back up inside, my knees buckled and her strong arm gripped the small of my back. Bent backward, all of me exposed to her, she fucked me with the rounded green of the fruit.

I begged for her fist, and on one knee she took me, her whole fist entering the tight cavity so fiercely I screamed in pain and clenched to push her, like the avocado, out. When she felt the squeeze of my muscles against her tightened fist, she growled and moaned at the same time, pulled out, the pink flesh of my lips following. She came out completely, and with each stroke entered me fresh, punched in with the full weight of her arm, and pulled out again. Her pace matched the yelling of men at the dock, counterpoint to the scree of gulls haggling over discarded fish heads. Tony changed pace, removed my blindfold to let me look, released my arm to let me feel the corded muscles of her forearm, her slippery wrist, and the length of her that plunged into me with each stroke, now faster, stronger, harder. My pleasure roared to a wave's peak, hovered as a white-tipped tidal wave, and ever so slowly curled inward, still reaching higher. As the cascade began, her arm ceased its pi stoning. I was filled, stilled, and hanging. My eyes pleaded that she let me come, but all at once she pulled out. I yelled from the ripping pain. Emptied, my pussy contracted sharply and I came; the long-held wave at last crested, broke, and thundered through my flesh. Tony ground and dragged my pussy lips into my legs as I bucked. Rode me till she came.

The leather glove was washed with my juices. I licked my own sweetness when she held it to my face.

The violence of her passion slaked, she could now take her time, tie me immobile, and cut me, in her own slow, stoking pace, with her cunt glued to my mouth.

Remembering the next part hurts more than anything else I recall of Tony. Her knives, razors, and needles danced on my skin. My fear changed the smell of me and spurred her on, her tongue licking the blood as it welled up, like a necklace of red jewels. Feeling the warmth of her tongue I moaned into that sweetest darkness, my own tongue thrusting. Her moan was the palest echo as she came with no sound, changed position slightly over my mouth, and cut again.

These times lasted hours. My mind detached from my body, and Tony touched and shaped the soul of me, seamlessly joined it to hers. That is the stuff of it, the acts of passion and the acts of loving, the stuff and the spirit of which I am now painfully bereft. There is no pain to match this, but the constant crash of sea onto rocks is its anguished echo.

As the months passed, she worked scrimshaw pieces of greater and greater complexity. Her enthusiasm for the work grew, verging on obsession. Tony began to talk about her finest work, the piece she'd never sell. Here at Dixie's Place with the rest of the guys, down to Marty's, even at the docks she talked to whoever would listen. But she wouldn't show it to anyone. Not till it's finished, she'd say. And then she'd wink at me, and that net around my heart would constrict.

The fire came before she finished. They don't know if the rummy started it lighting a cigarette and falling asleep or what, but she saw the flames from the shop late one night and ran down to the dock. She went down after the rummy, of course. Don't know if she saved him or if he had already crawled away from his shack, but he made it and she didn't. He'd inhaled smoke or something, and when he struggled to breathe clean air at the emergency room, her knife fell out of his pocket. The ER nurse is family, and she came over to my place the next night to give it to me.

Rescue workers never found her body. The part of the dock they'd dragged the rummy from was badly burnt, and most of it pretty much washed into the deep waters of the gulf before they even got there.

Now I'm a maudlin old femme. Time for me to go home, make it up to Danne.

At home Danne apologized in that halting butch way, words so few but the meaning there. She held me close, and I felt rough hands on my back, kisses compress my face.

Her passion stretched me against forces stronger than gravity, a part of me glued to the touching, a part of me away, held safe in the pulling, the tightening of that net.

All these years she wanted to mark me, but I never allowed her to. I knew if I allowed the marking, I would hate her for violating me, despise her for breaking me, revile her for saving me. And there would be no choice but to love her for reaching me.

I cried in her arms and let her kiss away the pain behind the rope burns at my wrists and ankles. In short, quick-breathed sentences, she told me she would never stand between me and the memory of Tony. That she loved Tony, too. That touching me, in a fucked-up way, was remembering Tony. That she missed Tony like hell, like it was an ache inside her that would never stop, a rip that never healed. But that it was me, me she loved. Me she wanted to be with, not the memory of who I was to another woman.

And the "you" echoed through my emptiness. When Danne said "you," my ears opened to swallow the "I love you's" clogged in them like wax these past five years. I slammed back down and into my body, and I saw her, maybe for the first time, no longer a view of us from somewhere up on the ceiling.

Through those many heart-torn words, Danne's big shoulders were hunched up around her neck. I touched them and they fell like a landslide, and all the wadded-up grieving of twenty years came out in the heart-twisting, pride-rending sobs of a butch.

A touch, then, a mingling of tears, the soft graze of teeth, and with trembling fingers I handed her Tony's blade. For the first time Danne held the blade in her construction-blunted hands, and I knew it would be the last time I'd ever desire its wicked caress.

Even today I undress slowly for my butch, like I did when a look from Tony's green eyes would move my arms to peel everything off in layers of perfection. You see, my skin makes keloids, a tough kind of scar tissue. The Scrimshaw Butch would touch those random keloid scars she'd made on my back, my arms, my butt.

Somewhere in our time together she must have figured that I was the perfect whalebone. She'd carve me lightly, and it hurt like her kisses. It took a lot of time. She studied how I scar and then worked with every mark she'd ever made, adding here and there to cover, here and there to augment. And I am beautiful, a tribute to her genius, her absent presence forever etched on my skin. I am her greatest work of art. And I am not finished.

Danne eased the razor through my skin, her touch light and stinging. The familiar net around my heart constricted, pulled hard. I gasped at the double sensation of pain from my skin and from my heart. Was this profane or sacred? My skin could not guess.

When she finished, my panting slowed, and she held out the mirror so I could look at her handiwork. A scrollwork "D" was red-etched around the faded "SB," flowering vines used the "SB" as a lattice to grow on, and my initial was the single rose grown from the vines, resting in the curve of the "D." While I was looking, my heart grew big, and all at once the space between the thin filaments of the net grew wider. First my heart, then my entire body slipped through its bonds.

Spread on our four-poster, pelvis up to meet my Danne's fisted thrust, I see the fluid and misty landscape of ecstasy, where the passage of time and death are not real things. All those years, and Tony waits for me again. Not for me to come with her, but to finally let her go. I see her wink. There is good-bye, a blurring of vision. Shards of glass fall like rain, and with Danne, comes the sun. Comes the sun.

Talkin' Trash
Elena Georgiou

I want the phone to ring.
I want the sound of your voice
to smack my body as waves hit rock,
grinding down mountains, opening up
secrets hidden between my shoulder blades.

I want you to beg me to let you come
over to wash my hair with rosewater.
When I refuse, I want you to hang up.

I want you to call back when I'm doing my laundry
and whine until I agree to let you be with me
the next time it's wash day,
so you can fold it.

I want you to ask me if I miss you.
And when I say: *Yes, I think about you
night and day*, I want you to know
I'm lying.

I want you to tell me you'd buy three bridges,
cross two oceans in a thunderstorm
to make my lie of missing you a reality.

I want to tell you that for a small
part of the Caribbean sea I'd turn into
a hungry anemone that sucks you closer.

I want you to ask me if this is all I want.
I want to tell you, no.

I want you to be my boy, my girl.
I want to paint your toenails gold,
massage your fingers with homemade oil
named after the smell of your neck.

I want to dust my mattress with baby powder,
lie on satin, tie ivory shells around my hips
and prepare myself for your coming.

I want you to call one last time,
ask me to unlock my door,
lie on my bed and wait.

I want to hear your bag drop to the floor,
the drag of your feet move to my bed.

 I want to feel the weight of your body
sink the mattress two inches lower.

I want your arms
to come from behind and hold
my breasts in an open prayer.

I want to hear you call on God
and give her credit for making me.

I want to watch you plead: *Lord
have mercy*, as you slide your mouth
from my navel to the back of my knee.

I want you to make me speak in tongues.
I want you to make me reach for things
you swear to me aren't there.

I want you to flip me, hold me
with one arm around my waist,
press your stomach to my spine,
fall and rise with me,
slide into night with me.

And when morning offers the hush of sleep,
I want you to open your tired eyes,
wrap my hair around your fingers,
pull me closer and murmur: *Yes, baby,
I promise I will be your toy.*

About the Authors

Donna Allegra is an African-Caribbean butch New Yorker. She writes fiction, essays, and poetry. Her most recent work appears in *Does Your Mama Know?*, *Hot and Bothered*, *MOM*, *Lesbian Travels: A Literary Companion*, and *Hers 3: Brilliant New Fiction by Lesbians*.

Toni Amato, a working-class butch dyke, lives in Vermont with her wife and two dogs. Recently, she has been reprimanded for not mentioning her cats. There are two of them, one of whom is particularly fond of having her butt whapped. Toni's work has appeared in *Leatherwomen II* and *Best Lesbian Erotica 1998*.

Teresa Cooper is currently working toward an MFA in fiction writing from Columbia University's School of the Arts. Her fiction has appeared in *Blithe House Quarterly* and *The Lesbian News*. She is also a freelance writer whose work has appeared in *Out*, *Parenting*, *Tribe*, and *Girlfriends* magazines, among others. Teresa is the editor and co-publisher of *The Fish Tank*, the quarterly 'zine for dykes.

Dawn Dougherty is a Boston-based consultant, writer, and educator. She is a die-hard femme whose work has appeared in *Paramour, Sojourner, Bay Windows,* and *Lesbian Short Stories.* In her spare time, Dawn likes to raise hell, collect unemployment, and take long, hot baths. She is currently studying belly dancing and hopes to shake her shimmy professionally one day.

Elena Georgiou is the recipient of the 1998 Astraea Emerging Writers Award in Poetry. She is also the co-editor (with Michael Lassell) of a forthcoming poetry anthology, *The World in Us: Lesbian and Gay Poetry at the Beginning of the 21st Century.* She teaches creative writing at City College, CUNY. She lives in the Nation of Brooklyn.

Gerry Gomez Pearlberg is the author of the poetry collection *Marianne Faithfull's Cigarette* (Cleis) and editor of *Queer Dog: Homo/Pup/Poetry* (Cleis), winner of a 1998 Firecracker Alternative Book Award. Her experimental prose piece, *The Fetish Papers,* is available as a handbound, limited-edition chapbook from Big Fat Press in Brooklyn, New York. Her writings have recently appeared in *The Writer's Voice Magazine, Lesbian Travels: A Literary Companion, Bark,* and *Poetry Nation.*

Sacchi Green lives in the five-college area of western Massachusetts, hardly the real world but interesting. After five decades of "research" she's finally writing things down and has stories in several recent or upcoming science fiction and fantasy publications, including the anthology *New Blood: Dark Erotica.*

Cynthia Greenberg is a displaced California poet and troublemaker living in New York City. She has an abiding interest in activism, literacy, language, and bodies of water. Her work has appeared in *Nice Jewish Girls: Growing up in America* and *Best Lesbian Erotica 1998.* She is currently at work on an anthology about lesbians and loss.

Nicola Griffith was born in England but now lives in Seattle with her partner, writer Kelley Eskridge. She is the author of three novels, *The Blue Place*, *Slow River*, and *Ammonite*, and editor of the *Bending the Landscape* series. Her homepage can be found at http://www.sff.net/people/Nicola.

Ilsa Jule has lived in New York City for the past nine years. She considers herself to be a native New Yorker (it's more a state of mind) and can't imagine living anywhere else. While attending Hunter College she founded *Sappho's Scribblers*, the 'zine for and by the dykes at Hunter. "Pornography for Miss X" is dedicated to Elizabeth Grainger.

Catherine Lundoff lives in Minneapolis with her wonderful girlfriend. Her writings have appeared in *Cherished Blood*, *Pillow Talk*, *XOddity*, and *Lesbian Short Fiction*. "El Tigre" was a prize winner in the WritersBloc Fiction Writing Contest in 1996.

Gayla Mann has been called a lot of things, but earthy, crunchy, leatherdyke is her favorite. Native to West Virginia, she lived ten years in Texas, and, after obtaining a master's degree, finally settled in Pennsylvania with her partner of three years. Currently Gayla is involved in growing a polyamorous pagan lesbian household, creating markets for her artwork, and developing web pages and databases. She is also working on a volume of S/M verse.

Skian McGuire, formerly a Philadelphian, is a Quaker sadomasochist who now lives with her dog pack and her partner of sixteen years in the wilds of western Massachusetts. She writes bad poetry and as-yet-unpublished science fiction, and is working on a novel called *Nights at the Bijou*, of which "Remote Control" is an excerpt. She has no plans to quit her day job.

Peggy Munson is a queer writer on disability who has published fiction and poetry in such places as *Hers 3*, *13th Moon*, *The Spoon River Poetry Review*, *Literature and Medicine*, and the *San Francisco Bay Guardian*. In her spare time, she plays electric guitar, anthropomorphizes her dog, and lures strange women to come nap with her.

Letta Neely is a black dyke living in Boston. She has written two chapbooks and one book of poetry, *Juba* (Wildheart Press). Her work has been included in the anthologies *Catch the Fire* and *Does Your Mama Know?*.

Carol Queen is the author of *The Leather Daddy and the Femme* (Cleis Press), *Real Live Nude Girl: Chronicles of Sex-Positive Culture* (Cleis Press), and *Exhibitionism for the Shy* (Down There Press). She co-edited *Switch Hitters* (Cleis Press) and *Pomosexuals* (Cleis Press). She lives in San Francisco.

Susan Rosenberg has been in federal prison for the last thirteen years for politically motivated, antigovernment activities. She was given the longest sentence in U.S. history for weapons possession. Since 1984, she has done years in lock-down/maximum security prisons, including the Lexington Kentucky High Security Unit (HSU) in the late 1980s. Susan is an AIDS advocate for women in prison. She is the recipient of five PEN Awards, including three first-place awards in the poetry, short story, and essay/memoir categories. Her writing appears in *Covert Action*, *Prisoner News Service*, *Fortune News*, *Prison Life*, *Columbia Journalism Review*, and the anthologies *Hauling up the Morning*, *A Loving Testimony*, and *In Defense of Mumia*. She is currently working toward a masters degree in writing from Antioch University. Rosenberg says, "I've become a writer as a means to continue living behind the wall and to continue to resist the deadening of prison." She is at work on a novel about Cointelpro. Letters to Susan should be addressed to her attorney, Mary O'Melveny, 2022 Columbia Road NW, Washington, DC 20009.

Carol Rosenfeld is a New York City-based writer, poet, and aspiring performance artist. "Q & A" is excerpted from *Fool's Mushroom*, her novel-in-progress. Her poem "Dyke-otomy" will appear in *Poetry Nation*, and she has self-published two chapbooks, *Poems I Can't Show My Mother* and *Poems That Will Never Make the Norton Anthology*. Carol co-chairs *In Our Own Write*, a cultural program of New York City's Lesbian and Gay Community Services Center.

Michele Serchuk is a writer and photographer. Her writing has been published in *Herotica V*, *Early Embraces*, and *Australian Women's Forum*. Her photos have been seen in *On Our Backs*, *Girlfriends*, *SECRET*, *Libido*, *Paramour*, *Pucker Up*, *Masquerade*, *Cupido*, and *Bad Attitude*.

Alison L. Smith grew up in Rochester, New York, where she attended twelve years of Catholic School. At Brown University, she studied playwriting with Paula Vogel. She has been a writer-in-residence at MacDowell and Ragdale colonies. She has worked in the theater for many years; her most recent project was directing Kate Baldwin's one-woman show *Living in Wonderland*. She lives in Northampton and is writing a novel about three generations of a Catholic family.

Laurie Stone won the National Book Critics Circle Award for Excellence in Reviewing as well as a grant from The New York Foundation for the Arts. She was critic-at-large on Fresh Air. She is the theater critic for *The Nation*, a longtime columnist for the *Village Voice*, and author of the novel *Starting with Serge*, the essay collection *Laughing in the Dark*, and the collection of literary memoirs *Close to the Bone*.

Cecilia Tan writes, edits, and publishes erotica in the Boston area. Her book of erotic short stories, *Black Feathers*, was published in 1998. Her work has appeared in *Ms.* and *Penthouse*, and in *Best Lesbian Erotica 1997* and *Best American Erotica* 1996 and 1999. She owns Circlet Press, publishers of erotic science fiction and fantasy. She does not like to be without a cat. She gets around.

Cheryl Boyce Taylor is a poet born in Trinidad. She is the author of a collection of poetry, *Raw Air* (Fly by Night Press). Her work has been featured in *The Maryland Poetry Review, In Defense of Mumia*, and *Aloud: Voices from the Nuyorican Poets Cafe* which won the American Book Award in 1994. She holds a B.A. in Theater, an MEd from Long Island University, and an MSW from Fordam University.

Andrea Tetrick dwells in Washington, D.C., but hails from the sleepy little burg of Bishop, California, nestled on the eastern slope of the Sierra Nevada Mountains. Andrea is indebted to her partner, Karen Robb, for urging her to take a year off work to write stories. She also thanks Crystal Reynolds, The Meat Joy vocalist/songwriter, for graciously allowing her to borrow the name Jimmi Veneer.

Shoshie Tornberg is a writer, poet, and poetry performer who has appeared in Boston's Amazon Poetry Slams and New York's Three Dollar Bill Poetry Slam. She was also a finalist in both the 1998 OutWrite National Poetry Slam and Boston's Network for Battered Lesbians 1998 Annual Poetry Slam. Her work has appeared in the annual publication *P'Town Women*. Shoshie lives in Jamaica Plain, Massachusetts.

Robin G. White is the author of the erotica play *Pantyliners*, produced by the Theater Offensive at the Boston Center for the Arts. Robin is the wordsmith, lead vocalist, and flautist for the Boston-based Rennaissance Soul band Sweet Black Molasses. Her work has appeared in numerous periodicals, and she has performed in plays, television shows and films, including *2 in 20*, *Ten Percent Revue*, *Mother Country*, *Gay Boston*, and *Drag Kings, Sluts, and Goddesses*. She lives in Atlanta.

Lucy Wikersham is the pseudonym/alter ego of a twenty-four-year-old dyke, New York City resident, and aspiring academic. In her copious free time she studies for the Graduate Record Examination and indulges her early '80s music habit. She has promised her friends that she will publish an entire collection of dirty stories under her real name as soon as she is tenured at a major research university.

Sarah Fran Wisby lives and works in San Francisco.

About the Editors

Chrystos has been a proud lesbian for thirty-two years. She is a treaty and prisoners' rights activist who performs her work internationally. She is the author of *Not Vanishing, Dream On, In Her I Am, Fugitive Colors, Fire Power,* and *Wilder Reis* (German translation of her work published by Orlanda, Berlin). She is widely anthologized and has received many awards and grants, including The Audre Lorde International Poetry Competition and The Sappho Award of Distinction from the Astraea National Lesbian Action Foundation.

Tristan Taormino is series editor of *Best Lesbian Erotica,* for which she has collaborated with guest editors Heather Lewis, Jewelle Gomez, and Jenifer Levin. The 1997 collection was a finalist for a Lambda Literary Award. She is the author of *The Ultimate Guide to Anal Sex for Women* which won a 1998 Firecracker Alternative Book Award. She is co-editor of *A Girl's Guide To Taking Over the World: Writing from the Girl Zine Revolution* and *Ritual Sex.* She is also a contributing editor to *On Our Backs* magazine, for which she writes "Adventure Girl," a sex adventure column. Her writing has appeared in several anthologies and publications, and she is the recipient of two 1998 Vice Versa Awards for excellence in gay and lesbian journalism.

The Best Lesbian Erotica!

Best Lesbian Erotica features the steamiest, most thought-provoking lesbian sex writing you'll find. Each year, guest judges selected from the queer literary world review the year's best erotica and choose the final collection, representing a wide range of styles and voices.

Best Lesbian Erotica 1999.
Selected and introduced by Chrystos.
Edited by Tristan Taormino.
ISBN: 1-57344-049-3. 14.95 paper.

Best Lesbian Erotica 1998.
Selected and introduced by Jenifer Levin.
Edited by Tristan Taormino.
ISBN: 1-57344-032-9 14.95 paper.

AVAILABLE AT YOUR FAVORITE BOOKSTORE
& FROM CLEIS PRESS
How to Order

- **Phone:** 1-800-780-2279 or (415) 575-4700
  Monday - Friday, 9 am - 5 pm Pacific Standard Time
- **Fax:** (415) 575-4705
- **Mail: Cleis Press** P.O. Box 14684, San Francisco, California 94114
- **E-mail:** Cleis@aol.com

  Turn the page for more great books from Cleis Press...

Hot Erotica from Cleis Press!

Annie Sprinkle: Post Porn Modernist — My Twenty-Five Years as a Multimedia Whore by Annie Sprinkle. ISBN: 1-57344-039-6 21.95 paper

Best Gay Erotica 1998. Selected and introduced by Christopher Bram. Edited by Richard Labonté. $14.95 ISBN: 1-57344-031-0

Best Gay Erotica 1997. Selected and introduced by Douglas Sadownick. Edited by Richard Labonté. $14.95 ISBN: 1-57344-067-1

Best Gay Erotica 1996. Selected and introduced by Scott Heim. Edited by Michael Ford. $12.95 ISBN: 1-57344-052-3

Best Lesbian Erotica 1999. Selected and introduced by Chrystos. Edited by Tristan Taormino. ISBN: 1-57344-049-3. 14.95 paper.

Best Lesbian Erotica 1998, selected by Jenifer Levin, edited by Tristan Taormino. ISBN: 1-57344-032-9 14.95 paper.

The Leather Daddy and the Femme: An Erotic Novel by Carol Queen. ISBN: 1-57344-037-X. 14.00 paper.

Queer PAPI Porn: Asian Gay Erotica edited by Joel Tan. 1-57344-038-8 14.95

Serious Pleasure: Lesbian Erotic Stories and Poetry, edited by the Sheba Collective. ISBN: 0-939416-45-X 9.95 paper.

How to Order Cleis Press Books
- **Phone:** 1-800-780-2279 or (415) 575-4700
  Monday - Friday, 9 am - 5 pm Pacific Standard Time
- **Fax:** (415) 575-4705
- **Mail: Cleis Press** P.O. Box 14684, San Francisco, California 94114
- **E-mail:** Cleis@aol.com

More Books from Cleis Press...

DEBUT LITERATURE

The Little School: Tales of Disappearance and Survival ,
second edition,
by Alicia Partnoy.
ISBN: 1-57344-029-9
14.95 paper.

Marianne Faithfull's Cigarette: Poems
by Gerry Gomez Pearlberg.
ISBN: 1-57344-034-5
12.95 paper

Memory Mambo
by Achy Obejas. Lambda Literary Award Winner.
ISBN: 1-57344-017-5
12.95 paper.

Queer Dog: Homo Pup Poetry,
edited by Gerry Gomez Pearlberg.
ISBN: 1-57344-071-X.
12.95. paper.

We Came All The Way from Cuba So You Could Dress Like This?: Stories
by Achy Obejas. Lambda Literary Award Nominee.
ISBN: 0-939416-93-X
10.95 paper.

Seeing Dell
by Carol Guess
ISBN: 1-57344-023-X
12.95 paper.

MYSTERIES

Dirty Weekend: A Novel of Revenge
by Helen Zahavi.
ISBN: 0-939416-85-9
10.95 paper.

The Woman Who Knew Too Much: A Cordelia Morgan Mystery
by B. Reese Johnson.
ISBN: 1-57344-045-0.
12.95 paper.

VAMPIRES & HORROR

Brothers of the Night: Gay Vampire Stories
edited by Michael Rowe and Thomas S. Roche.
ISBN: 1-57344-025-6
14.95 paper.

Dark Angels: Lesbian Vampire Stories,
edited by Pam Keesey.
Lambda Literary Award Nominee.
ISBN 1-7344-014-0
10.95 paper.

Daughters of Darkness: Lesbian Vampire Stories,
second edition,
edited by Pam Keesey.
ISBN: 1-57344-076-0
14.95 paper.

Vamps: An Illustrtated History of the Femme Fatale
by Pam Keesey.
ISBN: 1-57344-026-4
21.95.

Sons of Darkness: Tales of Men, Blood and Immortality,
edited by Michael Rowe and Thomas S. Roche.
Lambda Literary Award Nominee.
ISBN: 1-57344-059-0
12.95 paper.

Women Who Run with the Werewolves: Tales of Blood, Lust and Metamorphosis,
edited by Pam Keesey.
Lambda Literary Award Nominee.
ISBN: 1-57344-057-4
12.95 paper.

Sexual Politics

Forbidden Passages: Writings Banned in Canada,
introductions by Pat Califia and Janine Fuller.
Lambda Literary Award Winner.
ISBN: 1-57344-019-1
14.95 paper.

Public Sex: The Culture of Radical Sex
by Pat Califia.
ISBN: 0-939416-89-1
12.95 paper.

Real Live Nude Girl: Chronicles of Sex-Positive Culture
by Carol Queen.
ISBN: 1-57344-073-6.
14.95 paper.

Sex Work: Writings by Women in the Sex Industry, second edition, edited by Frédérique Delacoste and Priscilla Alexander. ISBN: 1-57344-042-6. 19.95 paper.

Susie Bright's Sexual Reality: A Virtual Sex World Reader by Susie Bright. ISBN: 0-939416-59-X 9.95 paper.

Susie Bright's Sexwise by Susie Bright. ISBN: 1-57344-002-7 10.95 paper.

Susie Sexpert's Lesbian Sex World, second edition, by Susie Bright. ISBN: 1-57344-077-9. 14.95 paper.

GENDER TRANSGRESSION

Body Alchemy: Transsexual Portraits by Loren Cameron. Lambda Literary Award Winner. ISBN: 1-57344-062-0 24.95 paper.

Dagger: On Butch Women, edited by Roxxie, Lily Burana, Linnea Due. ISBN: 0-939416-82-4 14.95 paper.

I Am My Own Woman: The Outlaw Life of Charlotte von Mahlsdorf, translated by Jean Hollander. ISBN: 1-57344-010-8 12.95 paper.

PoMoSexuals: Challenging Assumptions about Gender and Sexuality edited by Carol Queen and Lawrence Schimel. Preface by Kate Bornstein. ISBN: 1-57344-074-4 14.95 paper.

Sex Changes: The Politics of Transgenderism by Pat Califia ISBN: 1-57344-072-8 16.95 paper.

Switch Hitters: Lesbians Write Gay Male Erotica and Gay Men Write Lesbian Erotica, edited by Carol Queen and Lawrence Schimel. ISBN: 1-57344-021-3 12.95 paper.

LESBIAN AND GAY STUDIES

Case of The Good For Nothing Girlfriend: A Nancy Clue Mystery, 2nd edition, by Mabel Maney. 0-939416-91-3. 14.95

The Case of the Not-So-Nice Nurse by Mabel Maney. Lambda Literary Award Nominee. ISBN: 0-939416-76-X 9.95 paper.

Chasing the American Dyke Dream: Homestretch edited by Susan Fox Rogers. ISBN: 1-57344-036-1 14.95 paper.

A Fragile Union: New & Selected Writings by Joan Nestle. 1-57344-040-X 14.95

Nancy Clue and the Hardly Boys in *A Ghost in the Closet* by Mabel Maney. Lambda Literary Award Nominee. ISBN: 1-57344-012-4 10.95 paper.

Different Daughters: A Book by Mothers of Lesbians, second edition, edited by Louise Rafkin. ISBN: 1-57344-050-7 12.95 paper.

A Lesbian Love Advisor by Celeste West. ISBN: 0-939416-26-3 9.95 paper.

On the Rails: A Memoir, second edition, by Linda Niemann. Introduction by Leslie Marmon Silko. ISBN: 1-57344-064-7. 14.95 paper.

SEX GUIDES

Good Sex: Real Stories from Real People, second edition, by Julia Hutton. ISBN: 1-57344-000-0 14.95 paper.

The New Good Vibrations Guide to Sex: Tips and techniques from America's favorite sex-toy store, second edition, by Cathy Winks and Anne Semans. ISBN: 1-57344-069-8 21.95 paper.

The Ultimate Guide to Anal Sex for Women
by Tristan Taormino.
ISBN: 1-57344-028-0
14.95 paper.

WORLD LITERATURE

A Forbidden Passion
by Cristina Peri Rossi.
ISBN: 0-939416-68-9
9.95 paper.

Half a Revolution: Contemporary Fiction by Russian Women,
edited by Masha Gessen.
ISBN 1-57344-006-X
12.95 paper.

COMIX

Dyke Strippers: Lesbian Cartoonists A to Z,
edited by Roz Warren.
ISBN: 1-57344-008-6
16.95 paper.

TRAVEL & COOKING

Betty and Pansy's Severe Queer Review of New York
by Betty Pearl and Pansy.
ISBN: 1-57344-070-1
10.95 paper.

Betty and Pansy's Severe Queer Review of San Francisco by Betty Pearl and Pansy.
ISBN: 1-57344-056-6
10.95 paper.

Food for Life & Other Dish,
edited by Lawrence Schimel.
ISBN: 1-57344-061-2
14.95 paper.

WRITER'S REFERENCE

Putting Out: The Essential Publishing Resource Guide For Gay and Lesbian Writers, fourth edition,
by Edisol W. Dotson.
ISBN: 1-57344-033-7
14.95 paper.

Since 1980, Cleis Press has published provocative, smart books — for girlfriends of all genders. Cleis Press books are easy to find at your favorite bookstore — or direct from us! We welcome your order and will ship your books as quickly as possible. Individual orders must be prepaid (U.S. dollars only). Please add 15% shipping. CA residents add 8.5% sales tax. MasterCard and Visa orders: include account number, exp. date, and signature.

How to Order

- **Phone:** 1-800-780-2279 or (415) 575-4700
  Monday - Friday, 9 am - 5 pm Pacific Standard Time
- **Fax:** (415) 575-4705
- **Mail: Cleis Press** P.O. Box 14684, San Francisco, California 94114
- **E-mail:** Cleis@aol.com